THE MEDICINE GAME

A Novel

DARRYL BOLLINGER

JNB Press

This book is a work of fiction. Names, characters, places, and incidents are the product of the author's imagination or are used fictitiously. Any resemblance to actual events, locales, or persons, living or dead, is coincidental.

Copyright © 2012 by Darryl Bollinger

All rights reserved

JNB Press
Tallahassee, FL

www.jnbpress.com

Printed in the United States of America

First Trade Edition: January 2012

ISBN 978-0-9848432-0-6

In memory of my father, who told me that I could do anything if I put my mind to it.

ONE

Jack heard the voice and was confused. He wasn't sure if he was dreaming or awake. He thought he recognized the voice, then heard it again.

"Help. Please. Somebody—"

A crashing thud outside finished waking him from a deep sleep. It came from his right. He sat up in the berth, rubbing his eyes. The boat was rocking gently in the water. He strained to hear what was going on. There was no other sound but the clanging of rigging in the light breeze. Quiet. Still groggy and perplexed, he got up out of the berth wearing only his boxers. He stumbled through the cabin of his sailboat to the companionway. Barefoot, Jack went up the three steps to the cockpit.

It was dark with only the dock lights illuminating the marina. He stopped and looked over at the boat to his right.

What the . . . ?

He saw Peter, the old man who lived on the boat next to him, lying motionless on the deck of his sailboat.

Jack jumped out on the small dock that separated the two boats and over into Peter's boat.

"Peter? You okay?"

Peter's eyes were glazed over, and he was clutching his chest. He didn't respond.

Damn, he's had a heart attack. Jack jumped down into the floor of the cockpit and stretched the older man out on his back. He couldn't see Peter's chest moving, and when he placed his ear next to Peter's face, Peter wasn't breathing. Jack started chest compressions. One hundred per minute, at least two inches, let the chest come all the way up. He was glad he'd taken the CPR class, but realized he'd forgotten his phone. It was still on the shelf next to the berth back on his boat. He needed to call 911.

"Help!" Jack shouted. "Help! We need help out here." He continued yelling as loud as he could while he kept up the compressions.

Finally, across the way, a heavyset middle-aged man walked out of the cabin door on the trawler docked there. He looked across the dock at Jack with a puzzled look on his face. Before he could speak, Jack hollered out to him.

"Kevin. Call 911. Peter's had a heart attack, and I'm giving him CPR. Quick."

Kevin went back into his cabin. Seconds later, he came out with his cell phone and was talking into it. "Yes, this is Kevin Whitehead. I'm at the Fort Myers Yacht Basin, J dock, slip twenty-four. We need an ambulance. Someone had a heart attack. Our neighbor is giving him CPR right now, but we need an ambulance."

Jack kept up the CPR. In a few minutes, he heard a loud siren. The hospital was only a few blocks away. Less than a minute later, he could see the reflection of flashing lights and heard the commotion as the paramedics came running down the docks pushing a gurney. They grabbed their gear off the gurney and stepped over into Peter's boat. The petite young woman came over to Jack as her partner, a stocky bearded man, checked Peter's vitals.

"He collapsed out here, and I came over soon as I heard him. Found him lying here and started CPR. Probably less than a minute. He wasn't breathing," Jack said.

"I'll take over now, sir. Thank you," she said.

Jack made his last compression and moved out of her way. She took over and started a clipped dialogue with her partner. He brought out the defibrillator and shocked Peter. Jack heard the bearded guy say they had a pulse. They continued working on Peter, moving him to a stretcher and to the gurney.

"I'm going to follow them to the hospital and make sure he's okay. I'll be back in a few," Jack said to Kevin, standing on the dock behind Peter's boat. Jack went back to his boat to put on some clothes and shoes.

The paramedics wheeled Peter down the dock and out to the waiting ambulance, Jack not far behind. At the main dock, the paramedics went toward the ambulance as Jack turned and went to the marina parking lot to get his car. Unlocking his car, he heard the siren screaming and saw the flashing lights headed toward the hospital.

He drove the two blocks, parking in the visitors area next to the Emergency Department. The ambulance was backed up to the emergency entrance, lights still flashing.

At the triage desk, he identified himself and told the clerk he was Peter Stein's neighbor and wanted to know how he was doing.

She asked him to please wait, and as soon as she had any information, she'd let him know. Jack was too nervous to sit and paced the floor outside the door to the treatment area.

In a few minutes, a nurse in scrubs came out, recognized Jack, and came over to talk to him.

"Peter's stable, his vitals are okay. We'll transfer him to CCU for observation as soon as they're ready upstairs."

"Can I see him?" Jack asked.

She shook her head. "No, still kinda busy back there. He's pretty much out of it anyway, but he'll be fine. Nothing you can do tonight. Go on home and stop by in the morning."

Jack nodded and thanked her.

When he got back to the marina, a small crowd had gathered on J dock, circled around Kevin who was telling everyone what had happened. Seeing Jack, he stopped mid-sentence and asked, "How's he doing?"

The people gathered turned, saw Jack, and parted to allow Jack inside the circle.

"He was stable, and they're transferring him to the Cardiac Unit for observation. The nurse in the ER said he'd be fine. I'll check on him in the morning when I get to work."

Someone asked out loud, "Does Peter have any relatives we need to call?"

Jack shook his head. "Not that I know of. I've never heard him mention anyone, other than an ex-wife a long time ago."

Before long, the group dispersed and everyone went back to their boats. Kevin was the last to leave.

"Want a drink? I'm too wired to sleep," Kevin asked. He was a large man, thick around the middle. From New Jersey, he had lived here for seven or eight years.

"Me, too. A drink sounds good."

Jack followed Kevin onto the deck of the large trawler opposite Jack's boat.

Kevin stopped at the door to the cabin. "What's your pleasure?"

"Beer's fine, thanks."

Kevin disappeared into the cabin and soon came out holding two bottles of Bud Light.

Not Jack's favorite, but he kept quiet. He took a long swig from the bottle. It was cold and tasted pretty good under the circumstances.

Kevin swallowed and said, "What a night, huh? Good thing you heard Peter. I didn't hear a thing."

"I was sound asleep and heard him call for help. But when I got to him, he was unconscious. I just hope he's going to be all right," Jack said.

"I know. He was just in the hospital for some heart thing, wasn't he? Some kind of new treatment?"

"Yeah, he had a new drug called Clearart. From what I know, it's supposed to be the latest treatment for heart disease. Replaces open heart surgery. With it, they don't have to split your chest open like they used to. That's about all I know. I'm on the financial side of things, not the clinical side."

Kevin took another swig from his beer. "Yeah, Peter told me a little about it. He said it was like Drano for the arteries."

Jack laughed, thinking that sounded like Peter all right. "Good description, from what I know. They keep you for a day to monitor you while they're dripping that stuff in your veins. It's supposed to break up the plaque that clogs your arteries. From all accounts it works well."

"Expensive, though, from what Peter said. He told me that if it wasn't for Medicare, he wouldn't be able to afford it," Kevin said.

"No, it's not cheap. But still a lot less expensive than open heart surgery. And a lot quicker recovery time."

He thought back to when Peter was in the hospital. Jack remembered taking Peter to the hospital and bringing him back to his boat the day after the procedure. Jack slept in Peter's boat that night in case the old man needed something. Two days later, Peter had his whiskey and was chewing on his unlit cigar like always.

Jack finished his beer and stood. "Thanks for the beer, Kevin. And the help. I'm starting to feel sleepy all of a sudden. I guess the adrenalin has faded."

"I won't be long behind you. Keep me posted on Peter. Let me know how he's doing, will you?"

"Yeah, I will. I'll go by first thing in the morning and check on him. Thanks again."

He walked back over to his boat and went down below. He closed the companionway doors, turned, and went to the V-berth up front. Jack stretched out on his back and lay there, staring through the hatch above him. He was worried about his neighbor. Peter had just been in the hospital a few weeks ago, getting the cardiac treatment that Jack and Kevin were discussing.

Jack figured that Peter was good for another year. That was one of the drawbacks to Clearart from the patient's perspective. The treatment had to be done every year. Of course, from the drug company and hospital's perspective, that was a good thing; an ongoing revenue stream. Jack closed his eyes and figured he would ask Richard about it tomorrow.

TWO

Jack heard the alarm clock go off. He reached over, turned it off, and lay back in the berth. The boat was gently rocking. He felt like he'd just closed his eyes and gone to sleep. Another day. After a few minutes, he got up to put on his running shorts, t-shirt, and shoes.

He climbed the few steps leading to the cockpit of the Catalina 30 and the fresh air. Another beautiful day in Southwest Florida, he thought, looking up at the blue, cloudless sky. He gazed across the Fort Myers Yacht Basin at the river and yawned. The facility was operated by the City of Fort Myers and located downtown on the Caloosahatchee River.

This was his favorite part of the day. It was quiet and cool, at least for Fort Myers this time of year. He looked over at the Island Packet next to him, Peter's boat. Peter was a tough old bird, but Jack was still worried about him. Jack would check in on him as soon as he got to the hospital. He chuckled to himself as he pictured Peter sitting up in bed flirting with the nurses and asking when he could go home.

Jack said a silent prayer for him, stepped off the boat onto the dock, and walked toward the main dock. He stuck his earbuds in and turned on his iPod. It was loaded with classics, which to him were classic rock songs. Most days, he put it on shuffle, enjoying the surprises selected by the electronic roulette wheel. Today, though, he opted for Bob Seger to accompany him on his run.

When he got to the main dock that ran along the seawall, he stopped to stretch. A few people were stirring about, mainly those going out fishing or otherwise getting an early start on the water. He finished stretching and set out along the seawall, running slow and loose until he warmed up. Most mornings, he got three or four miles in. He ran south along the river, down Edwards Drive until it curved into First Street. Warmed up and hitting his usual pace of seven minute miles, he turned right on First Street. He ran past Ray's On the River and Palm View Condominiums.

After six or seven blocks, First Street curved and ended at McGregor Boulevard. Once at McGregor he turned right and ran down the sidewalk along the beautiful palm tree lined street that was well-known in Fort Myers. He passed the exclusive gated community where his best friend Richard lived. He kept running for another mile or so and checked his watch. Fifteen minutes; time to turn around and head home.

Twenty minutes later, after walking around the marina a bit to cool down, he was back at his boat, Wind Dancer. He refilled his water bottle and sat in the cockpit to cool off. Even though it was only seven in the morning, it was already getting warm. Another few weeks and it would be hot, even this early.

Most of the boats in the yacht basin belonged to weekenders, as the full-timers like Jack called them. They lived in Fort Myers and only came out to their boats on the weekend, if at all. There were probably a dozen full-timers who lived in the marina. These were people who lived on their boats. It wasn't a lifestyle for everyone. Space on a boat was at a premium, so there was not a lot of room for someone encumbered with a lot of stuff. Although everyone cited the freedom of being able to cast off the lines and sail the world, most full-timers tended to stay in one place for years at a time. This was true of those who lived here.

His neighbor Peter had been here for fifteen years. He was in his seventies, which was as much as he would tell anyone. Peter had sailed all over the world with the pictures and stories to prove it. As the unofficial mayor of the yacht basin community, he loved to regale the tenants with stories of his adventures. Sitting in the back of his boat almost every evening, barefoot and dressed in shorts and a t-shirt, he held court.

Although he'd quit smoking, he still chewed on a fat Cuban cigar. No one knew where he got the Cubans, and he never volunteered any information. He would occasionally offer one to his close friends. Jack tried one once, but it was too strong for him. As a non-smoker, it damn near made him sick. Peter always had a tumbler with a finger or two of Jameson Irish Whiskey, which completed the picture. He rarely took his boat out anymore except for maintenance. When he did go out sailing, Jack went with him.

Jack Davis was the second newest tenant. The newbie, a woman who arrived a year ago, lived over on the L dock. She replaced Jack at the bottom of the yacht basin ladder. Most people who lived on boats were either retired or content to work odd jobs and live on a shoestring. Jack was the only live-aboard here who worked full-time.

He worked a couple of blocks away at Rivers Community Hospital, which was what brought him to Fort Myers. He'd gone through a messy divorce in Jacksonville, where he grew up, and found a job as controller at Rivers. Fortunately, there were no kids involved, just a spiteful, vengeful, and basically psychotic ex-wife. In Jacksonville, he'd been on the corporate treadmill, climbing the career ladder along with everyone else that age. He had the BMW and went to the right restaurants and hung out with the right people. After the divorce, he decided to change his focus. He wanted a good job, but a different lifestyle. So, with what little money he salvaged from the wreck of a marriage, he bought a boat and headed south, ending up in Fort Myers.

It had been a good move for him. He liked the hospital and quickly made friends. His two closest friends were Richard and Molly. Five years ago, they had started at Rivers on the same day and gone through new employee orientation together. Though coming from completely different backgrounds, they had much in common and spent a lot of time together outside work.

He finished his water, grabbed a towel, and went to the bathhouse to shower. When he got back to the boat, he put on his work clothes. Most days this consisted of slacks and a golf shirt. Rivers Hospital was casual, typical of Fort Myers where few employers required a coat and tie. Ready for another day at the office, he set out to walk the two blocks to work.

Rivers Community Hospital was the oldest hospital in Fort Myers, located downtown at the intersection of Cleveland Avenue and Martin Luther King Boulevard. Their only competition was Lee Memorial Hospital, founded three years later. It was located a mile south of Rivers on the opposite side of Cleveland Avenue.

Rivers was established by Wallace Rivers, a wealthy industrialist who was a contemporary of Thomas Edison. Wallace Rivers's young wife had died in Fort Myers one winter before there was a hospital here. Wallace was heartbroken and set up a generous endowment for a hospital to serve the area. The Rivers Foundation operated the hospital for over ninety-three years as a not-for-profit community hospital serving the citizens of Fort Myers. Two years ago, the Foundation decided that operating a hospital had become too complicated. It was no longer a good fit with the Foundation's broader goals. They sold the hospital to HealthAmerica, a large publicly-owned hospital company.

HealthAmerica was the current darling of Wall Street. The acquisition had been a major coup for them, and Rivers was their flagship hospital in the Sunshine State. Their stock had been on a meteoric rise, and they were the chief proponent for competition in health care, claiming that was the path to reducing costs. Less known was the fact that quite a few of their officers had made tens of millions of dollars from the immensely profitable business of providing health care.

Jack wasn't sure about HealthAmerica. He had liked Rivers, but it was changing with corporate ownership. Everything was about the stock price. So far, he'd managed to stay out of the company politics, but didn't know how much longer that would last.

The hospital consisted of two towers, identical from the outside. The first was a large ten story building that housed all of the patient rooms. The second tower contained the administrative offices, including his and various support services like the lab, radiology, and so forth.

Jack went in by the Emergency Room, so he decided to stop by and find out what room Peter was in. He walked in through the hall door which led into the ER administrative area. Angie, one of the managers he knew, wasn't in her office. He walked out to the triage desk and saw her standing there talking to one of the techs.

"Well, well," she said as Jack walked up. "Sorry, but we don't have any money left to give. We're tapped out."

She was referring to their last encounter at one of Jack's infamous budget review meetings.

"Not looking for dollars this trip, Angie. Just wanted to check on a patient."

The tech excused himself, and Angie turned her attention to Jack.

"You know with all the privacy rules I can't give out confidential information." She was smiling as she said it.

Jack ignored her comment, but did lower his voice a notch.

"A friend of mine. My neighbor. Paramedics brought him in early this morning. Heart attack. I gave him CPR until they got there. Peter Stein. What room is he in?"

Angie started typing on the computer terminal in front of her. "I didn't come on till seven a, so let me check."

She stopped typing and frowned. "Seventy-three?"

"Sounds right. I didn't know his exact age, but that's close."

She walked around from behind the counter to face Jack. "I'm sorry, Jack. He didn't make it."

Jack felt as if he'd been punched in the gut. He didn't say a word. He just stood there. His eyes were locked onto Angie's as if to verify what she said.

"He crashed just before they took him to CCU. They did all they could, Jack. I'm so sorry." She reached out and took his hand.

He looked at the floor and shook his head. "I can't believe it. They told me he was stable and going to be fine."

He had a dozen questions, but knew there were no answers. There was nothing else to say.

"I'm sorry, Jack," Angie said again.

He looked into her eyes as if they held the answers to his questions. Her expression told him not.

"Thanks, Angie." He pulled his hand back and walked away in a daze.

Finding a restroom on the hall back to the elevators, he went in, locked himself in a stall, and sat down. It didn't matter that he was sitting on a toilet seat with his slacks on. He just wanted to be alone for a minute. Leaning forward, his elbows were on his knees and his hands together. His chin rested on his hands. A tear rolled down his cheek.

He couldn't believe Peter was gone. So sudden. He wished he'd been able to say goodbye.

A few minutes later, he took a deep breath and tried to compose himself. His phone vibrated in his pocket, but he didn't bother to check it. He washed his face and walked out to take the stairs up to the fourth floor.

Jack unlocked the door to the outer office where his assistant, Barb, worked. He was early as usual and walked past her vacant desk to his office. He opened his office door and went to his desk, where he sat in his leather chair, looking out the fourth floor office window. The bright sunlight reflected off the Caloosahatchee River only a few blocks away, just past the marina where he lived. It looked like another day in Fort Myers except Peter was no longer here.

As the controller at Rivers, Jack ran the accounting department and worked there before the acquisition. Although HealthAmerica had filled the senior management positions with their people, he was just below the radar and had survived the transition. He liked working at the hospital and tried to stay out of the politics. It was a good job and paid well. Plus, he liked living in Fort Myers.

Jack tried to quit thinking about his friend and turned his attention to the computer screen on his desk. Everything was computerized these days; his calendar, his mail, his news, everything. He scrolled through his appointment calendar, reviewing the day's schedule. Mostly meetings, he saw. One of those days. Seems like he spent more time in meetings than anything else.

He checked his email first thing in the morning before getting started on the work day. Fifty-seven new emails. It took longer than usual to get through them. He wasn't sure if email was a blessing or a curse. Most of the time it was a curse.

He scanned them all, responding to most and deleting some, though not enough. He looked at requests for information, notices of meetings, cover-your-ass emails, and other items that Barb had added to his calendar; the usual stuff. He looked at his watch, even though the time was prominently displayed at the top of his screen. Time for the first of many meetings. He grabbed his notebook and budget file and headed toward the small conference room downstairs.

Jack walked into the conference room and saw Richard Melton sitting at the table. Richard was the Director of Pharmacy at Rivers and one of Jack's closest friends. There was an empty seat next to Richard. Jack walked around the table to Richard and sat down. They had become best of friends since coming to work at Rivers almost five years ago.

Jack threw his notebook and file down on the conference table without saying a word.

Richard leaned over to Jack and whispered, "What are we meeting about today? Squeezing more blood out of the proverbial turnip to appease our corporate masters?"

It was no secret that Richard hadn't been happy since the acquisition. He resented what he perceived as the negative corporate influence on health care.

When Jack didn't respond with his usual snappy comeback, Richard knew something was wrong. He looked at Jack, who was staring down at his notebook without looking at it.

"You okay?" Richard asked in a low voice.

Jack shook his head. "No, not really. Peter, my neighbor—he had a heart attack last night. I just went by the ER to check on him, and they told me he didn't make it."

"Jesus, Jack. I'm sorry."

"You have a few minutes after the meeting?"

"Sure. Why don't we grab some lunch and go to my office."

Jack just nodded. "I guess we need to get started here."

He turned to address the large group of department heads gathered around the table. This was the first of the preliminary budget review meetings scheduled this week.

"Okay, everyone. Let's get going. The sooner we start, the sooner we finish." His voice was flat without the usual jocular tone. Several people around the table looked at one another, wondering what was going on.

Jack proceeded to go through the budget revisions, pointing out areas of concern passed down from the corporate office in Atlanta and encouraging everyone to sharpen their pencils. There was a lot of discussion and, of course, the usual moans and groans. Everyone wanted the cuts to come from another department besides theirs. He tried to be impartial, but it was a difficult task on a good day. Today was even tougher. It was a long meeting, but at last they finished the agenda for the session and adjourned.

They went through the cafeteria line and got lunch to go. When they got to the pharmacy door, Richard punched in the code and opened the door, waiting for Jack to enter. Richard shut the door behind Jack and led them back to his small office.

They put the Styrofoam containers on the desk and talked while eating a quick lunch.

"I'm sorry about Peter. Tell me what happened," Richard said.

Jack told him about waking up early this morning, hearing Peter fall in the cockpit of his boat.

"I should've stayed with him in the ER, but I thought he was going to be okay. They said he'd be fine, so I left."

Richard shook his head. "Nothing else you could've done. You gave him CPR, called the ambulance. It was just his time, Jack."

"Yeah, but he'd just been in for a Clearart treatment a month ago. Why did he still have a heart attack? I thought that stuff was a wonder drug?"

"Not unheard of," Richard said, reaching for a chip. "It's not one hundred percent effective. Nothing is. Bad things still happen in this business."

"I know that. But how does it work? I thought it cleaned the plaque out of the arteries so you wouldn't have a heart attack? I know it's expensive as hell, and we make a ton of money off it."

Richard nodded. "Yes, and so does Advanced Cardiac Meds. It's already their top grossing drug, but coronary disease is a hundred billion dollar a year market."

For years, the Holy Grail has been to find a non-invasive but effective treatment. A "magic" bullet like Clearart was worth billions of dollars.

"The heart doctors do well with it, too. I think with the volume of Clearart procedures they're cranking out, they're probably making as much as they were before," Jack said.

The cardiologists and cardiac surgeons hadn't been overly enthusiastic about Clearart, for good reason. They stood to lose substantial revenue with the shift from surgery and invasive procedures, which were immensely profitable to them.

But they were resourceful and quickly figured out they could make up their income with the volume of Clearart procedures. It seemed like everyone with coronary disease was a candidate for Clearart. The lobbyists convinced Medicare and other insurers to cover Clearart for almost every cardiac patient who came through the door.

Clearart, at $25,000 per treatment, still was half the cost of surgery. But it had to be repeated annually, which conveniently resulted in a continuing and growing revenue stream for Advanced Cardiac Meds, the doctors, and the hospitals.

Fort Myers, with its large population of retired people, was the ideal proving ground for such a drug. HealthAmerica, a pioneer in promoting Clearart, had partnered with Advanced Cardiac Meds, claiming it proved the efficacy of the competitive, free-market model. The extensive publicity campaign made no mention of the fact that HealthAmerica had already made hundreds of millions from the drug.

There were two issues with Clearart. The exact dosage was critical and hard to calculate in advance. Elevated doses could cause key enzymes in the patient to rise beyond accepted levels and therefore must be carefully monitored during administration. Plus, the loose chunks of plaque could cause problems. This was why Clearart must be administered intravenously on an inpatient basis, with three consecutive treatments given over twenty-four hours.

Second, Clearart was tricky and expensive to manufacture due to its complexity. As a biopharmaceutical agent, it had to be grown in a laboratory environment, requiring highly technical intervention and monitoring during the manufacturing process.

"So, that's the short course on Clearart. Did it help?" Richard said.

"Yes, it did. Thanks for the primer. Still in shock, I guess." Jack glanced at his watch. 1:03. "I'm late. Got to run. Later."

He grabbed his notebook and left for his next meeting.

After work, Jack walked back to the marina. When he got to his boat, he just stood there, looking over at Peter's boat, Left Behind. A fitting name, he thought. He realized he was hoping against hope to see his friend sitting there in the shade of the bimini top, chewing on a cigar and nursing a tumbler of whiskey. That was the way he usually found Peter when he came home after work. It was hard to believe he would never see Peter again.

He stepped onto Wind Dancer and sat there, facing Peter's boat, thinking back to when they first met. It was late in the afternoon, and Jack had just arrived in Fort Myers after an overnight sail from Key West. He was alone and backing Wind Dancer into the slip. A skinny, barefoot old man with thinning white hair, in shorts and t-shirt, was standing there to help tie him up. Jack eased the boat back toward the dock. Without saying a word, the man leaned over and tied the stern spring line off first, with a casual ease that only comes with experience. Jack shifted the transmission into neutral and went forward to tie off the remaining lines. Coming back to the cockpit, he handed the water hose and electric cord to the man, who plugged them into the utility box on the piling behind Jack's boat.

When he stepped up on the dock, the man reached out to welcome him.

"Peter Stein. I'm your neighbor," he said, pointing to the cream-colored Island Packet moored in the slip next to Jack.

Jack extended his hand. "Jack Davis. Thanks for the help." He nodded toward Peter's boat. "Nice boat."

"Thanks." Peter looked at the Catalina. "Wind Dancer, huh? Tell me you didn't come up with that?"

Jack laughed. "No, I know, not very original. But I bought the boat used, couldn't afford a new one, and I'm superstitious about changing a boat's name."

Peter nodded. "I don't blame you—that's asking for trouble. You're gonna take some shit for that name around here, though. Seems like everybody who comes to Florida and buys a sailboat names it that. Why don't you come over and have a drink. You must be thirsty," Peter said as he walked over to his boat.

Jack hesitated. "I probably need to check in first."

"Don't bother. They've already closed. You can take care of it tomorrow."

Jack shrugged and followed Peter. After a few beers, he ended up eating dinner with Peter, and they stayed up until midnight. Although several generations apart, they became fast friends, and Jack found it easy to talk to him.

A shadow passed over Jack and brought him back to the present. He looked up to see Kevin standing there.

"Mind if I come aboard?" he asked.

Jack nodded and waved him over.

Kevin had two beers in his hand. He stepped aboard, handing one to Jack, and sat opposite him.

"Hard to believe, huh? They told me up at the office. I thought he was doing so well." He held up his bottle. "Here's to Peter." Kevin crossed himself.

Jack reached over and tapped his bottle against Kevin's. "To a good friend."

They sat in the cockpit of Jack's boat drinking their beer, neither man saying a word for several minutes.

When they started talking, it was stories about Peter. Kevin told Jack about meeting Peter for the first time. Kevin had just come up from Naples and had never docked his new boat by himself. He damn near took out the J dock. Kevin was backing into the slip a little too fast, and Peter was standing there screaming at him to reverse the engines.

"Forward," he yelled.

Even after jamming both throttles forward at the last minute, Kevin had bumped the dock pretty hard.

Peter's first words to a shaken Kevin once his boat was secure were, "Damn. That calls for a drink. Come on over, son. We both need one after that."

They were laughing by the time Kevin was done. Jack told Kevin about his first sailing trip with Peter on Left Behind. Although Jack had lots of experience sailing smaller boats, he'd never sailed anything as big as the Island Packet. They were off Fort Myers Beach, in a pretty stiff breeze. Jack was at the helm, and Peter wanted him to jibe, a basic maneuver turning a sailboat with the wind coming from behind. Jack, being nervous and wanting to impress his friend, turned the boat a little too quickly, grazing a quick-thinking Peter in the head with the boom, knocking his hat into the water and damn near Peter as well. Peter took the helm and turned the big boat around while Jack managed to snag the hat with a boat hook.

Peter took the dripping hat, wrung it out, put it back on his head, and told Jack to take the helm.

"You sure?" Jack said.

"Hell, son. If you never made a mistake, then you're not reaching high enough. Besides, it was as much my fault. You did exactly what I told you; I just didn't think you'd move that fast."

Kevin and Jack both had tears in their eyes from laughing so hard. Finishing his beer, Kevin stood and said he had a dinner meeting to attend. Jack thanked him for the beer and told him he'd see him later. Kevin, still chuckling, stepped off the boat onto the dock and walked toward the marina office.

Jack sat there for a while even after he finished his beer, smiling as he thought of other sailing trips with Peter. He'd learned a lot from the salty old sailor. As far as Jack knew, he was the only one Peter ever let sail Left Behind. He once told Jack that he could tell that he, too, had the heart of a sailor.

As night approached, he got up to go below and change. He swapped his shirt and slacks for a t-shirt and shorts. Wanting a little music with dinner, he hit the shuffle button for Jimmy Buffett. When he heard the opening harmonica for "A Pirate Looks at Forty," Jack couldn't help but laugh, thinking how appropriate for Peter.

He looked in the small refrigerator, took out a cold Tecate and container of guacamole. Finding a bag of tortilla chips in the galley cabinet, Jack went back up topside with his meal. Seated at the cockpit table with Buffett playing in the background, he tipped his bottle toward Peter's boat.

He kept thinking about Clearart and his conversation with Richard. When he finished eating, he went down below, got his laptop, and went to the Advanced Cardiac Meds website.

The company was founded nine years ago by Michael Taylor, PhD, and backed by a private venture capital firm. With the FDA approval of Clearart two years ago, the company had gone public, and their stock had gone through the roof.

He went to the Executive Management section and scanned the typical cast of characters. Chief Financial Officer, Chief Legal Counsel—the usual lineup. He clicked on the Board section and looked at the list. Michael Taylor, as CEO, was listed along with an MD, an attorney, two industry titans whose names Jack thought he recognized, and . . . Victor L. Chaney, CEO of HealthAmerica.

Not too surprising, Jack thought, but he was curious about the connection. He scrolled through several more pages and saw a reference to a new plant in Cuernavaca, Mexico. It was a state-of-the-art plant that promised significantly lower costs and improved production times due to innovative new techniques, according to the blurb.

He decided to skip the Investor section, preferring to go directly to EDGAR, the system maintained by the Securities and Exchange Commission. All publicly-held companies were required to file numerous detailed reports with the SEC and EDGAR was the easiest way to access those.

Most people didn't bother to wade through the reams of detailed financial information contained in many of those reports. They were the realm of the accountants and serious investors. Like Jack, they realized that an incredible amount of information could be gleaned from them, if they knew what they were looking at.

He discovered that Chaney had been on the Board since the beginning and owned a modest number of shares. When he looked at the ownership, he saw that SA Ventures, Ltd. was listed as the biggest owner of ACM stock. Michael Taylor was the ACM executive who owned the most, not a surprise.

He wondered who SA Ventures was, but it was getting late and he was tired. It would have to wait for another day.

THREE

Cuernavaca, Mexico

Manny Garcia ran his hand through his long brown hair and scratched his beard. For the third day in a row, he'd been working for sixteen hours straight and was exhausted. Production was on schedule, and he was sitting at a computer screen staring at a 3D diagram of the Clearart molecule from the latest run. It was hard to believe that the position of one carbon atom could make a difference, but that seemed to be the case.

As the Senior Director, Staff Scientist for Antibody Engineering at Advanced Cardiac Meds, he was the perfect candidate for this job. After getting his PhD in Molecular Genetics and Microbiology from Duke University, he joined a small Silicon Valley biotech firm that had developed a revolutionary cardiac treatment drug called Clearart. His job was to guide the evolution from the research lab to production, not an easy task.

He succeeded, but the biggest investor was pushing to reduce the time for production and cut costs. So Manny had developed a method to "grow" Clearart using E.coli instead of the more expensive CHO, a cell line derived from a

Chinese hamster ovary. Since E.coli couldn't be used to grow more complex molecules, he had to tweak the Clearart protein, hence moving the position of one atom. It had worked, and the new plant was producing Clearart much faster and cheaper than the plant in California. MexC, as he dubbed the Mexican version, was a success. However, in looking at the patient data collected on initial users, the effectiveness seemed to be absent.

He and his lab tried to figure out a way to grow the original, which he referred to as CalC, with the E.coli. This was his last attempt, and it was a disaster. It was a classic case of he couldn't have it both ways. There was no choice but to revamp the facility to grow Clearart using CHO, a move that would take months and cost tens of millions of dollars.

He was flying back to California tonight to present his findings to senior management in the morning. It wasn't going to be a pleasant meeting.

The next morning, there were low clouds and fog in the San Francisco Bay area. Typical for this time of year, the temperature was around sixty. It was seven o'clock, and Manny was driving to ACM's campus in Mountain View.

Since it been just him last night, he flew back on ACM's small Gulfstream for the less than three hour flight. He had managed to sleep most of the way, exhausted from his failed efforts.

Bypassing the building that contained his lab, he drove to the building in the center of the campus that contained the administrative offices. The meeting was in one of the small conference rooms next to the CEO's office.

When he got off the elevator, he stopped in the restroom to check his appearance. Though ACM was casual, he wanted to make sure he hadn't missed anything crucial while dressing in his sleep-deprived state this morning. He had no idea who was going to be at the meeting, but knew it would be a small group. Satisfied that his shirt was buttoned and his fly zipped, he walked out and down the hall to the conference room.

He stepped in and Michael Taylor, the CEO, was seated at the head of the table. Next to him was a short, stocky man in a dark blue suit. He had silver hair and looked like someone Manny should know but couldn't place. No one else was in the room.

Taylor stood up to greet him. "Good morning, Manny." He extended his open hand toward the other man, still seated. "This is Vic Chaney. He's the CEO of HealthAmerica and on our board."

The short man sized him up and stood to shake his hand. Although Manny was six feet tall, Chaney was a good foot shorter. His handshake was firm and his eyes penetrating. "How was your flight?" he asked.

"Fine," Manny said. "I managed to grab a couple of hours sleep, so maybe I'll be coherent."

Chaney nodded and sat down. Manny took a seat on the other side of Taylor and put his file on the table. He knew the contents by heart, so didn't bother to open it. Last night on the plane, he'd emailed his PowerPoint presentation to Taylor's assistant to load on the conference room projector. He reached for the remote on the table and queued the first slide.

Manny wanted to start by showing the physical difference between MexC and CalC, to validate that there was a real distinction between the two molecules. He moved quickly, knowing that at this level, his audience had a limited attention span.

The next couple of slides highlighted the difference between the cultures used to grow Clearart. Then he put up the final slide. It compared the reported results for the two versions. Visually, the difference was stunning. The quiet in the room was palpable.

Chaney spoke first. "The only place we've shipped the Mexican stuff to is HealthAmerica, right?"

Manny nodded. "That's correct."

Taylor was watching Chaney, trying to gauge his direction.

Chaney continued. "So the new stuff isn't causing any harm; it's just not quite as effective?"

Manny shook his head. "If you're asking is it causing any further damage, then the answer is no. But MexC has no therapeutic value—it's not fixing anything."

Taylor sat back and clasped his hands together on his lap. "Isn't it possible that we don't have sufficient data yet? Maybe there are some QC issues in the new plant playing a part?" He looked at Chaney for a reaction.

Manny couldn't believe where this was headed. He'd been fully prepared to get chewed out for failing with MexC. But in his mind, the only option was to go back to the original production process. It never occurred to him that they would consider any other course.

Chaney ignored Manny and looked at Taylor, pointing his finger. "Mike, we've been friends for a long time. We've both invested substantial money in this. We have no choice but to make this Mexican plant work, *as-is*." The emphasis was on the last phrase and the message was clear. There would be no turning back.

Manny opened his mouth to object, but Taylor held his hand up. "Manny, I appreciate your efforts this week. I know you're exhausted. Why don't you go home and get some rest? Come back and see me in the morning and we'll chat."

He was furious. Manny grabbed his file and stormed out of the room without saying another word.

Vic looked over at Mike. "Is he going to be a problem? We can't afford to let this get out. You realize what it would do to the stock?"

"Manny's good. He's a company guy. I'll talk with him after he cools down. He'll be okay."

Chaney was agitated and rocking in his chair. "I don't know. Maybe we should get our friend to watch him for a while. I don't want to take any chances."

Mike thought about it and said, "Probably not a bad idea. I'll make the call. But we're fine. Hey, you heard Manny—it's not like the MexC is harmful. Probably just need to give it more time."

"You better give it plenty of time, make sure we keep a lid on it. We've got a lot riding on this, Mike. The new plant has got to work. Clearart tanks and we're fucked."

Squealing the tires on his Porsche, Manny Garcia drove the short distance to his office. Screw Michael Taylor and Vic Chaney. He had work to do, and he'd be damned if he was going home to "get some rest." Besides, he was so angry he couldn't sleep anyway.

Later that morning, he looked up and was surprised to see Michael Taylor standing in his doorway.

"I knew you wouldn't go home. Let's go for a walk, shall we?" Taylor said.

Manny studied him for a minute before getting up from his desk. This was Taylor's way of making amends. In the years that Manny had worked for him, Taylor always suggested going for a walk when he wanted to apologize and dial back the emotion.

They strolled through the small park next to the building, part of the ACM campus.

"I'm sorry for dismissing you like that this morning. Vic can be an obnoxious ass, and I didn't want the two of you getting into a knife fight that early."

Manny was still seething, but not about the dismissal. "So we're going to change the Cuernavaca plant to CHO, right?"

When Taylor hesitated, Manny had a sick feeling in his gut.

"It's not that simple, Manny." They walked a few more steps. "How much ACM stock do you have?"

Manny had to think. He wasn't sure, but he rounded it off in his head. "Two-hundred thousand shares, something like that."

"Stock closed at eighty-four yesterday." Taylor let that sink in. He waved his hand toward the buildings on the campus. "We have almost five thousand employees at ACM. Every single one of them has their entire 401(k) invested in ACM stock."

They walked another ten yards before Taylor spoke again.

"Things are never black and white, Manny. You did what you could. I was thinking it's time to move you and your lab to the Indus project. It's coming out of R&D and the production process is critical. Turn Clearart over to

Kim. She's not a developer like you; she's more of a mind-the-store type. Let her deal with Clearart."

Manny stopped walking and stood there, looking at his boss and mentor. He was trapped and he knew it. Resigned, he hung his head and nodded.

FOUR

The next day after work, Jack was meeting Richard and Molly at Ray's. Ray's On the River was a popular restaurant and watering hole in downtown Fort Myers. It was located on the Caloosahatchee River a few blocks south of the marina where Jack lived. The large tiki deck overlooking the river was a huge drawing card, and they had live music every weekend. It also offered some incredible sunset views. The food was good, nothing spectacular, but the beer was cold and the service friendly. Best of all, it was within walking distance for all three.

Jack was first to arrive. He saw Alex behind the bar and waved as he walked by the hostess stand and out to their usual table next to the water. She had long dark hair and a dark complexion. Tall and thin, Alex had been there since the trio first came to town. She and her husband had owned the place, having bought it from Ray some years ago when he retired. Four years ago, her husband died unexpectedly and left the place to her. Owning it free and clear, Alex decided to kept the place open and run it herself. Although she was the owner, she still managed the place and worked like a dog. When things were slow, as they were now, she always took care of their table. But at the moment she was behind the bar taking another order.

Jack went over to a table next to the water and pulled out a chair. He sat facing the river and turned slightly so he would be able to see the other two arrive. A few minutes later, Alex walked up.

"Hey, hon," she said, as she set down the frosty mug of Tecate. "Sorry to hear about Peter."

News traveled fast along the river. Occasionally, Jack had persuaded Peter to come with him down to Ray's for a burger.

"Thanks, Alex. He was a good friend." Jack changed the subject. "So, how's my favorite bartender?"

"Not bad. Same old crap. The snowbird crowds are starting to thin out. Where're your partners in crime?"

"On their way. You know us. We never arrive at the same time."

Alex laughed. "Well, at least you all leave together. I'll check back when they get here."

"Thanks," Jack said.

It had been a busy day. The beer was cold and tasted good after work, sitting outside on the water. It was a pleasant afternoon. Late spring was a nice time of year in Fort Myers. He watched a few boats going up and down the river and soon forgot about watching the entrance to the restaurant.

Two arms wrapped around him from behind. A soft, fragrant cheek was next to his. He saw long red hair near his face and reached up to put his hands on the freckled arms. It was always nice to be hugged by Molly.

Molly Byrne was a petite redhead with piercing green eyes and a fiery personality to match. She was a nurse manager in the Cardiac Care Unit on Five South at Rivers Hospital. Five South was a separate CCU set up to handle Clearart procedures and nothing else. Administration had determined that the volume was sufficient to justify such a move and was piloting the concept for HealthAmerica.

"I'm so sorry about Peter. Why didn't you call me? You okay?" she said. She sat on his left, facing the water.

Jack shrugged. "I'm fine. I just wanted to be by myself last night. Besides, I knew I'd see you this afternoon."

He watched her as she processed his answer. Her green eyes sparkled in the remaining sun, and he noticed a few freckles on her face. She was wearing a green halter top and white shorts, which meant she had changed before coming over. Easy enough. Her condo, Palm View, was right next door to Ray's. Satisfied that he was okay, she nodded.

Jack wanted to lighten the mood a bit. "You look beachy tonight. Or is that bitchy?" Jack laughed.

Smiling, she looked at him and flipped him a finger. "After my day, I don't need your crap."

"Whoa! Aren't we on edge? Rough day, huh?" Jack said.

Before she could say anything, Alex walked up with another mug, this one containing a cold Sam Adams. A holdover from Molly's Boston life, Jack figured.

"Once again, I see you're not choosy about who you drink with." Alex laughed as she set the beer down in front of Molly.

"Yeah, I know. I haven't had much luck with men. Obviously. Thanks, Alex."

Molly smiled as she lifted the beer.

"The way you two gig each other reminds me of my younger brother. And I thought we were bad." Alex shook her head and walked off.

Molly started telling Jack about her day. By the time they had finished the first beer, Richard walked up.

"Well, I see my two friends waited for me. That was thoughtful."

They turned and looked at the trim blond guy joining them. As usual, Richard had on his trademark golf shirt, neatly tucked inside his pressed khaki shorts. Completing the picture were spotless deck shoes.

Molly couldn't resist. "Damn, Richard. You look like an ad out of *GQ* magazine or something. Do you ever look like a slob?" She shook her head as Richard sat down.

Jack had to laugh. "She's right, you know. Just once, I'd like to see you in a t-shirt and ratty shorts wearing flip-flops. You probably don't even own a pair, do you?" Jack looked down at Richard's shoes. "Do you put on a new pair every day? I swear those have never been worn before."

"What on earth did you two talk about before I got here?" Richard asked, ignoring their questions. "The latest wrestling match? Who got booted off the island? I'm sure it was something intelligent like that," Richard said with mock disgust.

"No, we waited for you before we got into such lofty subjects, knowing you'd want to contribute." Molly taunted him. "We wanted to know what you thought about Traci getting kicked off the island."

Molly and Jack looked at each other and laughed. Richard just shook his head. He started to say something when Alex appeared with a cold Budweiser, his beer of choice. Neither Molly nor Jack could figure that one out. When it came to beer, they figured Richard would drink some exotic foreign brew or a trendy microbrew, but plain old "Bubba" beer, they would have never guessed. Yet, that's the only beer they ever saw Richard drink. Unless, of course, there was nothing else available.

Alex set the frosted mug of beer down in front of Richard and put her hand on his shoulder. "I see the civilized one has arrived. Thank goodness. These two need a referee."

Both Molly and Jack noticed that Richard put his hand on top of Alex's and gave it a squeeze. She left her hand on his shoulder and smiled.

"Thank you, my dear. You provide a breath of fresh air and make it tolerable to suffer these two," Richard said.

"Come over and join me at the bar if the burden becomes too great," Alex said, laughing. "I'll check on you later." She patted Richard's shoulder, turned, and walked back to the bar.

Molly saw Richard watching Alex. "You should ask Alex out. The two of you would make a good couple."

Richard was the only one of the three who had never been married.

Before Richard could say anything, Jack said, "Hey, what about me?"

"Not your type," she answered without taking her eyes off Richard, waiting for his response.

"Maybe I will," Richard said, surprising both of them.

Before they could grill him, he changed the subject and looked at Jack. "You doing okay?"

"I suppose. We're doing what Peter would have wanted." Jack held up his mug, and the other two touched their mugs to his. "He had a full life, and he wouldn't have wanted anybody to feel sad. He always told me he wanted an old fashioned Irish wake, even though he was as Jewish as they come."

They all chuckled and launched into a review of their work day. They had the ease seen in close friends, sometimes completing one another's sentences. They were close-knit, the only family any of them had anywhere near Fort Myers.

Richard looked at Jack. "Our discussion yesterday made me curious. So, I checked into some of the Clearart usage data. I found some interesting things that prompted a few questions. Yesterday I sent Steve Ingram, the Advanced Cardiac Meds rep, an email asking him to check into it. I'll let you know what he says."

"Now what are you two discussing about Clearart?" Molly asked.

"Nothing really," Jack said. "Peter had the Clearart treatment, and I was just wondering about it. So I sat down with the chemist here and got a quick education on it."

"That's right, I had forgotten. Peter was in, what, four or five weeks ago?" Molly said.

Jack nodded. "I guess I put too much faith in it. I figured he'd be fine after that."

Molly turned to Richard. "So what did you find out?"

"I haven't finished my analysis yet, so I'm not sure. But based on what I've seen so far, there may be an issue with the Clearart coming from their new plant in Mexico. So I asked Steve to check into it," Richard said.

"Which one did Peter have?" Jack asked.

Richard looked at Molly, and they both turned their hands up. "Good question," Richard said.

"I'll look it up," she said.

After the round they ordered dinner, which tonight consisted of typical pub food, wings and fries. They talked about current events, Florida politics, which was always interesting, and work.

As they finished eating, Richard said he needed to start winding down. He had a six o'clock in the morning, so he was calling it an early night. Jack turned around to catch Alex's eye at the bar and held up three fingers. Alex nodded and within a few minutes brought three beers to the table.

"Alex, would you close us out for tonight? Pops over there has an early meeting and needs to get his beauty sleep," Jack said.

Molly and Alex both laughed as they all gave Richard a pitiful look. The three friends were such regulars they kept a standing tab. Once a month, Alex would bring them the previous month's tab. They took turns settling up, figuring it would average out over the long run. It was easier that way, and they always left Alex a generous tip which she put in the tip jar for the employees to split.

They finished their last beer of the evening and stood to leave. Saying goodnight to Alex at the bar as they passed, they walked out to the parking lot.

"Still on for boating Saturday?" Molly asked.

"Of course," Richard said. "The weather should be perfect. We can meet over at my house, say around ten?"

Molly and Jack both answered "sure" at the same time. Richard owned a house on a canal a few blocks away. It was one block from the river, and he had a nice power boat tied to the dock behind his house. Though they occasionally took Jack's sailboat out, most of the time it was easier to meet at Richard's house and take his boat.

Molly's condo was on the right, next door. Richard's house was farther down off McGregor, and the city marina was four blocks the other direction. Since it was on his way,

Richard usually walked Molly back to the entrance of her condo when the three of them got together at Ray's.

They stopped in the parking lot. Jack put his arm around Molly's shoulders, and she gave him a hug.

"Sweet dreams. See you Saturday," she said.

"You, too," Jack replied. "Watch out for Pops there."

They all laughed. Although both of the guys had been up to Molly's condo many times, there had never been anything between them. Jack had even spent the night there on a couple of occasions after an especially long night, but slept on the sofa. Molly had left an abusive husband, her second, behind in Boston. Once that divorce was final, she swore off any serious involvement with men.

Molly turned to walk the short distance to her place with Richard by her side.

"Later," Richard said to Jack as they walked off.

Jack turned and headed toward the marina. It was a nice walk along the river with a gentle breeze blowing off the water. The lights on the water were always pleasing to watch. He didn't see another person on the short walk home. The gate was locked when he got to the marina dock. He punched in the code, opened the gate, and walked out to his slip. When he got there, he took off his socks and shoes. The boat rocked slightly as he stepped onto the side. He stepped down into the cockpit and keyed the padlock securing the companionway hatch.

As he unlocked the cabin door, he noticed a business card stuck in the crack between the door and the frame. He pulled it out and held it up in the light. J. Walter Dobbs, Esquire. The name of the firm, Dobbs, Hatch, Walters and Banks was listed below with a local phone number. Puzzled, Jack turned the card over. In a neat, uniform handwriting was a note saying "Please call me at your earliest convenience." The barely legible signature of J. Walter Dobbs was scribbled below.

Jack took the card with him down below and put it on the counter next to the sink. He wondered what that was about, but knew there would be no answer tonight. He was certain that J. Walter Dobbs was safely ensconced in his stately riverfront home by now. At least, if I was a J. Walter, Esquire, I would have a riverfront home, Jack thought. On the far bulkhead, a light was still on, casting dim shadows around the cozy cabin. He put his shoes underneath the small galley table and closed the companionway. Taking his clothes off, he collapsed on the V-berth up front. He fell asleep thinking about Molly.

FIVE

Thursday afternoon, Jack was still in his office at three thirty. He had a four o'clock meeting with J. Walter Dobbs and realized he needed to get moving. He walked out of his office and stood at Barb's desk.

"Hey, I've got a meeting this afternoon outside the hospital. Do you know anything about this firm and where they're located?" He handed her the card that he found on his boat.

Barb grew up in Fort Myers and knew everybody in town and everybody's business. She was Jack's personal guidebook to Fort Myers as well as his assistant. Whenever he needed local knowledge, Barb was the one he asked.

She took it out of his hand. Reading the card, she whistled. "Wow. I'm impressed. What did you do?" She handed the card back to Jack.

"What do you mean?"

"I mean, that's the biggest, baddest law firm in Southwest Florida. And Walter Dobbs is the biggest and baddest of the group. You're talking serious old money there."

"Really? Well, I have an appointment with Mr. Dobbs in thirty minutes. Where are they located?"

She didn't have to look up the address. "Dobbs, Hatch, Walters and Banks is located in the Southwest Florida Bank Building. Their reception desk is on the twelfth floor, although they own the building and occupy most of it."

Jack knew the building. It was the tallest in downtown Fort Myers and only a few blocks away.

"I guess I should be going. I certainly don't want to keep J. Walter Dobbs waiting."

"Whatever it is, it must be big. Call me when you get out and let me know."

After walking the two blocks, Jack entered the building and took the elevator to the twelfth floor. The elevator doors opened onto the main lobby for the law firm. Nice, he thought, as he stepped onto the dark green carpet and walked over to the mahogany reception desk where an attractive brunette asked if she could help him. The name of the firm was spelled out in brass letters on the paneled wall behind her. Jack said he had an appointment with J. Walter Dobbs. She asked his name and politely asked him to have a seat, saying she would let Mr. Dobbs's assistant know he was waiting.

He sat on the dark leather couch facing its twin across the waiting area. There was a couple waiting on the other couch and an elderly gentleman sitting in one of the wingback chairs. In a few minutes, another brunette arrived. She was model thin and wore a short but tasteful dark blue dress. Jack wondered where they got these people. Must be a store somewhere. She walked directly over to Jack. The receptionist must have given her a description of who to look for.

"Mr. Davis?" She held out a small slender hand. "I'm Amy, Mr. Dobbs's assistant."

Jack stood and shook her hand. It was cool to the touch.

"Please follow me," she said as she turned and walked toward the elevators.

He followed Amy into the waiting elevator, where they got in and went up two floors to the top floor. When they got off, she led him around the corridor to the river side of the building and walked into a corner office the size of Jack's boat. Make that twice the size of his boat, he thought.

Both outside walls were glass from floor to ceiling. The floor was a deep blue carpet. A small mahogany conference table with chairs for six sat in front of one window.

In front of the other window, facing the door, was a matching aircraft carrier-sized desk with only two chairs in front of it. The relatively sparse furnishings combined with two glass walls in an office this big made it appear even larger. A distinguished gentleman in a dark gray suit, white shirt, and red tie rose from behind the massive desk.

"Mr. Davis. Thanks for coming by on such short notice. Please, have a seat."

Jack sat and noticed that Amy had floated out of the room and closed the door.

"I want to express my condolences on the loss of our mutual friend, Peter Stein. It was quite a shock. I know he thought highly of you. Trust me, coming from Peter Stein, that was quite a compliment. Anyway, I know you're a busy man, so I'll get right to the point."

Jack wondered if he was just reading his usual script or being slightly condescending.

"I was a close friend of Mr. Stein, and have been for over forty years. I was also his attorney for most of that time. He appointed me executor of his estate, and I'm discharging those duties in accordance with Mr. Stein's last will and testament. Peter had no living relatives, at least not that I'm aware of. But he had specific bequests relating to you, which is why I asked to meet with you."

Jack started to interrupt, but decided to let the attorney continue. Dobbs looked at the file in front of him and read.

"The first item relates to final arrangements for Mr. Stein. He's stipulated that his body be cremated and his ashes scattered over the open water out of sight of land. He further asks that you be in charge of doing that at your convenience. He's provided for any costs related to this."

Dobbs took his glasses off and set them on his desk. He stared at Jack. "Is this acceptable to you, and are you willing to perform these duties?"

"Sure. He never spoke to me about any of this, but of course I'd be willing to carry out his last wishes."

"Very well. City of Palms Crematorium will have the ashes for you by Friday. I'll authorize them to be released to you."

He put his glasses back on and moved to the next page in his file. "The second item relates to Mr. Stein's boat, *Left Behind*, an Island Packet 370. Mr. Stein had sole ownership of the boat, and there are no liens outstanding against it. He's directed that the boat with all of its furnishings and equipment be assigned to you. Any taxes and fees required with such transfer shall be paid out of his estate."

Jack took a deep breath. An Island Packet 370 was easily worth over two hundred thousand dollars, four times what Jack's boat was worth. He'd lusted after such a boat long before he came to Fort Myers. It was what he called his lottery boat. If he ever won the lottery, that boat would be at the top of his shopping list.

"Excuse me, Mr. Dobbs. I don't understand. This is all news to me. Why would he leave his boat to me?"

Dobbs removed his glasses again and stroked his chin. "Mr. Davis. May I speak off the record here?" It was more of a statement than a request.

"I knew Peter a long time. He was perhaps my closest friend. He was a principled, some would say stubborn, man. Although he knew a lot of people around the world, he'd be the first to tell you that he had few friends. I can't go in to more detail, but suffice it to say that he'd been betrayed by many people over the years. As a result, he was guarded and trusted only a handful of people. So when I tell you that he spoke well of you and considered you his friend, well, that puts you in a small and select group.

"I asked him that very question when he came in here and changed his will several years ago. He told me that he liked you, and he knew you'd take good care of her, referring to his boat. That was enough for him and enough for me. Peter wasn't the kind of man who thought much of having his decisions second guessed."

Jack felt he'd been too harsh in his assessment of J. Walter Dobbs. Clearly the man was upset and cared deeply about Peter. Jack just nodded and didn't say anything else, watching as Dobbs struggled to control his emotions.

Dobbs put his glasses back on and returned to the file in front of him. "Item three. Slip twenty-five, J dock, at the Fort Myers Yacht Basin, where Left Behind is moored, is owned by Mr. Stein. He has stipulated—"

"Wait a minute. I thought the City of Fort Myers owned and operated the marina? How could Peter own his slip?"

"They do and he does, or did, rather. Before the city bought the marina, the previous owner was Peter Stein. He retained ownership of his slip in perpetuity as a condition of the sale. Shall I continue?"

Jack just nodded. There was a lot about Peter Stein that he didn't know.

"Mr. Stein has directed that free and clear title to slip number twenty-five, J dock, at the City of Fort Myers Yacht Basin be assigned to you. Again, any taxes and fees associated with such transfer will be paid out of his estate."

Dobbs closed the file and removed his glasses once again. "So, Mr. Davis. Assuming you agree, we'll need you to sign a few papers. If you have no further questions, I'll ask Amy to come back in with the paperwork and finalize this."

Jack just sat there stunned. "Of course. Forgive me, but I'm in shock."

J. Walter Dobbs laughed for the first time. "That's obvious. Don't try to figure it out, Jack. Just enjoy. It's what Peter wanted." He picked up the phone and buzzed Amy, asking her to bring the papers in.

A few seconds later, Amy glided back into the office with a stack of papers for Jack to sign. When he finished signing everything, Dobbs stood and extended his hand to Jack. With his other hand he handed a file to Jack.

"Congratulations, Mr. Davis. You're now the proud owner of a beautiful Island Packet sailboat and a slip in Fort Myers. We'll process the paperwork as soon as possible. In the meantime, if you should require proof of ownership, you have the necessary documents in this folder along with the keys. My card is in there with my personal cell phone number. If you need anything, please feel free to give me a call."

"Thank you, sir." Jack thought for a moment. "There is one more thing. I'd like for you to be there when we take his ashes out to sea."

Dobbs smiled. "I'd like that very much. Thank you. Just give me a call when you plan on doing it. I'll be there." He shook Jack's hand.

Amy escorted him back to the elevator and bade him a good afternoon.

Jack put on his sunglasses and walked back to the marina. It was all he could do not to skip. Barb was right; it was big. It was huge. He pulled his phone out of his pocket and called Richard. He didn't answer, so Jack left him a message telling him to meet at Ray's after work.

He called Molly's number, and she answered.

"Hey, what's up?"

"Meet me at Ray's after work."

"Oh, no hello or how are you or how is your day going? Just 'meet me at Ray's'? You sure know how to charm a girl."

"Well, wait till you hear what I have to tell you." He knew she wouldn't be able to stand it.

"What? Tell me."

"Nope. See you later." Jack smiled as he pressed End before she could respond. He knew this would drive her crazy, not knowing what was going on.

He was almost back to the marina when his phone rang. Pulling it out of his pocket, he guessed it was Molly calling him back to harass him. It was Barb.

"Hello, Barb. What is it?"

"You know damn well what it is! You deliberately waited for me to me call, didn't you?"

Jack laughed out loud as he could picture Barb tapping her foot as she was holding the phone. "No, I just got out of his office. And I was just about to call you."

"Right. Okay, then, talk."

"Well, Peter, my neighbor at the marina?"

"Yes, the one who had a heart attack Monday night, God rest his soul." She waited for Jack to continue.

"J. Walter Dobbs was his attorney and personal friend." Jack was deliberately dragging it out as much as possible.

"I'm impressed. He had friends in high places. But so what? Come on, Jack, you're baiting me. Get to it."

Jack couldn't help but laugh again. "Peter had a nice sailboat, an Island Packet 370. Mine is a Volkswagen. His is a Mercedes."

Barb shrieked, "He left it to you, didn't he? I knew it, I knew it."

"Yes, he did. And there's more," Jack teased her.

"Damn you, Jack Davis. If you don't tell me everything, and I mean everything, within sixty seconds, I'm coming down to your boat and I will embarrass you, I promise."

Jack was laughing so hard he had to stop walking. He knew Barb would make good on her promise. "Okay, okay. He left me his boat and the slip. He owned the slip at the marina. That's all of it, I swear."

"That's right, I had forgotten," Barb said. "He owned the marina before the city bought it. So he kept a slip?"

"Yes, that was part of his deal with the city. So you're now talking to the proud owner of an Island Packet 370 docked in its very own slip at the yacht basin."

"Wow. See, I told you it was big. That group doesn't handle little stuff. Well, congratulations! I'll see you in the morning, assuming you come down off your cloud by then."

"Thanks, Barb. See you in the morning." Jack ended the call and put the phone back into his pocket.

He decided to go by his boat and change before walking over to Ray's. On the narrow dock between the two boats, he paused. Left Behind was a beautiful boat, he thought, as he stood there next to the Island Packet, cream-colored hull with dark green bimini and sail covers. With all roller furling sails, she would be easy to handle. Whereas Wind Dancer had mostly fiberglass and stainless steel, Left Behind had lots of teak and brass. More maintenance, he thought. She was a boat that, before today, he could have only dreamed of owning. He silently thanked Peter and promised that he would take good care of her.

Turning around, he boarded Wind Dancer and went below. While he was changing, he felt guilty, like he was sneaking around on his faithful companion. Standing in the cabin, he looked around the place that had been his home for the last five years. She had served him well.

"I promise I'll find you a good home. I can afford to be choosy. Your new owner will treat you right and make you part of their family. But you'll always be part of me." Jack said the words out loud and it didn't seem strange.

He walked down to Ray's and out to the usual table out by the river. Neither Richard nor Molly was there. Alex saw him as he was sitting down and she waved. What a crazy week, he thought.

"Hi, hon," Alex said as she set the beer down on the table. "How are you?"

"Not sure. It's been one crazy week." He didn't want to tell Alex the news before Richard and Molly. "How's business?"

"Good. We had a great season. Things will slow down a little, but that's expected. How are things at Rivers?"

"About the same. Full during season, but starting to taper off."

"I'll be back when your buddies get here." She didn't even ask if they were coming. On the rare occasion when Jack did come here by himself, he always sat at the bar. Otherwise, it was this table or the next by the water.

A few minutes later he saw Richard coming toward the table. He pulled out a chair and sat facing the water.

"Sorry I missed your call. I was doing a performance review with one of my pharmacists. Of course, I'll never complain about having a cold beverage after work. What's on your mind?"

"You won't believe it. But let's wait for Molly. I don't want to repeat myself and, besides, she'll be pissed if I tell you first."

Richard nodded and laughed. She did have a temper, and neither wanted to give her an excuse. "No problem. I can wait. While we're waiting, I got a response back from Steve this afternoon."

Jack shook his head, not understanding.

"Steve Ingram, the Advanced Cardiac Meds rep? Remember, I sent him some data on Clearart usage? He took it to his boss, who kicked it up to corporate in California. They came back and told him there was nothing to it. They said the data was incorrect."

"So what happened? How did you get the wrong data?" Jack was surprised. He knew Richard was thorough and seldom made those kinds of mistakes.

"That's just it, Jack. I went back and checked my data. There's nothing wrong with it. Everything I sent them was right. So I dug a little deeper. I'm even more convinced they have a problem. Something doesn't make sense."

"What are you going to do?" Jack knew that once Richard latched on to something he wouldn't turn it loose.

"I told Steve I wanted to talk with someone from their quality group. So he set up a conference call for the first of next week."

"Probably a misunderstanding," Jack said. "Clearart is their cash cow. They can't afford any problems with it. I'm sure they have their best people on it."

"We'll see."

Molly walked up and, after giving each of them a hug, sat at the table. She looked directly at Jack. "Okay, Mr. Tease. What's so damn important?"

"Wow. And you busted my chops for skipping the small talk on the phone. Good afternoon to you, too."

She flipped him a finger just as Alex brought their drinks.

"Well, I see you two are at it again with the sign language. You know, if I didn't know better, I'd say you're siblings or lovers."

Molly and Jack blushed.

Richard laughed. "Alex, that's one of the things I love about you. You get right to the point. And you're so on target with that observation."

Molly responded by giving him the finger as well. Jack just sat there. He wasn't giving any of them ammunition.

Alex was still standing next to Richard as he lifted his beer and turned to Jack. "So what are we toasting tonight?"

Jack paused for effect and lifted his mug. "How about a toast to the proud owner of a new sailboat?"

Molly almost spit her beer out. "What? You bought a new sailboat? Where did this come from? You never mentioned getting a new one. Did you get a raise?"

Richard looked at Jack. "This is news. Like Molly, I didn't realize you were in the market."

"That's great, Jack," Alex said.

Jack was enjoying this. He decided to string it out a little longer and didn't say anything.

"Well, what did you get? Tell us about it." Molly had calmed down.

"It's an Island Packet 370, fully loaded with every available option." Jack took a swallow of beer as he watched his friends' reaction.

Richard knew enough about sailboats to be suspicious. "An Island Packet 370? That's a nice boat. Not to insult you, but definitely a few rungs up the ladder from your current home. Did you win the lottery?"

Molly looked at Richard, then Jack. Jack was doing his best to conceal a smirk, but Molly caught it. "Okay. I know I'm the least knowledgeable one about boats, but something's going on." She reached over and pinched Jack's bare leg.

"Ow! What'd you do that for?"

"There's more where that came from if you don't come clean. Now!"

Jack smiled and leaned forward, able to contain himself no longer. "The short version is that Peter left me his boat. And the slip."

This time it was Richard who almost choked on his beer. "He left you his boat? As in bequeathed it to you? *You?*"

Molly shook her head. "I can't believe it. You're telling me that Peter willed you his boat? But where's the slip?"

"At the yacht basin. Peter owned the marina years ago and sold it to the city. Part of the deal was that he retained ownership of his slip. So I have a beautiful Island Packet with a slip. End of story."

Jack was grinning from ear to ear.

"That's terrific news," Alex said. "Congratulations. The next round's on the house."

"No offense, my friend, but why you?" Richard said.

"His lawyer said he liked me and thought I'd take good care of his boat. See, sailboat people have a special relationship with their boats—"

"You're so full of shit," Molly said, shaking her head. "But I'm happy for you. And Peter was right. You will take care of it. You always wanted an Island Packet."

"Her. Boats are always referred to as feminine. Never thought I would own one, though."

"A female or a boat?" Richard asked, laughing.

Molly slapped his arm. "Enough from you pigs." She looked at Alex. "See what I have to put up with?"

"I think this calls for a round of shots, don't you, Alex?" said Richard.

"Absolutely, to celebrate Jack's new home. I'll be right back."

A few minutes later Alex returned with shots for everyone. She passed out the small glasses and stood next to Richard.

Jack picked his up, raised it, and spoke, "Thank you all. I'm extremely grateful to Peter, and I'll miss him terribly. He was a good friend and neighbor."

"Here, here," came the chorus from the group as they followed suit and drank the tequila shots in unison.

"Don't forget to invite me on the inaugural cruise," Alex said.

"Of course. I agreed to take Peter's ashes out on the Gulf, so as soon as I figure out a date, I'll let you know."

"Need to go check on the kitchen. I'll be back later." Alex walked away with the empties.

"So what were you two saying about Clearart when I walked up?" Molly asked.

Jack and Richard brought her up to speed on their conversation. Richard told her about his analysis and his discussion with Steve Ingram.

"What is it that looks off?" Molly asked.

"Based on what I've looked at so far, it doesn't seem to be as effective as it was originally touted to be."

"That's interesting. I haven't noticed any problems on the unit. But we don't do any type of follow-up; that's up to the patient's doctor."

Jack was listening. Without a clinical background he couldn't contribute much to the discussion.

Richard continued. "That's just it. According to the data I've looked at so far, the discrepancy isn't huge. It's not like everyone who's taking it is falling off the perch. The mortality rate for Clearart patients at Rivers is definitely higher. But it appears to be only related to the Clearart produced at their new plant in Mexico."

"That's strange," Molly said. "I went back and checked. Peter had the Clearart from Mexico."

"Coincidence?" Jack asked.

"Don't know. I told Steve I want to talk to their Quality Control people. Maybe they have a problem, maybe not, but somebody needs to take a serious look at what I've compiled. So we have a conference call scheduled for Monday afternoon."

"Anything I can do?" Molly asked.

"Not now. I want to go back through the data one more time. Let's see what happens with the call."

The conversation returned to Jack's new boat.

"So, when do we get to see the new home?" Molly asked Jack.

"I need to get my things moved over first, then you guys can come over. As I was telling Alex, the first trip is to take Peter's ashes out."

"What happens to Wind Dancer?" Richard asked.

"Putting her up for sale. Works out good, though. No rush. As soon as I get moved, I'll start trying to sell her."

"Let us know if you need any help moving."

"Thanks, but I think I can manage. That's one advantage of living on a boat—you don't have a lot of stuff."

SIX

Jack was sitting in the waiting area outside of Chuck Thompson's office. Chuck was the Chief Financial Officer at Rivers and Jack's boss. They had a budget meeting scheduled to review the first pass at next year's budget.

Mary, Chuck's assistant, was on the phone, so Jack flipped through his notes. In a few minutes, Chuck's office door opened, and a short, barrel-chested man in a dark blue suit walked out. His ruddy complexion stood out between his wavy white hair and pale blue shirt accented with a red-striped tie. He glanced at Jack as he passed, nodded, and kept walking. Chuck was standing at his door. He motioned for Jack to come in.

"That was Vic Chaney, wasn't it?" Jack asked.

He'd never met the man, but recognized him from the pictures. Vic Chaney was the CEO for HealthAmerica.

"What was he doing here, slumming?"

Chuck laughed and nodded. "I suppose you could say that. He was on his way to Sanibel and stopped by. He does that from time to time. Justifies taking the company plane down here."

"I understand he has a mansion out there," Jack said. "Have you ever seen it?"

Everyone in Fort Myers knew Chaney had a beachfront home on Sanibel Island. It had been featured in the local magazine last year. The place resembled a small hotel from what Jack remembered in the article. Of course, he'd never seen it.

"No, I'm afraid I'm not in his circle anymore. I worked for Vic in a previous life. We were at one of HealthAmerica's first hospitals. He was the administrator and I was the controller. But that was a long time ago. The only reason he stops by here is to make the rounds, that's it."

"Did you know he was on the board of Advanced Cardiac Meds?" Jack asked.

Chuck shrugged. "No, but I'm not surprised. Vic's probably on a dozen boards. He's way up the food chain in corporate America."

He sat down and moved on to business. "How's the budget coming? Are we there yet?" He was referring to the latest target handed down from corporate.

Jack sat on the other side of Chuck's desk. "We're close. Within eight mil, which is pretty good at this stage." Within eight million dollars on a billion dollar budget was close. Jack passed the two-page summary across the desk to him.

Chuck examined the numbers, asking a few questions about various revenue and expense items. Jack was well prepared. This was their third budget cycle together, so Jack was able to anticipate most of Chuck's questions.

They spent the next thirty minutes reviewing the numbers. Chuck put the projections on the corner of his desk, indicating he was done. "I know you, and you have a cushion somewhere in there."

Jack tried to remain expressionless.

"Don't worry. I did the same thing when I was in your position. All of the good ones do. Anyway, I wanted to give you a heads-up. I talked to one of my buddies at corporate this morning, and next Friday we're probably going to be told to come up with another fifteen."

Jack held his hands out. "Another fifteen? Fifteen more on top of the eight? You've got to be kidding me, Chuck!"

"I know, I know. Like I said, just giving you a heads-up. It's coming."

"That sucks," was all Jack could say.

"I need it by Thursday afternoon, Jack. I've got a conference call with corporate Friday morning."

"The eight I can do. You'll have it by Thursday. But another fifteen million? That's going to take a while," Jack said.

"I know. But that can wait. Right now, it's unofficial, so don't worry about it until we get the word from Atlanta."

HealthAmerica was based in Atlanta.

Jack shook his head and got up to leave. "I'll have it up here Thursday afternoon."

"Thanks. Hey, before you leave?" Chuck said.

Jack stopped with his hand on the door. "Yes?"

"You're good friends with Richard in pharmacy, right?"

"Yes, why?" Jack was curious as to where this was headed.

"Off the record, okay?" Chuck asked.

Jack nodded.

"I understand he suggested to his ACM rep there may be a problem with Clearart."

Jack shrugged.

Chuck hesitated. "From what I heard, the ACM rep kicked it upstairs and was told there was nothing to it. Now, Richard is requesting an audience with their QC group."

"You seem to know an awful lot about what's going on. Is there a problem?" Jack asked.

"I've been around HealthAmerica a long time, Jack. Let's just say that corporate isn't thrilled about our pharmacy director poking around in ACM's business. If there's a problem, go through channels and let them handle it."

"What are you trying to say, Chuck?" Jack felt his face flush. He didn't like the implied threat in Chuck's voice.

"Nothing, Jack. Just passing along gossip out of corporate, okay? Richard brought it to ACM's attention, which is what he's supposed to do. Now that he's done that, he needs to let them handle it. Turn it loose. I'm just trying to help. You know how corporate is. That's all I'm saying."

Jack relaxed a little. "Richard can be a little obsessive. He just feels like ACM isn't taking him seriously, that's all."

"They take anything related to Clearart very serious, I can assure you. Tell him to chill. If there's anything there, their people will be all over it."

"So you want me to pass the message along, indirectly, of course?"

Chuck shrugged. "Just thought you'd want to know." He turned his attention to his computer screen, the conversation finished.

Jack opened the door and went back down to his office. He was puzzled. It was unusual for Chuck to say something like that. He knew Jack didn't give a rat's ass about the politics. If Chuck felt compelled to say something, then somebody was pressuring him or had said something to him. Richard must be ruffling some feathers in Atlanta.

When Jack got back to his office, he dialed Molly's extension. Getting her voice mail, he left a message telling her he would stop by tomorrow morning around ten to pick her up. He pulled up the budget worksheets on his computer and worked through some areas to meet the new targets for next Thursday. After a few hours, he looked up to see Richard standing in his doorway.

"Something you said the other night at Ray's kept me up," Richard said.

"What're you talking about?" Jack's mind was still working on budgets.

"When we were talking about Clearart. You said something to the effect that Advanced Cardiac Meds couldn't afford to let anything happen to Clearart; it was their cash cow. Remember?"

Jack thought for a minute. "Vaguely, I guess. Why?"

Richard closed the office door, came over, and sat across from Jack. "Well, you're right. That's what kept me up. ACM isn't going to let anything happen to Clearart. They'll protect Clearart at all costs.

"Look at Tylenol. In 1982, six or seven people died after taking Tylenol that had been deliberately poisoned. Johnson & Johnson had to recall thirty million bottles off the shelves. That's how we ended up with over-the-counter medicine that's triple-sealed and tamper-proof. It cost them over one hundred million dollars.

"Think about it, Jack. That was for a product that sold for a buck or two at the time. And it cost them that kind of money? Think about what would happen if there was a problem with Clearart. This is a drug that retails for ten thousand dollars a pop. A problem that forced a recall of Clearart could cost ACM hundreds of millions of dollars. Hundreds of millions."

Jack thought back to his discussion with Chuck. "Which is all the more reason they would be on top of any problem with their blockbuster drug, right?"

"Maybe."

"I know you, Richard. You've got a burr about this thing. You think they didn't take you seriously. But, hey, you're on record. You brought it to their attention. Now it's up to them to check into it."

Richard looked at his friend for a long time before speaking. "Sounds like you're trying to tell me something."

Jack knew he had to proceed with caution. "All I'm saying is you shouldn't get too hung up on this. You pointed it out, and their corporate office has the ball. You've got an audience on Monday. Don't get sucked into something here."

"Jack, listen to me. I've run the data, and it doesn't lie. All I can tell you is there's a problem." Richard leaned forward and pounded his fist on the desk. "Advanced Cardiac Meds is killing people in this hospital."

Jack didn't doubt that Richard believed what he was saying. But Jack thought there had to be a flaw somewhere in his logic. This was just too outrageous.

"Wait a minute. So you're sitting here telling me that ACM knows they have a problem with Clearart? And they're deliberately covering it up?"

Richard sat back in his chair. "That's exactly what I'm saying."

Jack shook his head. "You've been reading too many John Grisham novels. How could they possibly do that?

Come on, get real. We're not the only hospital that uses Clearart. Something would show up somewhere. Plus, doesn't the FDA or somebody check on the drug manufacturers?"

"Jack. You're telling *me* to get real? I know this world, okay? Yes, in theory, the FDA monitors drug manufacturers. Most people don't realize it, but the majority of the monitoring is voluntary on the part of the manufacturers. And yes, problems should be showing up elsewhere. But the problems I've found seem to be related only to Clearart manufactured in Mexico. How much monitoring do you think goes on there?"

"That makes no sense at all. The proverbial fox guarding the chicken coop? It can't be that simple. Plus, think about it from a financial perspective. ACM has a terrific annual revenue stream from Clearart. You said that patients have to have treatments every twelve months, right? So why would they jeopardize that? Sorry, pal, but I just don't see it."

"I know you don't believe me on this. Like I said, I don't have all of the answers, and I still have a lot of questions. But I can tell you without a doubt that ACM has quality issues with Clearart from their plant in Mexico. I'd bet my life on it."

Jack took a deep breath. "Look. I believe you've found something. I know you too well. You don't make those kinds of mistakes. But see how the call goes Monday. All I'm saying is that ACM has a lot of incentive to fix any problems with Clearart."

Richard considered what Jack said. "Okay. I hear you. You're right. They do have a big incentive to fix any problems. I just don't trust these big corporations. So we'll see how the call goes Monday."

Richard got up to leave. "You and Molly are coming over around ten in the morning, right?"

"Looking forward to it. Anything I need to bring?"

"No, I'll stop by the market tonight and pick up a few things. We should be set. I was going to ask Alex to come with us." He waited for Jack's reaction.

Jack raised his eyebrows and shrugged. "Sure. Fine with me."

"You think it'll be okay with Molly?"

"I don't see why not. She's the one who suggested you ask her out, remember?"

"I know, but Molly can be a little . . ."

Jack laughed. "Unpredictable? Yeah, I know, but she'll be fine. I'll mention it to her when I pick her up."

"Thanks. See you then."

"Later," Jack said as Richard walked out.

Jack wondered what was going on with Richard and Alex. Like Molly, he thought they made a good couple. He wanted to ask more, but figured Richard would tell him later.

Relieved that he seemed to get through to Richard, Jack turned his attention back to the budget. He was looking at the revenue projections. Curious, he drilled down to see how much revenue they got from Clearart procedures. He shook his head when the numbers flashed up on the screen. Twelve percent of Rivers's revenue, over a hundred million dollars, came from Clearart alone.

Jack knew the number was big, but didn't realize it had grown that much. He thought back to his research on ACM. What was the name of the stockholder he wanted to research? He'd written it down somewhere and hopefully transferred it to his phone. He pulled up the Notes section and scrolled through it. Most of the entries were cryptic and hard to follow. There it was—SA Ventures.

He looked up SA Ventures, but found little. They were a private venture capital firm based in Silicon Valley and concentrated on biotech start-up companies. ACM was their most successful investment as far as he could determine. There were a few articles in business publications referring to SA Ventures as investors, but other than that there was no information about the firm.

Right now, he needed to get back on budgets. With Thursday's deadline approaching and another fifteen million in cuts coming, he had a lot of work to do.

SEVEN

Saturday morning, Jack stopped his car under the canopy at the entrance to Palm View, Molly's condo complex. He wouldn't be long, so he left the car at the curb past the front door. It was walking distance to Richard's house, but they both had assorted gear with them. He went up to the eighth floor to get Molly.

They were back downstairs in the lobby five minutes later, carrying the lunch basket that Molly prepared, towels, and a clothing change. Earlier that week they discussed taking Jack's new boat up to Cabbage Key for the weekend, but Jack insisted he needed more time to get moved in. He also thought the first trip on Left Behind should be to disperse Peter's ashes, so they had agreed to take Richard's boat up for the day.

As they were loading Jack's red Mini, he said, "Richard invited Alex to go with us."

Molly stopped what she was doing. "No shit? When did this come up?"

"Not sure. He mentioned it to me late yesterday afternoon. Wanted to know if it was okay."

"Why wouldn't it be?"

"He just seemed to be a bit nervous about it. My guess is they've been seeing each other, but I don't know any more than what I just told you."

"Well, I think it's great. I like Alex, and they make a cute couple. I hope it works out." She closed the car door, and they drove the short distance down McGregor Boulevard to Richard's house.

Although it was a gated community, they had the access code and were soon pulling into Richard's drive. The community was small but exclusive, sandwiched between McGregor and the Caloosahatchee River on some of the most expensive real estate in Fort Myers. It consisted of only half dozen or so two-story homes, all custom and all Mediterranean style. The houses surrounded a wide deepwater canal that offered direct access to the river. Every one of the homes had a dock and at least one boat.

Richard's home sat at the end of the canal, facing the river. Technically, the back of the house faced the river, but the orientation of the home was to take advantage of the unobstructed river view and not the street. Behind the house on the canal side was the requisite pool and screened enclosure common in Southwest Florida. Next to the pool cage was a dock that ran the entire width of the lot. Tied to the dock was a twenty-five foot Boston Whaler cabin boat with twin Mercury outboards.

They hauled their stuff from Jack's car through the gate on the side of the house. As they walked down the narrow path to the dock, they saw Richard on the boat stowing his gear. He had on a pink golf shirt tucked into khaki shorts.

"Good morning. Should be a great day out on the water. Need any help?" he said.

"Thanks. We've got it," Molly answered.

She and Jack lugged their gear down to the boat. They passed everything over to Richard, and he put it in the small forward cabin. They made one more trip back to the car to get the last few items, and they ran into Alex coming out of the house.

She was dressed in white shorts, deck shoes, and a green halter top. With her long dark hair and olive skin, she looked lovely. She was carrying a picnic basket.

"Hey guys," she said.

"Hey Alex," Molly said. "Glad you could come with us." She gave her a big hug.

Jack walked over and hugged her as well. "Me, too. Maybe you can keep Richard in line. Where was your car? I didn't see it out front?"

Even with her complexion, Alex blushed and looked over at Richard.

"Uh, I told her just to put it in the garage," he said.

They both looked like the cat that swallowed the canary. Jack turned around and winked at Molly as if to say I told you so.

Changing the subject, Alex asked, "You need any help?"

"No, we've just got a few more things. Go help Richard get everything stored," Molly said. It was all she could do to keep a straight face.

As soon as she and Jack got around the corner of the house, Jack said, "I told you."

"She spent the night here, didn't she?" Molly asked, grinning from ear to ear.

"Duh! Did you see the looks on their faces?"

The sight of Richard acting like a teenager on a first date made them both giggle.

They brought the rest of the gear out to the dock, and after handing the things over to Richard, took off their deck shoes and boarded. Richard's boat was spotless, like everything of his. They accused him of spending more time cleaning the boat than his house.

Molly automatically went up front to cast off the bow line. She was the least experienced of the group, but had learned a lot from the guys over the last few years. No way was she going to let two men outdo her. Richard started the engines and let them warm up. Alex sat in the seat next to Richard.

Jack was in back with the stern line. He grew up in Jacksonville, spending his childhood fishing, surfing, and boating in the waters off Jacksonville Beach. The boats he grew up with were substantially older and more rickety than this one. Most of his boating experience came from trial and error, the best teacher.

Richard was like Jack in many ways. He grew up in Charleston and was also a child of the ocean; same ocean but a different world. His boating experience was carefully taught. He was the product of sailing schools and professional instruction. He and Jack both knew the correct nautical terms and were adept at reading the weather. They both could handle a boat with ease, something Molly was still struggling to learn. But there was an inner confidence Jack possessed that came from learning things the hard way.

The engines warmed up and idling, Richard said, "Okay."

Molly and Jack cast off their lines and coiled them up. Richard maneuvered the boat away from the dock and turned toward the river. They idled down the canal, passing the large homes on each side. Once they cleared the entrance to Richard's neighborhood, he inched the throttles forward to move the boat at the highest slow speed he could get away with. Slow speed was a nebulous term, not as objective as no wake, which applied in the canal. Slow speed meant that the boat wasn't going fast enough to get up on a plane or on top of the water. These days, it seemed like most of the Caloosahatchee River in Fort Myers was a slow speed zone, due to the preponderance of manatees.

In the channel leading from Richard's canal to the main channel of the river, they passed a small boat anchored in the shallow waters just outside the marker. An old man was fishing and waved at them as they went by. Jack thought it was ironic. Here was this exclusive gated community, yet anyone could go into the canal from the river in a boat.

They discussed where they were going and decided to head up to Cayo Costa Island. Cayo Costa was the last of four barrier islands between the Caloosahatchee River and Charlotte Harbor. Sanibel, the largest and most well known, was first. It was a boomerang-shaped island facing south, not west, which was a surprise to most visitors. Next was Captiva, linked to Sanibel by a small, two-lane bridge. Only Sanibel and Captiva were accessible by car. Just beyond a narrow, tricky opening called Redfish Pass lay North Captiva, which was private and home to a limited number of residences.

Cayo Costa was owned by the state and home to Cayo Costa State Park. Since the park was accessible only by boat, it was less crowded than Sanibel and Captiva. The four islands were separated from Pine Island and the mainland by a large shallow expanse of water called Pine Island Sound.

As soon as possible, Richard advanced the throttles forward, bringing the heavy boat up onto a faster, more efficient plane. They headed west down the river toward Sanibel.

Out of habit, Jack looked up at the sky, bright blue, with a few puffy cumulous clouds scattered around, a light breeze out of the west. The temperature was already warm and would be hot later. Maybe a few thunderstorms this afternoon, typical for this time of year. It was a nice day to be on the water.

Barefoot, Molly went up front, gripping the rail as she went. Jack stood in the cockpit on the other side of Richard, watching her as she went forward. Molly was thin, but not unhealthy. She had on a red stripe halter top and black shorts. He knew she was wearing a bikini underneath. She always did when they went boating. She sat next to one of the rail support posts near the bow, hanging her legs over the edge. Her eyes were invisible behind the large round sunglasses. Tilting her head back slightly, she was soaking up the wind blowing in her face. Her long red hair blew behind.

They sped up the waterway, gradually curving north up through Pine Island Sound. Sanibel was on their left, though there wasn't much to see from this vantage point. There was a lot of traffic on the waterway today, boats of all shapes and sizes. This was a popular route, like an interstate highway for boats. They passed sailboats, large trawlers, fishing boats, and a couple of what could only be described as yachts.

Several speedboats passed them, engines roaring and going twice as fast as they were. The locals called them dick boats, this being an unflattering reference to the implied inverse relationship between the size of the boat and the male owner's body part.

Then there were the FOP boats. The acronym was an uncomplimentary term that stood for freaking old people. These were pontoon type boats with a flat deck and usually had an awning. People would place their lawn chairs under the canopy, much as they would on a lanai at home.

They continued north, careful to stay in the well-marked Intracoastal. Captiva was on the left, and soon they could see South Seas Island Resort. South Seas was a popular upper-end destination resort that occupied the northernmost tip of Captiva Island.

Finally they came to the south end of Cayo Costa. The Intracoastal went between Cabbage Key and Useppa Island, two small islands much farther apart than the two hundred yards that physically separated them. Useppa, to the east, was an exclusive enclave off limits to mere mortals. It was a private island club, members only, and consistently touted as one of the top-ranked island retreats in the world.

Poles apart, Cabbage Key, between the intracoastal and Cayo Costa, was everyman's island. A popular gathering spot for the Jimmy Buffett wannabes, it was open to everyone.

Just past Cabbage Key, they turned left off the Intracoastal on to the small well-marked channel that led to Cabbage Key and Cayo Costa State Park. They passed the crowded dock at Cabbage Key and idled on to the state park dock. Only three other boats were there.

Molly and Jack put out the fenders and stood at opposite ends of the boat. Richard gently brought it next to the dock where his crew secured the boat. He switched the engines off, and together the foursome unloaded a cooler with wheels, beach umbrellas, towels, and sunscreen. Slipping on sandals for the short hike, they gathered their supplies for the day and headed down the sandy path across the narrow island to the Gulf of Mexico side.

Arriving at the beach, they paused and looked for a spot to claim. With nine miles of beach and relatively few people, it wasn't difficult to find an unoccupied piece of sand. Richard pointed to the right, and they walked that direction. After a few more steps, the entourage soon stopped, satisfied this was a good location to set up camp. Jack and Richard each grabbed a large beach umbrella to plant in the white sand.

Molly pulled the cooler between the umbrellas while Alex unfolded the low slung beach chairs. She put towels on each one. They kicked off their sandals and stripped down to bathing suits. Molly, as Jack predicted, was wearing a bikini, a green one today. She had the figure to wear one with confidence. Not especially large up top, she still had the proportions to turn heads, including Jack's. She applied a generous coating of sunscreen. With red hair and fair skin, she was susceptible to burning in a short period of time in the intense Southwest Florida summer sun.

Alex was wearing a stunning black bikini. Jack had never seen her in a bathing suit before, but she did it justice. She was tall and slim and, with her dark skin, didn't bother to apply sunscreen.

Both of the guys were in good shape. Not muscle bound, but fit with no belly yet. Richard, with the blond hair and blue eyes, had the same problem as Molly. He had his sunscreen and was mimicking her, liberally applying it over any exposed skin.

Jack, like Alex, was more sun-tolerant. With brown eyes and hair to match, his skin was already several shades darker than Molly and Richard. He smeared a light layer of Molly's sunscreen on his face and called it good.

Suitably prepared, they sat back in the shade of the umbrellas, inches above the hot sand. To a stranger, they seemed to be mismatched. The dark-skinned Alex sat next to a blond Richard, while the fair-skinned Molly was with a tan Jack. Based on appearance, the casual observer would suggest they switch partners.

Except for a few puffy white clouds scattered about, the sky was the definition of blue. The sun was almost overhead and reflected off the white sand and turquoise water beyond. The sea was flat, and a gentle breeze was blowing off the water. Beach umbrellas of various colors dotted the landscape on each side of them. To their right, an older couple holding hands was walking in ankle-deep water, the gentle waves washing past them. On the left, a family with two small kids was playing in the edge of the water. The kids, looking to be eight or nine years old, were squealing with delight.

Molly and Alex were sitting in the middle between the umbrella poles, the cooler separating them. "How 'bout a cold drink?" Molly asked.

She opened the cooler and glanced around to make sure the coast was clear. Since it was a state park, officially no alcoholic beverages were allowed. But, as long as the park visitors were discreet and behaved, the rangers tended not to look too hard for violations. In the confines of the cooler, Molly opened the first beer and poured it into the red plastic cup. She handed the first one to Alex, who passed it to Richard. Repeating the process until four cups were filled, she closed the cooler and sat back to relax.

"I met with Chuck yesterday," Jack said, "and it looks like Atlanta is going to want another fifteen million in budget cuts."

"Greedy bastards," Richard said.

Molly took a sip of her beer. "No different than the doctors. I think they're doing Clearart for every cardiac patient that walks in the door."

"Hey, they had to make up for all that lost income. I looked up Advanced Cardiac Meds; they're a high flyer these days. Wish I'd bought some of their stock. The website said they're moving all their Clearart production to the new plant in Mexico," Jack said.

"That's what Steve, the ACM rep, told me. Find out anything interesting?" Richard asked.

"Yeah. I found out they were backed by a venture capital firm that's well below the radar. SA Ventures, based in Silicon Valley, concentrates on biotech firms. And . . . guess who's on the board of ACM?"

They looked at Jack with blank faces.

"Vic Chaney. He's been a director since the beginning."

"Interesting. The bulldog himself," said Richard.

Everyone called Vic Chaney the bulldog, off the record, of course. It wasn't a flattering comparison. Physically, he even resembled a bulldog. And he had the reputation of never turning loose. Wall Street loved him. HealthAmerica employees loathed him.

"Did I tell you I saw him in Chuck's office last week?"

"What was he doing at Rivers? Was he lost?" Molly asked.

Jack laughed. "I asked Chuck the same question. He said Chaney stopped by to justify his trip to Sanibel."

"Did the Grand Pupa acknowledge your presence?" Richard asked.

"He nodded. That was all. I guess I shouldn't look for an invite to the Sanibel mansion, huh?"

"He's a crook, you know that," Richard said. "What did you find out about the venture capital firm? Never heard of them."

"Me either. Nothing on the Internet about them. When I get a chance, I'll check with some of my contacts in the finance world, see what they know."

"Now I'm curious," Richard said. "Let me know what you find out."

"Enough about work," Molly said. She turned to Alex. "These two will talk about work the entire time if we let them. So how did you end up in Fort Myers?"

Alex told them how she came to Fort Myers, and they all started talking about everything but work. After a while, they went for a swim in the warm Gulf waters. When they came out of the water, Richard and Alex went for a walk on the beach while Molly and Jack went back up to the umbrellas.

"He's crazy about her," Molly said as they watched the other couple.

"And how do you get that?"

She turned and looked at Jack, shaking her head. "Men are so clueless. It's obvious. And she's crazy about him."

Jack looked down the beach at the couple, then back at Molly. "Looks like a couple walking down the beach to me."

"No, there's something there between them, it shows—at least to a woman. You can tell by the way they look at each other."

Jack looked out at the Gulf, afraid to look at Molly, afraid that his face would give away too much. What could she see by looking at him?

"Water's calm today. Wouldn't be much good for sailing," he said.

"When are you moving over to Left Behind?"

"Probably tomorrow. Need to get that done."

"Need any help?"

Jack thought about it. He didn't really need any help.

"Sure, if you're not busy. Can always use an extra set of hands."

"I'll come down after I've had my coffee in the morning."

Before long, Alex and Richard returned from their walk. Molly brought out the sandwiches she'd made, and they ate lunch. It was a relaxing day at the beach. A few more people arrived after them, but it was still not crowded. They rested a bit in the shade and went back out into the water, tossing a football around, looking for shells and walking the beach. Clouds started to build in small clumps out over the water.

Around five, after drying off, they decided to pack up and head back to Fort Myers. The group headed back to the dock on the same path as they came. They loaded the boat, Alex stowing everything in the small cabin. Jack and Molly both noticed that Alex seemed to be familiar with Richard's boat. They concluded this wasn't her first time.

Richard turned one key, then the other as each of the big outboards started with a puff of blue smoke. Molly and Jack assumed the crew positions and cast off the lines. Richard backed the boat up, then nudged the throttles forward, moving the boat at idle speed up the channel toward the Intracoastal.

Without even asking, he turned toward the dock at Cabbage Key. There were at least fifteen or twenty boats there. Bo, the dock master, was out on the end giving directions to arriving boats, telling them where to dock. Otherwise it would have been complete chaos. He recognized Richard and waved. Bo pointed to the opposite side, and Richard acknowledged, turning the Whaler that direction. Bo didn't bother to go over and help them dock the boat. There were plenty of others coming in that needed all the help they could get, and Bo turned back to his job directing traffic.

The music was playing as they walked up the hill to the bar. Situated on a forty foot shell mound, the Cabbage Key bar was probably one of the highest spots around. Everything was so flat in this part of Florida that it looked like a considerable hill. The bar was a popular place, especially on the weekends. Local legend was that Jimmy Buffett's famous song, "Cheeseburger in Paradise," was based on Cabbage Key. Parrotheads know better, but it made for a good story.

They went inside, where the walls and ceiling are lined with years of mostly dollar bills that have been pinned up in every available space. Each is autographed by its previous owner, many with booze-inspired words of wisdom. It was a tradition for the tourists. Molly spotted a group just leaving, and they walked over to the table to claim it. A server came over and bused the table before they sat down. She took their drink order, margaritas all around. When she brought their drinks, they ordered food.

After cheeseburgers and margaritas, it was getting late. Wanting to get back to Richard's house before dark, they made their way back down to the boat and prepared to leave. Bo was on the other dock now, still helping the tourists come and go. He saw the four and waved. They got into the boat, and Richard handed Jack the keys. Jack took them without a word and sat in the right seat and started the engines. Alex went up front, so Molly stood next to Jack while Richard took Jack's place in the stern. They looked at Jack and, when he nodded, they cast off. Jack paused when they got to the Intracoastal and stared at the southern sky. A few scattered thunderstorms had formed while they were inside, but nothing of any consequence.

They turned and headed south on the Intracoastal. It was close to dark now and would be night before they made it back to Richard's.

Jack didn't mind driving the boat in the dark. He was comfortable on the water and knew his way around this area well. Although there was still some light, Molly pulled out the floodlight and plugged it into the console. She stood between the two guys and prepared to light the markers if directed by Jack.

Alex was stowing gear and tidying up. Twilight came fast. It was dark by the time they made the turn to the east up the Caloosahatchee. Before long they were back at Richard's. Jack snuggled the Whaler next to the dock where Richard and Molly secured the lines. Jack switched the outboards off and pressed the switch to tilt the props out of the water. He removed the keys and handed them to Richard, then went to help Molly unload their gear. Alex was putting covers on the instruments while Richard checked everything and prepared to wash the boat down. It was late as they convened in Richard's kitchen.

"Well, that was a good day. Anyone care for a nightcap?" Richard said. He uncorked the decanter of

Glenlivet and poured himself a couple of fingers before anyone could respond.

"I'll just take a sip of yours," Alex said.

"Not for me. I'm bushed," said Molly.

"No, nothing else for me either. I'm done." Jack turned to Molly. "You ready?"

"Let's go."

Everyone exchanged hugs and goodnights, then Richard walked Molly and Jack to the door to say goodnight. They noticed that Alex made no pretense about leaving. Smiling at one another, Jack and Molly climbed into the Mini and drove off toward Molly's condo.

EIGHT

Monday after work, the three friends were sitting on Jack's new boat enjoying a cold beer. Jimmy Buffett was playing in the background. Molly was sitting on one side of the cockpit table and Richard the other. Jack was sitting behind the helm, with his feet propped up on the stainless steering wheel.

He had just given Richard his first tour of Left Behind. Yesterday, he and Molly spent the entire day moving all of Peter's possessions over to Wind Dancer while moving Jack's things over to Left Behind. That way he could go through Peter's belongings at his leisure.

"Nice digs, I must say," Molly said. "Are you going to change the name?"

"No, I like it. Besides, sailors consider that bad luck." He chuckled as he remembered Peter's reaction to the Catalina's name. "If I wasn't superstitious, I would've changed Wind Dancer's name a long time ago. God knows I've caught enough flak for that."

"I always wondered about that one. Glad to hear you didn't come up with it," Richard said.

"Nope. She was a used boat—I couldn't afford a new one—and that was her name. I always wanted to name a sailboat Unole, but doesn't look like I'll be buying a new one anytime soon."

Molly and Richard both wrinkled their foreheads and looked at Jack.

"It's Cherokee for strong wind. Always thought it would be a good name for a sailboat. But I like Left Behind."

"This one's first class. I'm impressed. I see you already have a For Sale sign on Wind Dancer." Richard nodded to Jack's boat behind him.

"Yes, but I'm not in a hurry. I want to find her a good home."

"My God. You sound like you're talking about a person," said Molly.

This time Jack flipped her the finger. "I've told you before, sailors and their boats have a special relationship."

Molly shook her head. "I guess I don't understand. In all fairness, I've never owned a boat, so I wouldn't know."

Richard pointed his thumb over his shoulder. "Maybe Jack would make you a deal?"

She laughed. "Why do I need a boat? Each of my good friends here owns one. What's that saying about the only thing better than owning a boat is having a friend with a boat?"

They all laughed at Molly's comment.

"Or the two best days of a boat owner's life are the day he buys it and the day he sells it," Richard added.

More laughter ensued.

"Or the definition of a boat?" Jack asked.

Richard nodded knowingly while Molly looked puzzled.

"A hole in the water into which you pour substantial sums of money."

Again, they howled in laughter.

"Well," Richard said on a more serious note. "I had my conference call with Mountain View this afternoon. The Advanced Cardiac Meds Quality Control boys. They had two of their big guns on the call. I recognized their names. Each of them has more initials after their name than I can interpret. It was interesting."

Jack looked at Richard. "What did they say?"

"I won't bore you with the entire replay. The short version? I'm basically a lowly pharmacist in Fort Myers, FL. What could I possibly know about interpreting multifarious data relating to the efficacy of complex treatment protocols involving state-of-the art biopharmaceutical agents? I think I quoted that verbatim, but I'll have to get back to you on some of the words. I'm still looking them up."

Molly looked over at Jack. "What did he just say?"

"I think you and I would've just summed it up as screw you and go away."

"Oh, okay. Now I understand. Thanks for translating, Jack."

Richard had to laugh at his two friends. "Only the two of you could make me laugh about that. I suppose that's why I hang around you. You do make the bullshit tolerable."

"What now?" Molly asked.

"I'm thinking about flying out to San Francisco to pay them a personal visit."

Jack almost spit out his mouthful of beer.

Richard laughed when he saw Jack's reaction. He saw the puzzled look on Molly's face. "Just kidding. Captain Jack here thinks I'm being too stubborn about this. He wants me to back off. Seriously, I haven't decided. But I'm not going to go away. The more I look at the data, the more I'm convinced there's a problem."

Jack was afraid this would be Richard's reaction. He had an idea. "Who have you told about this Clearart issue?"

Richard thought. "You. Molly. Steve Ingram with ACM. I suspect he's told his boss. The brass in ACM's Quality Control department. Why?"

"Have you told Larry?" Larry Carlson was the VP for Clinical Operations at the hospital, Richard's boss.

"No, I haven't."

"Well, why don't you take it to him? Show him what you have and see what he thinks. Larry seems to be straight up. Get him to take a look at it." Jack was thinking about Chuck Thompson's comment. "Besides, don't you need to pull him into the loop if there is something going on?"

Richard paused before answering. "You're right. I suppose I should. He probably needs a heads-up on it. Besides, he might have some ideas on where to take it next."

Jack was relieved that Richard seemed to be calming down a bit. Maybe Larry could talk some sense into him. Jack was surprised that Richard was so adamant. He wasn't the type to jump to conclusions; in fact, just the opposite. Richard was usually the level-headed one, methodical and pragmatic. He was usually the one calming Jack and Molly down.

"On a different subject, I was thinking about having Peter's service this Saturday. The weather is forecast to be decent," Jack said.

They both nodded.

"Who are you inviting?" Molly asked.

"Walter Dobbs, the attorney. Alex. You two, of course. And Kevin," he said, pointing to the large trawler across the

J dock from them. "That's it. Peter had no family that I knew of, besides some crazy ex from years ago. He wouldn't have wanted a large group."

Molly looked at Jack. "We can identify with the crazy ex concept, right?"

Jack held up his beer in acknowledgment.

She turned to Richard. "How did you ever escape that?"

Richard shook his head. "Just lucky, I guess. Came close one time."

"Really?" Jack said. "I didn't know that."

Richard took a swig from his beer. "Right after I finished pharmacy school. Mother had it in her mind that it was time I should settle down. Of course, I should marry a proper Charleston lady. And she just happened to know one, her best friend's daughter."

"What happened?" Molly asked.

"We dated for a while, even talked about getting married. She was an interior designer in Charleston. But in the end I decided that we were doing it for the wrong reasons. So I broke it off. Ashley moved on and married a doctor in Charleston. But I don't think Mother has ever forgiven me."

"You know, in the years we've known you, we've never heard that story. And I thought I kept things close," Molly said.

Richard shrugged. "No secret, just never had come up before. What about you?" He looked at Molly. "I know you've been married twice, but that's about it."

Molly shifted in her seat. She didn't like the spotlight shifting to her. "Not a lot to tell. The first one was when I was young and stupid."

Jack couldn't resist. "So now you're just stupid?"

She kicked at his foot with hers. "I'm the youngest one on this boat, mind you. Plus, you have no room to talk based on what you've told me about the witch you left in Jacksonville."

Jack nodded in agreement. "Can't argue about that. But right now we want to finish hearing your story."

"As I was saying before I was so rudely interrupted, the first one was just a way for me to get out of the house. Dumb with a capital *D*. It lasted a couple of years before I got tired of him going out with the boys every night. So I left him, buckled down, and finished nursing school."

"What about number two?" Richard prodded.

Molly's face turned serious as she thought about her second husband. "That one's not so simple."

Jack didn't kid her this time. He could tell she was struggling. Finishing the last of his beer he said, "Time for a refill."

Molly shook hers to verify it was empty, and Richard took the last swallow from his bottle. Jack gathered the empties and went below. A minute later, he emerged with three beers.

Setting two bottles on the table, he took his back to the stern and reclaimed his seat.

Molly had summoned up her courage and continued her story. "I'd started a new job, my first as a Registered Nurse, at Mass General.

"For the first six months, I was totally absorbed in my new job. Trying to impress everyone and make my mark. Hey, I was a poor Irish-Catholic girl and determined to prove I was as good as anyone in the place."

Jack had never heard this tone from Molly before. Growing up in what he thought at the time was a middle-class neighborhood but later realized was lower middle-class at best, he could identify with what she was saying.

"Anyway, I caught the attention of a last-year resident, Ambrose Clark. He was older, bright, one of the brightest in that group. He was Beacon Hill, everything I wasn't. I was flattered that he was interested in me."

Molly took a few sips from her beer. She had a faraway look in her eyes. It was the look of someone remembering things she had tried to forget.

"Molly," Jack said in a gentle tone. "You don't have to if you don't want to. We're friends here. We've all been through some things we'd rather not resurrect."

She shook her head in a defiant way. "No, Jack. Thanks, but no. I need to tell this, okay? And it's because you're my friends. I've never talked about this with anyone. It's time."

She took a long deep swallow from the bottle and set it back on the table. "Anyway, when he finished his residency, he was offered a position at Mass General. We were elated. A few months later, he asked me to marry him."

She looked at Richard. "I think his mother was related to yours." She forced a laugh, but it was hollow.

"Mrs. Clark didn't approve. But Ambrose convinced me she would come around and we married anyway. Big, fancy wedding—the works. It didn't help. In fact, it got worse. His relationship with his mother grew more strained, not less. He started blaming it on me."

Jack had an awful feeling about where this was headed. He was sorry they had gone down this path. The look on Richard's face told him that Richard knew the plot, too, from the other side; the Clark side. Jack wished he could wave a wand and reset the clock back to the beginning of the evening, take a different road. But Richard and Jack were obligated to go with her, however unpleasant it turned out to be.

Molly picked up the beer and took another drink. This time she held it in her hand, as if for support. A seagull cawed nearby, but the marina seemed quiet, as if everyone and everything was avoiding this spot. Her eyes were blank, and she was seeing the past. She took a deep breath and continued.

"At first it was just verbal. He criticized everything I did. I couldn't please him anymore. My clothes, my hair; nothing was good enough, and he didn't mind telling me, in private, of course. When we were with others, he was the model husband. Attentive, charming. It would make me sick inside. We'd go out and he'd be this pleasant person whom I'd married, but when we got home, the dark side would show itself. He would curse me. Tell me I was trash and that I didn't deserve him. What's so sad, looking back, is I believed him. I began to think it was my fault. If I could somehow change, I could please him and win back his love."

A tear slid down Molly's cheek. This was like watching a train wreck about to happen, Jack thought. He didn't want to watch, but he had to.

"Then one night, he came to my bed. I was almost asleep. By then, I couldn't stand the thought of anything physical with him, and I was sleeping in the spare bedroom. He'd been drinking and decided he wanted sex. It was my duty, he said."

By now tears were streaming down Molly's face. But she was determined to finish her story.

"He raped me. The son of a bitch held me down and raped me. I tried to resist, but he was bigger and stronger. He punched me when I wouldn't do what he wanted. He used me and, when he was done, he went to his room. The next morning, I had bruises where he'd hit me. But he was smart enough to hit me where they wouldn't show. Besides, what was I going to do?"

Jack and Richard had their heads down, feeling Molly's pain, embarrassed at the actions of another man as if it somehow tainted their own existence.

"I was too dumb to leave. I thought I could fix it, that it was my fault. There was no one I could talk to. After all, I had the perfect marriage as far as anyone outside could see. No one would've believed me. He knew it and I knew it. The beatings got worse. The sadistic bastard was enjoying it. He was truly pathological. I was a nervous wreck, walking on eggshells, afraid that I'd do something to trigger his rage.

"One night, I took a butcher knife into my bedroom. When he came in, I pulled it out and threatened to kill him. You know what he did?"

Molly gritted her teeth as she remembered that night.

"He fucking laughed at me. Laughed in my face. Told me if I so much as scratched him with that knife, I'd go to jail for the rest of my life. That he and his family would see to it. Then he turned around and started to walk out of the room.

"When he got to the door, he stopped and looked right at me and pointed. I'll never forget that look. It was the face of the devil. Pure evil. He told me he'd be back. And what he'd done so far paled in comparison to what he would do to me next time. I could count on it. He slammed the door, and I heard him leave the house.

"That was the last time I ever saw the bastard. I knew that if I stayed, I'd kill him. Or he would kill me. Either way, I had to go. I packed my things and left that night. Drove south till I hit Savannah, GA. Spent the night there, got out a map, and looked at Florida. I wanted to be as far south as I could get, but I didn't want to even be on the same coast as him, so I picked Fort Myers. Moved here, got a job at Rivers. Hired an attorney and got a divorce. I didn't ask for anything but my maiden name back. His mother was happy to oblige."

Jack moved to one side and Richard the other. With tears in their eyes, they both put their arms around her, holding her close. Molly reached up and pulled their faces close to hers. No one said a word for the longest time. The three of them just sat there, their tears mingling together on Molly's face.

At last the wave of emotion began to ebb. She squeezed their faces once more, then patted them each on the leg.

"Thank you," she said. "I've been carrying that around for way too long. You two are the best friends in the world. Thanks for listening. I love you both." She kissed each of them on the cheek.

Neither said anything. Words were inadequate at a time like this. Nothing they could say could erase the pain that had been inflicted on her.

Molly sighed. "I'm exhausted. Have you got anything to eat down there?" she said to Jack as she pointed to the cabin.

"I always have chips, salsa, and guacamole. It's what I live off of. Goes well with beer, too."

"Sounds wonderful," she said.

"Captain, I never expect fine dining on board one of your fleet. But as long as you have more of this dreadful beer, I suppose that will have to do for dinner," Richard said.

Jack went down below and brought up food and more beer. They ate as if famished. Molly invited them over to her place Saturday night, making good-hearted fun at the food before them, promising a more refined dinner.

It felt good to laugh again, and Jack didn't mind that it was at his expense. They asked if they needed to bring anything. Although she said no, Richard volunteered to bring the wine as a defensive move to avoid Jack's potential selections, which of course resulted in more laughter. After that was settled, Molly decided to call it a night.

Jack walked them to the gate at the main dock, and Molly threw her arms around his neck, hugging him tight. He put his arms around her waist and held her close.

"Thank you, Jack," she whispered. "Good night."

"Night, Molly," Jack whispered in her hair.

At last they separated, and she turned to go home.

"Good night, Jack," Richard said.

"Night, Richard."

Jack watched his two friends disappear into the shadows. He was tired, too. It had been a draining night.

NINE

Jack got off the elevator on the eighth floor and walked down the hall to Molly's condo. He stopped at the door marked 805 and knocked. Richard opened the door and had a bottle of Bud in his hand.

"Come in. We're outside watching the boats on the river. It's entertaining, as usual."

Jack walked inside and saw Molly standing out on the balcony. He went by the kitchen and opened the refrigerator; nothing but Budweiser and Sam Adams. He helped himself to a cold Sam Adams, twisted off the cap, pitched it into the trash can under the sink, and walked out onto the balcony.

Richard and Molly were leaning on the rail, beer in hand, watching the evening boat traffic on the river. Boats of all shapes and sizes were scurrying back and forth, trying to get to their destination before dark. It was always amusing to watch the near-misses, boats running aground and other close calls.

The sun was near the horizon. The sky was a palette of orange, yellow, pink, and purple set against a vivid blue background, painting another magnificent Southwest Florida sunset.

"Nice way to end the day," Jack said as he took a swallow of beer.

"I know. I don't ever get tired of the view," said Molly. She turned to Jack. "How was your day?"

"Meetings all day long. I met with Chuck again on the budget. It's official. Corporate is looking for another fifteen million out of our budget."

Richard and Molly groaned.

"Speaking of work, something's been bothering me," Richard said.

"Let's go inside," said Molly. "We can get a refill and get some munchies."

They all walked into the kitchen. Jack got three more beers while Molly and Richard put cheese and crackers on a plate. They sat at the small round table in front of the open sliding glass door.

Jack looked at Richard. "You sound serious. What is it?"

Richard finished a cracker and cheese before speaking. He leaned back in his chair and shook his head.

"I met with Larry, Tuesday after we talked on your boat," he said, nodding at Jack. "It went well, I thought. I showed him what I had on Clearart, and he said he'd talk to Atlanta."

Jack was hopeful. That was a positive sign. He waited for the other shoe to drop. It did.

"Larry called back today. He told me in so many words to drop it. He talked to corporate, and they weren't interested. Told him that was the FDA's job, and any questions on Clearart should be passed along to Advanced Cardiac Meds. Let them handle it. It was their responsibility, not ours. End of discussion."

"Sorry to hear that. You tried. Now what? It sounds like your options are pretty limited at this point," Jack said.

"I'm not sure. But that's why I wanted to show you what I've found. Maybe you'll have some ideas. Something definitely doesn't look right."

"What do you mean, doesn't look right?" asked Molly.

"Let me show you. Where's your computer?" Richard pulled a small white thumb drive out of his pocket.

"My laptop's in the bedroom. Hold on and I'll get it."

Molly went into the other room. She came back and put the laptop computer on the table in front of Richard and turned it on.

After it booted, he plugged the USB drive into the port on the side of the computer. Manipulating the touch pad on the keyboard, he brought up a bar chart on the screen. There were about a dozen brightly colored bars.

"This chart shows Clearart mortality rates for the last three months. Rivers, the first bar, is compared to fourteen other hospitals in our peer group. The peer group is composed of similar size hospitals with similar Clearart usage.

"What do you notice about this chart?" Richard said.

The other two leaned forward to look. They looked at each other and shrugged. Richard waited.

"All the bars are about the same height. That's all I see," Jack said.

Molly agreed.

"Precisely. And that's where most people stop. It's where I normally would've stopped. As you astutely pointed out, all of the bars are about the same height. Meaning, the data suggests no aberrations. Mortality rates for all of the hospitals in our peer group are about the same. End of story, right?

"But after Peter died, Jack asked me about Clearart, and I was curious. So I started playing around with the data. I didn't expect to find anything, but I wanted to take a fresh look at it."

They knew Richard was leading them; they just didn't know where. He was enjoying this, the professor in him coming out.

"Now look." Richard clicked on the touch pad and brought up a second chart labeled *Clearart Plants*. It was another bar chart, but with only two bars. On this chart one bar was noticeably bigger than the other.

"Well, duh. The bar labeled 16592 is way higher than the one labeled 21734," Molly said.

"Interesting. It looks like that plant has some obvious quality issues. But why didn't that show up on the other chart?" Jack said.

Richard smiled. He was pleased to watch his class catch up. "That's where you need to dig deeper. At the moment, Clearart is manufactured in two plants. ACM has one plant in California, plant 21734 and a new one in Mexico, plant 16592, where they intend to shift all of their production. I won't bore you with all the details, but two points.

"First, since the Mexico plant is only shipping to HealthAmerica hospitals, it wouldn't show up on any other hospitals that use Clearart. And the production from Mexico is small compared to the total production. Bottom line, any defective drugs coming from that plant would get lost in the overall totals."

"That's interesting; so the Mexican stuff is only being shipped to HealthAmerica. Why?" Jack asked.

"Not sure," Richard said, "but it's normal with a new plant to initially limit distribution in case of any problems."

"But isn't it normal for a new plant to have production issues?" Molly asked.

"Sure. Anytime you start up a new plant, there are problems. Especially with a drug as complicated to manufacture as Clearart. That in itself isn't unusual. I also went back and verified that our mortality rate at Rivers has increased since we started getting shipments from the new plant. No doubt there's a problem with the Clearart from Mexico, at least here at Rivers."

"But why wouldn't somebody have noticed? What you're saying is that Clearart patients at Rivers are dying at a higher rate than elsewhere, right? So, wouldn't physicians or patient families or somebody notice?" Jack asked.

Molly had years of experience on a cardiac care unit. She answered for Richard. "Probably not. Think about it, Jack. Most of the patients on Clearart are older. They have advanced cardiovascular disease. And most of them have other health problems as well. So an eighty-five-year-old patient who dies after receiving Clearart isn't unusual, especially if it happens several weeks or months later. These patients are at pretty high risk already."

Richard nodded. "Precisely. So it'll be a lot harder to see these patterns in the data with all of the other noise surrounding those patients. The only reason I found it is I was looking for something.

"The second reason is I'm not sure the data is valid."

Molly slapped her hand on the table and shook her head. "So . . ."

"Wait a minute, Richard. You just got through convincing us that the Clearart from ACM's new plant in

Mexico is bad. Now you're saying you don't know the data is good? I give. Which is it?" Jack asked.

"I think the data is valid. But to make sure, I'd want to match it up on a patient-by-patient basis. Verify that the data in the hospital computer is accurate. Make sure there's no system glitch that could be skewing the data. That would be the next step.

"Then I'd want to do the same analysis on the data from other HealthAmerica hospitals," Richard said.

"And how would you do that?" Molly asked.

"I'd have to get in touch with my counterparts at the other hospitals. Since corporate refuses to get involved, and I don't have access to any other hospitals' data . . ."

Jack sat back and thought. Questions were racing through his mind. How long had this been going on? Did Advanced Cardiac Meds know? Were they covering it up? He did know that if Richard contacted the other HealthAmerica hospitals, all hell would break loose.

"Did you share all of this with the QC group from ACM?" Molly asked.

"Yes! And they told me that my analysis was faulty. They couldn't verify that I had the correct data. Which is why I need to match it up manually on a patient-by-patient basis."

"So there's a possibility that the data is—"

"I think it's unlikely," Richard said.

"Can we do this without attracting any further attention?" Jack asked.

"Probably not. And I want to do one more thing," Richard said.

Molly and Jack looked at each other.

"Molly, can you get me a couple of empty bags of Clearart? Specifically one from each plant?"

She thought a minute. "Maybe. But what would you want with an empty IV bag?"

"It'll have enough residue in it for what I need. I have a friend at an independent laboratory in Atlanta. I want to send it to him, have it analyzed and compared."

They talked for the next thirty minutes about how to proceed, continuing the discussion over dinner. Richard was convinced there was an issue with Clearart and ACM was ducking responsibility. But Jack and Molly convinced him to proceed with caution.

In the end, they agreed to try and get the data for the Clearart patients. With much hesitation, Molly also agreed to get empty Clearart bags for Richard, only after making him promise not to involve anyone else until the three of them had a chance to talk first.

The next day on the unit, Molly checked to see which patients were getting Clearart from Mexico. She'd already gotten an empty bag from the California plant.

She looked on the computer. Only two patients were getting the Mexican Clearart. One was almost done, Mr. Satterfield. He was Theresa's patient. Molly looked at the clock. It was five minutes before noon.

She walked out to the nursing station in the middle of the unit. An overweight older woman with a round face framed by short blonde hair was sitting at the desk entering information on the computer.

"Theresa, why don't you go on down and get some lunch. I'll cover for you."

She looked up from the computer and saw Molly. "Okay. I need to disconnect the bag on Mr. Satterfield first. He's almost done."

"Why don't you go ahead? I can do it. Don't want to get too rusty," Molly said. She was just as capable as any nurse on the unit. They knew it and so did she.

It was an easy sell. Theresa was ready for a break. "Sure. Want me to get you anything while I'm downstairs?" Theresa asked.

"No, thanks. I've got to go down for a meeting when you get back. I'll get something then."

Theresa logged off the computer and walked out of the unit. Molly walked into the bay where Mr. Satterfield was.

"Just going to unplug you here," she said.

The older man in the bed was half asleep and didn't acknowledge her. She clamped off the line, disconnected the IV tubing, and disposed everything except the IV bag itself in the red biohazard receptacle. She took the IV bag off the pole and carefully folded it up in a towel she took from the sink.

"I'll be back in to check on you later," she said to the man who still had his eyes closed.

She went back to her office and put the towel in a tote she used to carry notebooks and such to meetings. Thirty minutes later, when Theresa got back to the unit, Molly picked up the tote bag and left the unit to go downstairs. She knocked on the pharmacy door and, when the young tech admitted her, she walked straight to Richard's office, closing the door behind her.

She placed the tote on his desk. "What you asked for."

Richard took the towel out of the bag and unfolded it enough to confirm the contents.

"Thanks, Molly. That should be sufficient. I'll overnight it this afternoon. We should have the results by next Wednesday."

She picked up the tote. "Got to run. I have a meeting in a few, and I want to grab a sandwich on the way. Later."

She turned and walked out.

TEN

It was a slow Wednesday evening at Ray's, so Alex spent more time at the table with Richard and his friends than she did behind the bar. Now that their relationship was no longer a secret, the two seemed to be more relaxed, Jack thought.

Richard had summoned a meeting after work.

"I talked to Terry, my friend at the Atlanta lab, this afternoon. He finished analyzing what I had sent him."

Jack and Molly leaned forward to hear what Richard had found out.

"He said the two samples were nearly identical."

"*Nearly* identical? What does that mean?" Molly asked.

"He said there was something different between the two, but the difference was too small for his lab to identify. His guess is the discrepancies are at the molecular level, which is too minute for his lab to fully differentiate. You'd need more advanced equipment to pinpoint the difference."

"So where does that leave us?" Jack said.

"By itself, nowhere. Terry asked what the samples were. All I would tell him is they were some hi-tech meds from a California biopharmaceutical company. That's when he told me I should call Manny, a former classmate of ours at Duke.

He said Manny was some big shot at a firm like that in Silicon Valley. I wasn't surprised; the guy was a genius. So he gave me Manny's number. Guess where he is?"

"You're kidding—ACM?" Molly said.

Richard nodded. "Manny Garcia is a lead scientist at ACM."

"You called him yet?" Jack asked.

"Yeah, but he was at lunch. That was just before I left the office to meet you guys. Thought I'd call him back tonight."

"And?" Molly said.

"Don't know. I'll play it by ear. See what he'll tell me."

Jack said, "I did a little more research on SA Ventures, the venture capital firm that bankrolled ACM. Nothing. Talk about private, there's zilch out there on that company. So I called an investment banker friend of mine in New York, asked him. He'd never heard of them either, but said he'd check around and get back to me."

"We don't seem to be making much progress," Molly said.

"Something will turn up. Maybe Manny can help."

Later that evening, after Richard got home, he took out the number for Manny Garcia and dialed it.

"Garcia." Manny answered on the third ring.

"This is Frank Jones with the Duke Alumni Association. I noticed on your profile you didn't check the box for Mexican or American, so I had a few questions to ask about your immigration status," Richard said, trying to keep his voice professional.

There was a long pause on the other end, then a roar of laughter. "Richard Wasp Melton, of the Charleston Meltons.

How the hell are you?" In North Carolina, it had been an ongoing joke between the two unlikely friends.

"Manny, how'd you know it was me?"

"'Cause you're the only dumb-ass I know who would make up something as lame as that. Where are you? You're not on the West Coast, are you?"

"No, no; Southwest Florida, Fort Myers."

Richard graduated from pharmacy school at the same time Manny got his PhD. Manny had moved back home to California and Richard had gone back to Charleston. They had lost contact with each other after that.

"What are you doing in Fort Myers? Running the city? Bank president or something?"

"Director of pharmacy at one of the big hospitals here. Got out from under the Charleston coattails. I hear you're the next Steve Jobs?"

"Just one of about a million scientists in the Valley, trying to make a living. How'd you find me?"

"Terry Horton. I was talking with him, and we got to reminiscing and your name came up."

"TH. Yeah, I see him every once and a while when I get through Atlanta."

They continued to chat about old times and other classmates, catching up on missing years.

Manny brought the conversation back to Terry. "So how did you end up talking to Terry?"

Richard chose his words with care. "I've been doing a little research on the side and Terry thought you could help me."

"Research? What kind?"

"What can you tell me about Clearart?" Richard said. As soon as the words left his lips, the connection chilled.

"What about it?" All friendliness had disappeared.

Richard tried to keep it light. "Just curious, really. Wondering about the stuff coming out of the new plant in Mexico, that sort of thing."

"Sorry, Richard. That's proprietary information. I'm not allowed to discuss it. You know how it works."

"I understand. I'm not asking you to tell me anything out of school." Richard decided to throw another bone out. "It's just that some of the data I'm looking at, well, the Clearart from Mexico seems to be less effective than that from California."

There was a long period of silence on the other end.

"If you have any more questions about Clearart, I'd suggest you go through your ACM rep. Listen, it was good talking to you, but I've got to run. Take care."

The line went dead.

Richard looked at the phone. That was weird. So much for getting any help from Manny.

In a small office in a non-descript building in Mountain View, CA, the man replayed the conversation one more time to make sure he hadn't missed anything. Taylor and Chaney were right; they had a problem—a big problem. The good news is that it was contained at the moment.

He picked up his disposable cell phone and dialed Michael Taylor's private number.

"You've got a problem," he said when Taylor answered. He relayed the conversation he'd just overheard, along with the results of his surveillance the last week.

"Shit. Vic was right. What do you suggest?"

"How many times have I told you? No names." He let that sink in before continuing. Even though his phone was disposable and he changed phones frequently, Taylor's wasn't. "Send your guy south Friday. One last trip to wrap things up."

"I don't like the sound of this. I mean, he didn't say anything," Taylor said.

"I've been watching this guy, and I told you about the conversation. It's a matter of when. Right now, it's under control. But that could change quickly."

"Why don't we monitor it for a few more days?"

Taylor was weak, the man thought, always had been.

"Hey, I don't care. I'm just telling you in my professional opinion, your guy is about to go over the wall. We handle it now, it's easy. But once he goes over, the damage is done. No putting it back in the bottle."

"Why M—" Taylor remembered in time. "Why there?"

Some days he could strangle Taylor, but he bit his tongue. "Lots of drug-related crime. It's dangerous. A person gets a little careless, in the wrong place at the wrong time, you never know . . ."

"I need to check with . . . our friend in Georgia."

"Let me know by the end of the day."

"Soon as I talk with him I'll let you know."

Taylor hung up, pulled up Vic Chaney's number, and pressed Send.

"Yeah?" Chaney didn't waste words.

"You were right." He remembered the previous caller's admonition. "My guy's a problem. Our friend thinks he's about to go over the wall, as he put it."

There was a pause. "Now what?"

"Our friend will take care of it, but he needs to move soon. I told him I'd check with you and get back to him."

Another pause. "Sounds like the only option. Just make sure there are no loose ends."

"I'll tell him." Taylor ended the call and swore under his breath before re-dialing the previous number. He hated this cloak and dagger crap.

The next morning at work, Richard called Jack and suggested they meet in the cafeteria and have lunch.

After they went through the line and sat at a table alone in the corner, Richard took a bite of his sandwich.

"I called Manny last night. Interesting conversation. We chatted about old times, old friends catching up on things. But as soon as I told him what I was looking at, he clammed up."

"What did he say?" Jack asked.

"That's just it. He was all talkative and glad to hear from me, but when I mentioned Clearart, he got quiet. I suggested that it appeared the stuff from Mexico wasn't as effective. He got formal, told me if I had questions I needed to go through my rep. Then he said he had to go and hung up. Odd."

Jack stopped eating. "So what's your take?"

"I don't know. Manny's a good guy, but he knew something he wasn't telling me. He never denied what I said about the Mexican Clearart not being as effective, which was strange. I'm thinking about calling him back, but I don't think it'll do any good. He was pretty adamant."

"Maybe somebody got to him."

ELEVEN

Peter's wake promised to be a huge success, if a wake could be thought of that way. Even though it was cloudy, it was a great day for sailing. A weak front had gone through that night, and there was a decent breeze out of the north.

Everyone invited had accepted and was on board Left Behind by nine that morning. Jack pulled away from the dock a few minutes before nine, and they were soon headed west on the river. With the wind direction, they could have sailed downriver, but he decided to wait. He was still getting familiar with the boat and didn't want to risk running aground before they had completed their assigned task.

So they motored all the way out to the Sanibel Causeway. As soon as they passed under the Sanibel Bridge and could clear Sanibel Island, Jack hoisted the sails, switched the diesel off, and turned west. He thought it would be heresy to have the engine running on Peter's sailboat out in the Gulf. Peter's ghost would probably make an appearance if they had done so.

It was the first time Jack had ever sailed a boat this big by himself. When he had sailed Left Behind before, Peter had always been with him. He had bailed Jack out on more than one occasion.

Jack was always surprised at how easy she was to manage. The Island Packet was considerably heavier than Wind Dancer, outweighing her by more than four tons. This made the boat less sensitive to minor fluctuations in the breeze and waves. After the first ten or fifteen minutes, he had the sails trimmed the way he wanted, and he released his crew. With full sail up, they were making an honest six and a half knots. As if to show her appreciation, Left Behind tracked steady and true.

Jack loved the wind in his face and the thought of a vessel this size being powered solely by the wind. They could sail to Mexico if he wanted. Molly had gravitated to the bow, where she always liked to ride. She was sitting alone on the windward rail holding on to the top lifeline. Her legs were underneath the bottom line and hanging over the side of the boat.

Farther back, next to the companionway, Richard and Alex were sitting next to one another on top of the cabin. He watched them with interest. They appeared to be engrossed in a serious discussion. Molly was right. They did make a handsome couple.

Back in the cockpit, Kevin was engrossed in conversation with Walter Dobbs. Kevin was gesticulating, and they broke out in raucous laughter. No doubt Kevin had told him one of his favorite jokes.

An hour later, Jack motioned to Walter and asked if he'd like to take the helm. Walter grinned and made his way back to the helm next to Jack. Walter was delighted. He'd told Jack earlier that he loved sailing. He'd been out with Peter before and occasionally took the helm with Peter directing him.

Jack stood beside him for a few minutes, giving him a few pointers on the way she handled. After he was convinced that Walter knew what he was doing, he left Walter and went up front to sit next to Molly. He noticed that Alex and Richard were still talking and barely acknowledged his passing.

He squeezed in next to Molly and gave her a hug. "What do you think?"

"She," Molly said, emphasizing the pronoun for Jack's benefit, "sails marvelously, don't you think?" She had a big smile.

"Yes, she does. Easy to handle. You'll have to take a turn at the helm."

"Not today. I'm just enjoying the ride. But I'll get my shot next time, right?"

"Absolutely." Jack liked the sound of that.

"I can't believe you gave up the helm to Walter. You looked like you were in heaven back there."

Jack laughed. "I was. But I'll get lots of other chances to do this. I knew Walter wanted to take the wheel, but he was too polite to ask."

"That was sweet of you."

They looked back at Walter, who was enjoying his turn.

"He looks pretty happy, kind of like you did. It must be a sailing thing. How did you learn to sail?" she asked.

He could only laugh as he thought back to his childhood. He told her about a friend who worked at a rental place on the beach. On a slow day, he let Jack take out a small board boat known as a Sunfish. Jack had been around boats all his life, but never a sailboat. It looked easy enough, and he wanted to try his hand at it. His friend helped him drag it out into the water and told Jack to have fun. Jack remembered asking what to do, and his friend said, "It's easy. You'll get the hang of it in no time." As soon as Jack got on top of the little boat, he pulled the single sail in to catch the wind. His friend had neglected to give him further instructions. As soon as the sail caught the full force of the breeze, the boat promptly flipped over, spilling Jack out into the Atlantic Ocean.

Molly started laughing as Jack told her. But, as his friend had forecast, Jack did get the hang of it. The Sunfish was a good boat to learn on. Mistakes were punished promptly and usually involved a dunking. But he learned to get a feel for the wind, a feel that was never lost. It was like riding a bicycle—he never forgot how to do it.

Jack looked behind the boat toward Sanibel; no sight of land. According to his watch, it was almost one o'clock, about what he had predicted. They had full sail up and were still making a steady six and a half knots. Jimmy Buffett music was blaring out of the speakers in the cockpit.

"It's about time," he said.

He stood and reached down to help Molly. They made their way to the rear. Molly stopped to gather Alex and Richard. In the cockpit Walter was still at the helm. Jack went below for the whiskey.

Jack figured Walter was probably the only whiskey drinker on board, but decided for this occasion everyone would have one in Peter's honor. Peter would have appreciated the gesture. Besides, this was supposed to be an Irish wake, and what could be more Irish than Jameson?

Although there was a nice stiff breeze blowing, the heavy boat didn't heel much on a broad reach. He came back out with a bottle of Jameson Irish Whiskey and six shot glasses. He handed Molly the bottle and set the stack of glasses on the cockpit table. Molly opened the Jameson and started pouring as Jack went back down for the urn containing Peter's ashes.

Peter's urn was secure on the bookshelf. He unfastened it and set it on the table. Jack looked over to the humidor. The Sunday he'd moved onto the boat, he'd found it on board. It was flush with Cuban cigars. He opened the box and grabbed a handful. He found the clipper and lighter and stuck them in his pocket. Clutching the cigars in one hand, he climbed back up to the cockpit.

Only Walter and Kevin took him up on the offer of a cigar, with everyone else waving him off. Jack turned the autopilot on so that Walter was relieved of manning the helm. He clipped three of the cigars and handed one and the lighter to Walter. Walter turned out of the wind and managed to light his. Jack handed the lighter and a cigar to Kevin. After several tries Kevin managed to get his lit and passed the lighter to Jack. Jack took the last clipped cigar and put it in his mouth. He took the lighter and remaining cigars back down below and grabbed the urn containing Peter's ashes.

In the cockpit, he turned the music off. Holding the urn, he stepped to the back behind the wheel. He was wearing shorts, t-shirt, and had an unlit cigar in his mouth. In Peter's honor, he hadn't lit the cigar. Plus, he didn't want to smoke it, figuring it would make him ill as it had before.

"I'll keep this short. Peter would like that." Jack smiled and everyone chuckled.

"I think it fitting that we're out here on the open water, under sail, to celebrate his passing. I know he would approve. Peter was an interesting man, somebody whom I was lucky to know for a little over five years. He was totally unselfish and never hesitated to help someone in need. All of you know he left me this boat, for which I'm eternally grateful. But this will always be Peter's boat to me. I'm just the caretaker for what I hope is a long time. Now, before we disperse the ashes, Walter Dobbs would like to say a few words."

Jack stepped to the side, and Walter made his way behind the helm. He took a puff of his cigar and exhaled.

"I had the privilege of knowing Peter Stein for over forty years. Never have I known a more principled person. He was unyielding when it came to truth and justice, regardless of who he was up against. I learned a lot from him and strive every day to live up to the standard he set. He was my best friend, and I miss him."

Walter rubbed his eyes and moved back to his spot on the side.

No one said a word as Jack carefully took the urn and removed the top. He paused for a minute, saying a silent prayer, and turned to pour the ashes overboard. As he did, he said, "We commit his body to the depths. Ashes to ashes and dust to dust."

He watched Peter's ashes disappear into the wind and water behind them. He set the urn down in the floor of the cockpit and turned around to face the group. He picked up his glass of whiskey, and everyone followed his lead. Jack held his glass up high.

"To Peter. Peace be with him."

In unison, the group repeated Jack's toast, and they all drank their whiskey together. Jack was surprised to see

Walter take the bottle and pour another round. When he'd finished, Dobbs raised his glass.

"To my best friend Peter."

Everyone raised their glasses and followed once again.

The group was quiet for a few minutes, then Jack went down below, taking the urn with him. Coming back through the companionway, he smiled and put the cigar back in his mouth.

"Peter would have liked this," he said out loud to no one in particular. He turned the music back on.

His official duties done, he walked back behind the wheel, turned the autopilot off, and shouted, "Ready about."

Richard and Molly took their stations as Jack prepared to turn Left Behind back toward Fort Myers.

"Hard alee," he shouted as he turned the wheel all the way to the right, swinging the bow through the wind.

Richard and Molly did a good job of managing the sails through the tack, and in minutes they were headed east with the wind on their port, or left side.

Sailing back in, they took turns sharing Peter stories. Of course, Walter, having known Peter the longest, had the most interesting stories. Jack was surprised at how relaxed he was with this group. Dobbs was all right and not the stuck up attorney that Jack had thought at first.

Everyone had decided to stick with the whiskey in Peter's honor, and no one was feeling any pain by the time they arrived back at the yacht basin before six. As soon as the boat was properly tied up, Jack jumped off to personally bid his guests goodbye and thank them for coming. Walter was the last to leave. Jack handed him the humidor filled with cigars.

Walter was stunned. "I can't take that, Jack. That's full of fine Cuban cigars. You keep it."

"Walter, I don't smoke these things. It would be a shame to waste them. Watching you, I could tell. You appreciate them. Besides, Peter would want you to have them."

He took the box from Jack, handling it as if it were a priceless treasure. "Thank you, Jack. For these and for today. I hope you'll keep in touch."

"Thank you for coming. And yes, I promise to stay in touch. You know where to find me."

TWELVE

Early Wednesday afternoon, Richard was sitting at his desk when a FedEx envelope arrived. He looked at the return address and saw it was from Manny Garcia.

Curious, he opened the package and pulled out a small stack of papers. A handwritten note was clipped to the front.

> Richard,
> Sorry about the other night. Be careful.
> They are watching.
> Manny

He started reading the material. An hour later, he was finished and couldn't believe what he held in his hands. It confirmed everything he'd suspected. He called Manny's number, but was transferred to voice mail, so he hung up and dialed the main number for Advanced Cardiac Meds.

"Manny Garcia, please," he said when the operator answered.

There was a hesitation, then the voice on the line said, "I'll put you through to his assistant."

"This is Holly Alford. How may I help you?"

"Holly, this is Richard Melton. I'm a friend of Manny's and was wondering how I could get in touch with him."

There was silence on the other end. For a minute, Richard thought they had been disconnected. The voice that responded was no longer chipper and confident.

"I'm sorry, Mr. Melton. Manny—Mr. Garcia was . . . he was killed in Mexico Friday evening."

Now it was Richard's turn for silence. He looked at the envelope and the ship date. Monday's date. The package was marked for two-day delivery.

"That's impossible," he said. "I just got a package from him that was shipped out Monday."

"A FedEx package?" Holly asked.

"Yes, why?"

"We had a mix up in the mailroom Friday. The FedEx packages that were supposed to go out didn't get picked up until Monday."

Richard was in shock. "What happened? To Manny?"

"Friday afternoon, he flew down to our plant in Mexico. He went out for a late dinner, and they think he was mistakenly shot in some drive-by gang thing."

"My God," Richard said. He couldn't believe Manny was dead. And he certainly didn't think it was an accident.

"Have . . . arrangements been announced?"

"No, not yet. I'll call you when they are if you'd like."

He gave her his cell phone number and hung up his phone.

Stunned, he tried calling Jack and Molly, but neither was available. He read Manny's note again and stuck it in his shirt pocket. Now he was nervous about holding the package. It needed to be somewhere safe, not in his office. His first thought was the safe deposit box, but access was too limited. The house was probably not secure enough. After a few more minutes he came up with a plan and left the office to make the arrangements and put it in a safe place.

When he got back to the hospital, he called Molly and Jack again. Still not available. He looked at his watch and knew he would have to leave soon. Steve Ingram, the ACM rep, was meeting him downtown for drinks and dinner. Rivers Community Hospital was ACM's biggest customer, and Steve came to Fort Myers every six weeks or so to take Richard out to dinner.

He took a white USB drive out of his briefcase and wrote a number on it. On his way out of the hospital, he went upstairs to Jack's office.

"Where has he been hiding all afternoon?" he asked Barb.

"Budget meeting with Chuck. Probably be there till late this evening sometime. You need something?" she said.

He handed her the white thumb drive. "Just make sure he gets this, please."

"Will do."

"Thanks, Barb."

Later that night, after midnight, Richard was walking to his car in downtown Fort Myers. He was just leaving the restaurant bar where he and Steve had a couple of nightcaps. On top of the wine with dinner and preoccupied with thoughts of Manny, he was less aware of his surroundings than usual.

Earlier that evening, when he parked on the street two blocks from the restaurant, downtown had been busy. Now, the streets were deserted, except for a homeless man Richard noticed shuffling along the wide sidewalk coming toward him. He was stooped, with a long unkempt beard, wearing threadbare shorts and a faded t-shirt with holes in it. There were sandals, or at least what was left of them, on his feet. The man had a black garbage bag slung over his shoulder and looked down at the pavement as he limped by, dragging his right foot. He stayed near the buildings.

Richard edged closer to the street as they passed, giving him as wide a berth as possible without being obvious. The homeless man didn't even look up at him. He just kept shuffling along as Richard passed. Even though Richard stayed near the street, he detected a distinct aroma coming from the man. It was the smell of someone who hadn't showered in a while.

Richard saw his car a few spaces away. He pulled the remote out of his pocket and clicked the unlock button. The car's headlights flicked on and off. The sharp toot of the horn echoed off the empty street. He never heard the person coming up behind him. Just before Richard got to his car, he felt a sharp object poking him in the back. He dropped his keys.

A deep flat voice said, "That's a knife in your back. Stop and don't say a word or it goes in your kidney. Don't turn around."

Richard froze, wondering where the man had come from. His eyes darted from side to side, looking for help. There was no one on the dimly lit streets this late. Fort Myers wasn't an urban town. After dark, not many people would be found walking the streets downtown. He wondered if the homeless man was watching. Richard doubted it. He seemed out of it and in another world.

"Hand me your wallet, real slow. Don't even think of trying anything. I won't hesitate to kill you if you don't cooperate."

The voice was calm and practiced, not nervous at all. Richard had never been robbed before, but thought that unusual. This guy wasn't an amateur. Richard had a feeling he wasn't the man's first victim.

He reached slowly into his back right pocket, easing his wallet out. He was sober enough to know to oblige the robber. As soon as it was clear of his pocket, he felt a gloved hand touch his. The hand took the wallet. He heard, or thought he heard, the man open the wallet and look through it. Richard never carried a lot of cash, and he was afraid the man would be disappointed. The point of the knife was still pressed against his back.

The robber didn't say anything. That was odd. Richard tried to think. There was ten or fifteen dollars in his wallet, no more.

Suddenly, Richard felt the man's powerful left arm around his neck, shutting off his airway and vocal cords. He tried to struggle, more of a reflex than anything else. Richard grabbed the man's arm and tried to pull it away. The attacker was strong, too strong for Richard. Then he felt the knife go into his right kidney. He screamed, but the sound was lodged below the man's left arm and couldn't escape. The dim street started getting darker, and that was the last conscious thought Richard Melton had.

After Richard collapsed on the street, the homeless man searched Richard's pockets, finding a small sheet of folded paper in his shirt. He opened it, glanced at it in a hurry, then stuffed the note in his own pocket. He finished searching

Richard's clothes, not taking anything else. He looked around, stood, and vanished down the alley.

THIRTEEN

After his morning run, Jack got dressed for work. Since this was the first Thursday of the month, they had a management meeting this morning. When he got to the auditorium, he looked around for Molly and Richard. He didn't see either of them, so he got a cup of coffee and stood at the back of the room for a few minutes, chatting to his colleagues as they filed in for the meeting. Sipping his coffee, he saw Molly over on the left side of the room, about halfway back. There was an empty chair on each side of her.

He walked up the aisle and across the row. Molly saw him as he got closer and smiled. She already had her cup of coffee in hand.

"Hey. Where's Richard?" Jack asked as he sat next to her.

"Haven't seen him." Molly looked him up and down. "Who dressed you this morning?"

Jack looked down and saw one of his shirt buttons was unbuttoned. He buttoned it. "Thanks. I know I can always depend on you to critique my fashion skills."

"Be glad it wasn't your fly. Then I wouldn't have said a word." Molly laughed.

"Friends like you . . ." Jack just shook his head.

William Hart, the CEO, walked up to the podium, preparing to get the meeting underway. Jack looked at his watch. 7:58. William was punctual, as always. The crowd started taking their seats, and the noise level dropped.

Jack turned around to look at the back of the room. Still no sign of Richard. That was odd. Richard was always on time. He looked at Molly, and she just shrugged.

William tapped on the microphone and cleared his throat. "Let's get started, shall we." He waited a beat as everyone made their final seating adjustments and ended their conversations.

"I'm afraid I have some bad news," he said, struggling to keep his emotions in check.

Everyone in the room looked around at each other. No one seemed to have a clue.

"Earlier this morning, I received a call from the Fort Myers Police Department." William's voice lost some of its strength and started to crack.

"I . . . I'm not sure how to say this. Bear with me, this is difficult."

He paused to try to regain his composure. People looked at one another and around the room, trying to see if anyone had a hint as to what was going on. They were worried now.

"Richard Melton was killed late last night."

The words echoed like a shot. There were gasps across the room. Molly grabbed Jack's hand and squeezed it hard. She looked at Jack, her eyes conveying a mixture of disbelief and shock. Jack's mouth was open, but no sound came out. The room was buzzing with whispered conversations.

"They don't have a lot of details, but apparently it was a robbery downtown late last night. They think his assailant approached him when he got to his car parked on the street."

William took off his glasses and rubbed his eyes. "As soon as the arrangements are finalized, we'll share that with you. I'd like for us to observe a minute of silence."

Jack watched the scene as if in another dimension. Except for the sniffles across the room, he could have heard a pin drop. Time stood still. Molly clutched his hand, as if it were the only thing keeping her from slipping over the edge. She didn't realize it, but she was the only thing keeping Jack out of the abyss.

After what seemed like an eternity, William cleared his throat again. "I know it's impossible to concentrate after getting news like that, so I think we'll adjourn."

Jack and Molly didn't hear a word William said. They sat there in silence, squeezing each other's hand. Each prayed the news would go away by the time William finished, that it was all just a bad dream. It wasn't. William adjourned the short meeting and walked away from the podium. People were getting up out of their seats, whispering among each other.

They continued to sit there, stunned, not knowing what to do or say. It had to be a mistake. Then Molly put her arms around Jack's neck, broke down, and wept. He held her close as the tears ran down his cheeks. People walked around them on their way out, not knowing what to say. He could feel her chest heaving against him as sobs racked her body.

They stayed that way as the room emptied. William came over and put his arms around both of them.

"I'm so sorry," he said. "I know how close you were."

After a few minutes, he released them. "Go on home. Take whatever time you need."

After William left, they walked out of the hospital, headed toward the river. Jack thought about going to his boat, but didn't want to risk running into anyone at the marina. When they got to McGregor, he steered Molly left toward her condo. At her door, she fumbled for the key with shaking hands. Jack took the key from her and unlocked the door.

Once inside, she walked out to the balcony, opened the sliding glass door, and sat down, staring at the river. Jack went to the kitchen and opened a couple of beers. He took them out to the balcony and sat down. Neither had said a word since leaving the hospital.

Molly didn't touch her beer. When Jack finished his, he started in on hers.

Two beers later, Molly spoke in a whisper. "I can't believe this, Jack. Why would someone kill him? He was the kindest, most generous person. Who would do that?"

There was no answer, so Jack remained quiet. His heart ached, like a piece had been torn out. Richard was like a brother to him, and he wasn't ready to let him go. It wasn't fair. Why? He knew the question would haunt him for the rest of his life.

He got up to get another couple of beers. "Want anything, Molly?" he asked in a tender voice.

She just shrugged.

He took that as a maybe and walked into the kitchen. He opened the refrigerator and this time noticed the Budweiser on the top shelf; Richard's brand. He started crying and was still crying when he walked back out onto the balcony carrying two Sam Adams.

Molly looked at him and saw the tears running down his face. She started crying again. Jack tried to explain, but couldn't get the words out. Finally, he just shook his head. This time, Molly took one of the beers and took a swallow.

By late afternoon, they had finished all of the Sam Adams in Molly's condo, trying to dull the pain. They couldn't bring themselves to drink the Bud, and every time one of them opened the refrigerator, it started a new round of crying.

Though neither was hungry, they decided they should try to eat something and soak up some of the alcohol. They rummaged around the kitchen, finding enough ingredients to make a couple of sandwiches. Molly grabbed the chips and sandwiches, and Jack fixed them two glasses of water.

Eating made them feel a little better, though it had no effect on the heartache each of them felt. The sun was starting to set as Jack cleared the table. They were still sitting out on the balcony where they had been all afternoon. Jack brought back an unopened bottle of Patron, along with two shot glasses, a salt shaker, and a saucer with slices of lime.

Molly tried to smile. "I bought that for this weekend."

If they had any more tears left, they would have cried again. The three of them had different tastes in beer, but they all liked Patron.

"We should have bought stock in this company years ago," Jack said. He opened the bottle and poured two small shots. They each licked their left hand and poured some salt on it. He handed a glass to Molly, and they each grabbed a lime.

He held his glass up. "To Richard."

Molly touched her glass to his and repeated, "To Richard."

Licking the salt on their hand, they tossed the shots back and sucked on the lime. They only thought there were no more tears. As they set the empty glasses down on the table, both had tears streaming down their cheeks.

The stress and the tequila had an interesting effect on the two. One minute they would be laughing as they shared stories about Richard, the next they would be crying as they realized he would never be around again to create new stories. This went on until over half of the bottle was gone. By this time, they were totally drunk. They could barely walk, and their speech would have been mostly unintelligible to a sober person listening in.

Molly announced that she had to pee and was going to bed while she could. Jack followed her into the condo and plopped down on the couch.

She stopped in front of him, and in a sober moment, reached out and said, "No, sleep with me tonight, please."

Jack wasn't sure what to say, but reached up and let Molly help him to his feet. They almost fell in the process. Together they stumbled back to Molly's bedroom. Molly went into her bathroom, and Jack could hear the tinkle and was surprised to see that she hadn't even bothered to close the bathroom door. He pulled the covers back and collapsed on her bed. As he lay there trying to stop the room from spinning, he saw Molly climbing into the bed. She had on a t-shirt that went down to the middle of her thigh. He wondered if she had on anything else. It didn't matter. Even if he had known, it wouldn't have made any difference.

She backed up next to him in a reverse spoon position. She nestled up close and pulled his arm over her, holding it tight against her chest. The last thing Jack remembered that night was how good she fit up next to him.

Jack cracked open his eyes and saw that it was daylight. His head was throbbing, and he closed his eyes. He was aware of hair in his face. That's odd, I must need a haircut, he thought, still in a drunken stupor. Then he realized there was someone up next to him, and he had his arm around her. What the . . .

The person stirred, and he was frantically trying to figure out who it was, where he was, and what the hell had happened. He risked opening his eyes a bit and saw that he was in someone's room. Although it felt like it was rocking, it was definitely not the boat. And the hair in his face was red, which ruled him out.

Oh shit, he thought, as the pieces started coming together and a few synapses connected. Molly. He was holding Molly next to him. And they were in a bed. Must be hers. That's right, they were drinking tequila last night at her place. Explains the damn headache. Explains a lot of things.

He strained to remember the details of last night, but they had been drowned in tequila. He thought back to earlier yesterday. Richard. Richard was gone. Forever. Pieces were starting to come back; the pieces he didn't want to come back.

Molly stirred next to him, and he was aware of her bare legs touching his. His arm was thrown over her, resting on her t-shirt-covered chest. At least they had some clothes on; that was good. A few more synapses fired. This is going to be awkward. He felt Molly's body stretch out. She was waking up. Jack was trying to figure out how he could get out of Molly's bed and back to his boat without . . .

Molly rolled over, and her face was inches away from his. She peered through barely open eyes, and it registered that she was lying in bed with Jack. Maybe. The eyes opened wider.

"Jack?"

"That would be me. Expecting someone else?"

"What—oh shit."

If his head didn't hurt so much, he would have enjoyed watching her go through the same process he did a few minutes earlier. She closed her eyes again. Turning away from him, she started the painful process of getting up out of bed.

"I have to pee," she said.

As she got up, Jack got a glimpse of her tush, just before she remembered to pull the back of her t-shirt down.

"Crap," she said as she walked to the bathroom, closing the door behind her.

Jack figured the honorable thing to do was to get up out of bed, go into the kitchen, and make coffee. Easier said than done. Just sitting up on the edge of the bed was a major effort. He sat there a moment as he heard water running in Molly's bathroom. He needed to get out of the bedroom. It would be more awkward if he was still there when she came out.

He summoned his strength and wobbled toward the kitchen, making sure he still had on his shorts. His shirt and slacks were somewhere, but thank God he at least had on his boxers. The khaki pants were on the floor next to the bedroom door. He bent over to pick them up and almost fell. As he stumbled around putting them on, he glanced around looking for his shirt. It was on the foot of the bed. He grabbed it and slipped it over his shoulders, trying to find the sleeve openings with his arms. Getting dressed was exhausting with a hangover. In the kitchen, he fumbled around looking for coffee to go in the coffee maker.

"Good morning. I think." Molly stumbled into the kitchen. She was wearing the same t-shirt, but he could see she now had on a pair of gym shorts underneath.

"Morning. Trying to find coffee." His mouth felt like he had swallowed a dozen cotton balls, and his head was throbbing.

Molly stopped as if she first had to assimilate the words, then think hard about where it could be. "Pantry."

The two struggled to make coffee, careful not to touch each other in the process. They managed to load the coffee maker and get it started. Too disoriented to sit down, they leaned against the counter until the coffee was ready. After pouring two large cups, they staggered out to the balcony. Thankfully, it was shaded in the morning. The balcony door was still open from last night.

After drinking their coffee in silence, they began to wake up.

Molly broke the ice. "Thanks for staying last night. I just didn't want to be alone." She took another sip of coffee.

Jack breathed a sigh of relief. "I understand. I wanted to be with you, too." Jack thought about how that came out. "What I mean is—"

"Shut up, Jack. I know what you meant. Just drop it. My head hurts too much to think this early."

Jack tried to laugh, but that made his head hurt more. "Want me to get you some Tylenol?"

"No, thanks. I took some when I got up. Just hasn't kicked in yet."

Jack went in to refill their coffee cups, and he toasted them each a bagel. He brought it out to the balcony, but forgot the cream cheese. They concluded it was too much effort to go back inside and get it, so they ate the bagels without anything on them.

Molly went in to get the next refill and toasted two more bagels. She remembered to bring the cream cheese out. Sitting down, she said, "You know, it would've been much easier to bring the carafe out here. Then we wouldn't have to go inside for refills."

Jack looked at her as if she'd just said the most profound thing. "Now you think of that," was all he could manage.

They spread the cream cheese on the bagels and nibbled on them along with their coffee. It was a workday, and they discussed going into the hospital. They decided it would do them good. But given how slow they were moving, they also agreed to wait until tomorrow.

Jack said he was leaving to go back to his place for a shower and a nap. "I'll come back later or you can come over to the boat," he said.

Molly nodded and walked him to the door. At the door she hesitated, then threw her arms around his neck and kissed his cheek. "Thanks, Jack."

He hugged her back without saying a word. The embrace reassured them both. They still had each other and now needed one another more than ever. She pulled away, and Jack held her shoulders.

"See you later," he said as he turned and walked away.

FOURTEEN

The funeral had been Saturday. Richard's parents had decided to have a service in Fort Myers for the benefit of his many friends in Florida. His body would be taken back to Charleston where he would be buried in a private service in the family plot at the cemetery there.

They flew in Friday with the priest from their church. Although the Meltons were Episcopal, Richard wasn't a member of any church in Fort Myers. So they decided to have the local service at Palms Cemetery, which had the largest chapel in town.

It was an overcast day, with showers off and on, fitting for the occasion. Molly and Jack rode to the service with Kevin, who offered to drive. The service was standing room only. Not only was there a large contingent from the hospital, but many of Richard's friends came from all over the country.

When they got to the chapel, one of the first people they saw was Alex. She looked like a different person, eyes bloodshot, and her face had an odd, pale shade to it even with her dark complexion. She was inconsolable and started crying as soon as Jack and Molly walked over.

They sat together, Jack, Molly, and Alex, with Molly in the middle holding each of their hands. The priest, an older man, had known Richard as a teenager and supplied anecdotes that made the service touching in a personal way. By the end of the service, there wasn't a dry eye in the building.

It had been a long weekend.

Monday morning, after he got to work, Jack called the Fort Myers Police Department and asked to speak with the detective handling the Melton case. The person answering the phone asked him to hold while he transferred the call.

"Budzinski," a gruff voice answered.

Jack explained why he was calling and asked for an appointment to come in and talk with the detective. The detective told him to come in at two. Jack thanked him and hung up the phone.

It was his first day back at work. Although he and Molly had discussed coming in Friday, they weren't ready and took Friday off as well. Coming back to work was harder than he thought.

Barb walked into his office. "You okay?"

He shrugged. "It's hard."

"I know. Just don't be afraid to grieve, Jack. You're not Superman."

He felt his eyes tear up. "Thanks," he said and picked up some papers on his desk, more as a prop.

She handed him a white USB drive. "With all that's happened, I forgot to give this to you. He stopped by last Wednesday afternoon and said to give it to you."

Puzzled at first, he realized she was talking about Richard. He took the drive and looked at it. The number

C157 was written in black on one side. He assumed it was budgets and laid it on the desk.

He had a difficult time concentrating on work. After the funeral, he and Molly had talked well into the night Saturday and most of the day Sunday. They were determined to pick up the pieces on Clearart. They owed it to their friend.

At a quarter of two, Jack walked into the Fort Myers Police Department. He stopped at the officer's desk guarding the entrance and told him he had an appointment with Lieutenant Anthony Budzinski. The sergeant asked to see his ID. Jack pulled out his driver's license and handed it to the sergeant. The officer looked at the license, looked up at Jack, and handed it back. He pointed to the clipboard on the counter and told him to sign the visitor's log.

As he handed him a visitor's badge, he said, "Wear this at all times in the building. Be sure and turn it back in to me and sign out when you leave. No exceptions. Elevators are behind me to your right. Fourth floor, turn right. Room 422 will be down on the left."

He thanked the sergeant and clipped the badge to his shirt as he walked toward the elevator. When he got to the fourth floor, Jack walked off the elevator and turned right. Three doors down, he came to a door marked 422 and knocked.

The same gruff voice he heard on the phone said, "Come in."

Jack entered the small office and saw a stocky man with short gray hair sitting behind a well worn metal desk. The man was dressed in a gray sport shirt with a badge on a chain around his thick neck. Jack noticed a picture of Wrigley Field on the wall behind the man.

"Lt. Budzinski?" Jack asked.

"Yeah?"

"Jack Davis. I spoke with you earlier on the phone."

"Oh, yeah. Have a seat." He motioned to the lone chair in front of the desk.

Jack sat down and looked up at the photo. "Cubs fan, huh?"

Budzinski's face relaxed a bit. "Always. I grew up a few blocks from there."

"How did you end up in Fort Myers?" Jack asked.

"Got tired of shoveling snow. Didn't have enough years in to retire, so got on with the city down here. Of course, there are only two or three thousand of us like that in Chicago. I was one of the lucky ones, had an uncle to put in a word."

He stopped talking and waited for Jack to pick up the conversation.

"Lieutenant Budzinski—"

"Call me Tony."

"Okay, Tony. I'm not sure why I'm here. Curious, I guess. I wanted to ask you about a murder last week. Richard Melton. He was a good friend of mine, probably my best friend."

Budzinski nodded.

"I read the papers and saw the news report, but I guess I just wanted to hear it from the horse's mouth. Bottom line is I'm having a hard time believing my friend was murdered by a homeless man just a few blocks from here."

"It happens," Budzinski said, spreading his hands. He watched Jack.

"Yes, but it doesn't make sense. I know Richard, and I know he wouldn't resist. If someone threatened him, he would have cooperated. He would have given him his wallet."

Jack paused and shook his head. "And on top of that, you're telling me a homeless person overpowered Richard and stabbed him to death? Richard was strong and in good shape, know what I mean?"

Jack looked at Tony for answers.

Tony leaned forward and put his elbows on his desk. "I'm sorry about your friend. I know how hard this is for you. I spent twenty years working the streets in Chicago. You ever seen anyone hyped up on meth?"

Jack shook his head.

"I've seen scrawny little kids on that stuff. Kids that weighed a hundred twenty pounds, dripping wet. It would take four or five officers to get them down and cuff them. Makes people superhuman. That's one of the things they like about it. So, to answer you, yes, it is unfortunate, but a wasted homeless guy on meth could do it. The meth problem isn't confined to the big cities. It's in Fort Myers, too, believe me."

Jack sat back in his chair, deflated.

"I'm sorry, Mr.—Tony. I appreciate you seeing me. I know you're busy and I don't mean to waste your time. I guess I'm just having a hard time with all this. It just seems so unbelievable."

Tony studied the young man in front of him for a long time. He looked down at his desk and back up at Jack before speaking.

"I probably shouldn't tell you this, but there is something unusual about your friend's case."

Jack perked up and leaned forward. "What? Tell me."

"I went down and talked to all the street people I could find, trying to get a lead on his killer. Seems like this new homeless guy showed up a few days before your friend was murdered. According to the others, this new guy just appeared out of nowhere. Kept to himself, didn't socialize with the others at all. He didn't camp with any of the other groups that I could tell. Nobody I talked to knew where he slept. And after the attack, nobody could remember seeing him again, not even later that morning. Like he vanished into thin air."

"I don't understand. What's unusual about that?"

"Mr. Davis, I've dealt with a lot of street people. And they do move around. So it's not odd that someone would just appear one day and be gone the next. Neither is the fact that a new guy would be standoffish, at least initially. Most of them have some sort of mental issues, but who doesn't, right? But these people are observant, and some of them are pretty smart. They don't miss much. Remember, you're out on the street trying to survive. You're prey. So you pay attention to your surroundings, keep an eye out, know what I mean? So nobody I talked to saw where this new guy came from, where he slept and where he went. That strikes me as suspicious. And lay the timing over it? Something smells."

"What are you saying? Did they give you a description of this guy?"

"Look. I don't have anything concrete here, okay? No one could give me a good description, nowhere close. I'm just telling you what my gut is saying, and I probably shouldn't be even telling you all of this. But something doesn't ring true about this. Alarms are going off in my head, and I intend to keep digging. That's all I'm saying."

He looked at Jack. "And if you have anything, anything at all that could help me, then tell me. Even if you don't think it's connected. Let me look for the connection."

Budzinski paused and handed Jack his card. "Do you know of anyone who may have had an issue with your friend?"

Jack took the card and looked at it. For a few seconds he debated whether or not to say anything about Clearart. He decided he wasn't ready to go there yet.

"No. Everyone liked Richard. He was that kind of person. I never heard anyone say anything bad about him. Not too many people I know of that I could say that about, including me."

"Did your friend have a computer?"

"A computer? Sure, he had a laptop. Why?"

Budzinski ignored the question. "Just a laptop, no desktop or anything else?"

"He had a desktop at work. We all do at the hospital. Can't do anything without one anymore. That was the only other one I know of. Why are you asking?" Jack was curious.

"Just wondering, that's all. Thinking there might be something on his computers that could help us. Wanted to make sure we had all of them."

"Like I said, the only one I knew of was his laptop at home. We, Molly Byrne and I, were over at his house quite a lot. I never saw any computer other than that. Was there anything on it?"

Budzinski hesitated. "Don't know. The computer wasn't at his house. Any idea where he usually kept it?"

"What do you mean, it wasn't at his house? He always kept it on his desk by the printer. It wasn't there?"

Tony shook his head. "No. Maybe he took it to work. I was going by the hospital this afternoon to check."

"Lieutenant. I never knew Richard to take his laptop to work. The only reason he got a laptop was so he could use it in different rooms at home. But to my knowledge, it never left his house."

Budzinski wrote something down on the notepad on his desk. "Interesting. I still want to check his office. You know what kind it was?"

"Yeah, it was a Dell, a new one, top of the line, loaded. He just got it a few months ago."

The detective wrote again on the notepad. "Anything else?"

"No."

Jack started to ask why anyone would take Richard's laptop computer, but he thought he knew the answer. "Was anything else missing from his house?" Jack asked.

"Not that we could tell." Budzinski looked at his watch. "I hate to cut you short, but I have another meeting. If you think of anything else, give me a call."

"Thank you. I will. I appreciate your time." Jack got up to leave and shook Tony's hand.

Tony watched Jack leave and thought, where the hell was Melton's laptop? Melton's parents had brought it up when they went to the house. They had a key to the house, and Tony had accompanied them after their son's murder. They walked around the house, his mother touching various sentimental things she saw as they walked around. It looked like a place where the owner had just stepped out and was coming back any minute.

It was Mrs. Melton who brought it up.

"I don't see his computer," she said. "He has a laptop. Most kids do these days. I don't see it anywhere."

That got Tony's attention. He asked her about it, but she didn't know any of the details. She just remembered him saying when she would call him at home he would say he was on his computer. And she remembered him saying he got a new one a couple of months ago and was talking about how much faster it was than his old one.

Yet there was no sign of the computer in the house. There was a printer on a desk in a bedroom that had been converted to an office. But no computer. All of this matched what Davis had just told him.

The detective tore off the top page of his notepad, folded it, and stuck it in his pocket. He was still going by the hospital to check Melton's office, but he didn't expect to find the computer there. There were a lot of unanswered questions about this case, he thought, as he walked out to go to his next meeting.

Jack went downstairs and was still thinking about what Budzinski said and almost walked past the desk sergeant.

"Hey! I need your visitor badge and you need to sign out," the sergeant bellowed at him.

"Oh, sorry." Jack stopped and unclipped the badge. He handed it to the sergeant and signed out. "Thank you."

The sergeant grunted, and Jack walked out.

He called Molly on his way back to work. "Hey, I just talked to the detective handling the case."

"What did he have to say? Any suspects?"

"No suspects, but he did tell me something interesting. I don't think he believes it was a homeless man who did it."

"The newspaper seemed pretty sure about it. Why would he say that?"

"Tony, the detective, seemed to think it didn't sound right, the whole story about the homeless guy. He talked to some of the street people, and there was a new guy around for a few days. Now he's gone and nobody knows anything about him."

"Sounds weird."

He heard her talking to someone else in the background.

"Hey, Jack, I've got to run. Let's get together tonight and we'll talk some more, okay?"

"All right. Come on down to the marina when you get off. See you later."

He pressed End on his phone. Maybe Molly could help him make sense out of this.

He was at his desk when his phone rang.

"Jack," he said.

"Jack. Brian Christopher. How are you?" Brian worked for an investment banking firm on Wall Street.

"I've had better days. A good friend of mine was killed last week, and this is my first day back at work."

"Sorry to hear that. Got a minute, or would you rather call me back?"

"No, no. Now's as good a time as any. What's up?"

"Remember you called me a couple of weeks ago? Asking about a venture capital firm? SA Ventures?"

With all that had happened, Jack had forgotten until now. "Yes, what did you find out?"

"That was a hard one. I had to dig deep on it. My guess is they don't want anyone knowing anything about them. But I made some calls. Nobody will go on record, so I don't have anything concrete, okay?"

"Okay."

"There's like three layers of offshore ownership. Bottom line, all fingers point to it being bankrolled by V. L. Chaney, your boss. Where did you come across SA Ventures?"

Jack was speechless and ignored the question. "You sure about this, Brian?"

"Hey, like I said, no neon signs pointing the way and nothing you can print. But talking to my contacts on the street, that's the consensus. Where did you run across them?"

"They backed a biopharm company I was researching, Advanced Cardiac Meds. Heard of them?"

"Who hasn't? But not on my plate, so haven't checked up on them."

"Well, not only did they back them initially, they're still the largest stockholder."

"Sounds cozy. Any problem?"

"No, just some routine stuff I was doing for a friend," Jack said. He didn't want to get Brian's antenna up. "Thanks for checking it out."

"No problem. Let me know if anything turns up on that."

"Sure; like I said, just some sideline research for a friend, that's all. Take care."

Jack hung up before he said too much.

Later that evening he and Molly were sitting out under the bimini on Left Behind.

"I've been thinking," Jack said.

"Uh-oh, that's dangerous."

He ignored her remark. "Something doesn't fit on this. Richard starts nosing around on Clearart. Then he's supposedly killed by a homeless man. But the homicide detective doesn't buy that. And guess what else?"

"What?"

"Richard's laptop is missing."

"Missing?"

"Budzinski said it wasn't in the house."

"That's strange. I never saw him take it anywhere."

"Neither did I. That's what I told the detective. And this afternoon I find out that SA Ventures, the largest stockholder in ACM, is pretty much a front for Vic Chaney."

"What?"

"My friend Brian, the investment banker, called and told me that. What's strange is that Chaney is going to great lengths to keep that a secret."

"So Chaney is the biggest investor in ACM? That doesn't sound right."

"It's not. All afternoon I kept thinking about a conversation Richard and I had about Clearart. How ACM would do anything to protect their blockbuster drug. Of course, I was referring to making things right if there was a problem. But there's another possibility. Maybe somebody is trying to cover up something. What if Richard was really on to a major problem with Clearart?"

Molly got a serious look and narrowed her eyes. "I'm not sure I like where this is going. Do you really think ACM would resort to . . ." She couldn't finish the sentence. Molly didn't want to think about the possibilities.

"I don't know. It's hard for you or me to think that way. But where billions of dollars are at stake? I think anything may be possible. All I know is Richard was convinced there was a problem with Clearart. We've got to revisit that. Take another look. So what do we have so far?"

"Not much. Richard showed us that information about the Mexican plant. It showed problems with the drug manufactured there."

"Yeah, and he wanted to get patient-specific information and match it up, remember? To verify what was on the computer."

"Jack." Molly leaned across the cockpit table and lowered her voice even though no one was around. "He talked to someone at ACM, remember? After he got those empty IV bags analyzed."

"That's right! What was the guy's name? He was some big shot at ACM."

Molly sat back. "I don't know."

They debated on how to solve the problem. They couldn't remember the name of Richard's contact. With all of the confidentiality measures in place, it would be difficult to bluff their way to the right person.

"I've got it," Molly said. "Alex. She would know, right?"

"You know, you're just too clever." Jack held up his hand for a high-five.

Molly slapped his hand and grinned. The pair was excited about making progress.

She pulled out her phone and called Alex. No answer. She left a message asking her to call them back.

"How about the patient information he was talking about?" Jack asked.

"Not sure. Without knowing which patients he had, we'd have to start at square one with all the patients who had Clearart, then narrow it down to those who got the drug manufactured in Mexico. It sure would help if we had access to the information that he'd already gathered."

"We need to think on that one. At least tomorrow we can track down his friend at ACM. That's a good start."

Molly finished her beer. "I think I'm going to call it a night. I'll help you clean up."

"No, don't worry about it. Not that much to do. Come on, I'll walk you home."

"I'm a big girl, Jack. You don't have to walk me home. Besides, it's not that far."

Jack ignored her and put his shoes on. She knew it was no use arguing with him and let it go.

Engaged in conversation as they walked, they failed to notice the man walking behind them. He had watched them on the dock from the marina parking lot. Dressed in a nondescript t-shirt, shorts and baseball cap, he blended into the Fort Myers cityscape. Once they had turned toward Molly's place, he fell in behind them keeping a safe distance, where he stayed until he watched them get to the lobby of her condo building.

FIFTEEN

The next evening Jack was back over at Molly's condo. She was cooking dinner, and they were in the kitchen.

"I went by Ray's this afternoon to see Alex," Molly said, "since she never called me back. She's not doing well."

"Sorry to hear that. You were right that day on the beach at Cayo Costa. You said they were crazy about each other."

She looked at Jack, surprised at how serious he was. "You remember?"

He nodded. "What's she going to do?"

"She's going back to Indiana for a while. Summer's slow. She said Joey can handle things while she's gone. She's not sure she wants to stay here. She did give me the name of Richard's friend at ACM, Manny Garcia."

"Manny Garcia—that's right. We'll have to look him up. Maybe he'll be willing to talk once he hears about Richard."

"Dinner is almost ready if you want to set the table," she said.

When she came out with dinner, Jack was sitting at the dining room table holding a white USB drive.

"What's that?"

"I'm not sure, but Richard gave it to Barb the day he was killed. Told her to make sure I got it. I thought it was budgets, so it's been sitting on my desk at work all this time. It was in my pocket."

She took it from him and looked at it. "It's Richard's thumb drive," she said.

Neither spoke for a minute. They stared at the drive as they thought back to the last time Richard had been here with them. It was like they were looking at his shadow.

"That was the night he showed us the data he had on Clearart," he said. "It was on a white thumb drive. Let's take a look at it."

Molly set the drive down on the table. In a few minutes, she came back and set her computer on the table. She turned it on and, once it finished booting, she plugged the USB drive into her computer and pulled up the directory. They ate while she scanned the drive.

There were a dozen or so folders on the device. She clicked on the one titled Clearart Patients. A list of fifteen or twenty files popped up on the screen. They seemed to be organized by month. Molly clicked on the first one listed. It appeared to be a list of patients by patient number followed by a five digit code. They recognized the code for the ACM plant in Mexico, 16592, beside some of the names. The only other code was 21734, which was the plant in California. There was a third column which contained a single letter *D* for some of the entries.

"Can you merge the files to get a total for each plant?" Jack asked.

"Sure. Give me a minute." Molly clicked on the mouse several times, typed in a few commands, and in a few minutes had a merged file with totals by plant.

"What do you think the *D* is?" he asked.

Molly studied it and thought. "Deceased," she said.

"Makes sense. He was looking at the mortality rate for the Clearart patients taking the Mexican drug versus the other."

She tapped a few more keys and in a minute had two percentages next to the plant number. The percentage for the Mexican plant was four times the number for the California plant.

"So you're telling me that a patient taking Clearart from the Mexican plant was four times more likely to die than those who took the drug manufactured in California?" Jack wanted to make sure he was interpreting the numbers correctly.

"Based on the data here. That's why he wanted to track it back to the actual charts to make sure the data was valid."

"How do we do that?"

"We'd need access to the medical records for all of these patient numbers. I only have access to the patients on my unit."

"Don't all the Clearart patients go through your unit?"

"They do now, but remember, we only started that program a few months ago. Before that, they could have been spread across several different units."

They went back to the main directory. There was a folder labeled Boats. Jack told her to click on it and underneath was several files. They both noticed a file labeled Left Behind. Why would Richard have a file named after Jack's boat? Molly clicked on it and the computer asked for a password. The file was password protected.

The number C157 was written on the thumb drive in black ink.

"Try C157."

She did and again, the document wouldn't open. They tried Richard's birthday, each of their birthdays, and still nothing.

"Damn, Molly, what could it be? We're missing something here. Think."

They tried several other possibilities that came to their head. Nothing worked. Fortunately, it was a Microsoft Word document and there was no limit on the number of tries. It kept saying "The password is incorrect. Word cannot open the document."

"Try the date we started at Rivers," he said.

They had all started on the same day almost five years ago.

Molly entered the date and clicked OK. The document was opened. They looked at each other.

Jack pulled up a chair next to Molly, and they both read what was on the screen.

> Jack and Molly.
>
> I wanted to put this where you could find it. Sorry for the cloak and dagger routine, but I have reason to suspect that my actions are being monitored.
>
> I know who is behind it and have the proof to back it up. It is in a safe place. I know the two of you can finish what I have started. Don't give up. This is my logon and password at work.

"We've got to get the medical records for patients who received Clearart. Can we get that with Richard's hospital logon?" Jack asked.

"Should be able to, if it's still valid." She went to the hospital's website and logged on with Richard's information. "It still works." She typed and clicked and, after a few minutes, looked up to Jack. "How about dates, patient IDs, and status for all patients receiving Clearart for the past six months?"

"It's a start." Jack watched as Molly clicked the mouse a few more times.

"Okay, done. I downloaded it and printed it. Hang on and I'll get it." She got up and left to get the pages off her printer in her bedroom. Holding the pages in her hand, she walked back to the dining room. She handed Jack a couple of pages, and they started checking the patients against Richard's list. When they had finished, the two lists matched up exactly.

They went in and checked the medical record for the first patient listed. It was a male, 87 years old, who had died less than thirty days after his Clearart treatment. Molly pulled up his electronic MAR, or Medical Administration Record. Sure enough, all three bags of Clearart he'd received were from plant 16592, the plant in Mexico.

It was two a.m. by the time they had finished checking every deceased patient on Richard's list. The mortality rate for the patients receiving Mexican Clearart was indeed over four times that of patients receiving Clearart produced in California.

That was significant. Now they had to figure out what to do with it.

Molly must have been reading his mind. "So what do we do with this?"

Jack sighed. "Stay out of there. I was just thinking that. What do you think about taking it to Larry?"

Molly wrinkled her nose. "Richard's boss? No way. I don't trust him, Jack. He was too quick to tell Richard to drop the whole thing. He's corporate all the way. How about the detective, what's his name?"

"Budzinski? I trust him. That's not it. I just don't think he'll latch on to it, you know? He's a Fort Myers detective, probably has a desk full of stuff he's working on. I can't see him taking this up, not with what little we have."

"But this is huge. I mean, if they, whoever the hell they are, if they did what they did, we're way out of our league."

Jack thought about it. She was right, of course. But he wasn't quite ready to take it to Budzinski yet. They needed to fill in a couple of gaps first. He wanted to hand Budzinski enough substance that he couldn't afford to ignore it.

"Not yet. We have to have a compelling story, one that he can't walk away from. Look at it from a distance. What do we have? A bunch of data that more or less proves Advanced Cardiac Meds is playing loose with the numbers on Clearart. The data indicate, *indicate* being the operative word, that the Clearart from Mexico isn't effective. Maybe a bunch of old people are dying as a result, maybe not. Remember, we can only show a correlation, not a cause. He's not going to be interested in that. Now if we can give him something to show that Richard was killed by someone because of it, then he'll be all over it."

They discussed other people. For every name they mentioned, they didn't trust the person or didn't know him well enough.

Finally, Jack said, "What about Chuck, my boss? He's always been straight with me. Plus, he's the one who gave me the gossip line about getting Richard to back off. And he has a lot of contacts in HealthAmerica."

She didn't immediately veto the idea. He could tell she was considering it. "I honestly don't know him well enough. I don't know that much about him. But I trust your judgment. He's the best we've come up with so far."

Jack's gut told him that Chuck could be trusted. He tried to think of reasons against it, but came up empty. They decided to sleep on it and, if they felt the same way tomorrow, then Jack would take it to Chuck.

We have an advantage here in front of us, Jack thought. Nobody knows that we have this information. Advanced Cardiac Meds thinks they got it when they snatched Richard's computer. As far as they know, it's over. But we have to be careful.

"Have you got another USB drive?" he asked.

"Sure, in my bedroom. Hold on a minute." Molly went to her room and came back with a similar sized device that was red.

"Copy everything from Richard's drive to your hard drive and to the other USB drive."

Molly inserted the red USB drive into another port on her laptop. She clicked her mouse several times and copied the files as Jack had requested. "Done," she said.

Jack reached over and pulled out the two drives. He handed Molly the red one and put the white one in his pocket.

"Hide it somewhere here in your condo. Not around where you keep your computer. I'll take the other one and hide it on the boat. That way we'll at least have copies in two different locations in case one of them disappears."

"Don't you think you're being a little paranoid?"

"Maybe. But this is all we have right now. And I don't want to take any chances on it disappearing. We're going to find out who's responsible. And I hope they burn in hell.

"Before you turn the computer off, let's Google Manny Garcia," he said.

Molly typed it in and they looked at the screen. The third entry was an obituary from a Bay Area newspaper. She clicked on it and they read it together.

> *Manny Garcia, of San Jose, died Friday evening in Cuernavaca, Mexico. Authorities there think he was an accidental victim of gang violence. Mr. Garcia was a scientist at Advanced Cardiac Meds in Mountain View. Arrangements have not been announced . . .*

They looked at each other in disbelief. Jack checked the date of the obituary. It was the Sunday before Richard died.

"This is getting too weird, Jack. What's happening?"

All he could think about was how all of this was connected. It had to be—this much coincidence was unbelievable. What in the hell is going on here?

"I don't know, Molly. Something's going on—I just can't figure it out. It's getting late. I think we've done enough tonight." Jack got up to leave, hoping she'd ask him to stay.

Molly followed him to the door and gave him a hug. "Be careful."

"I could stay, you know?" He started to add that he could sleep on the couch, but he saw the hesitation in her face and decided to say no more.

"I'm fine, Jack."

He nodded. "Okay. See you tomorrow."

Jack walked out the lobby door of Molly's building and started walking toward the marina. He walked past the parking lot at Ray's, and it was mostly empty; not a lot going on a Wednesday night. No one was on the street this late. He reached into his pocket and could feel the USB drive. They needed a plan. Now that they knew what they had, they needed a plan.

The news about Garcia was disturbing. Richard talks with him, and a week later, they're both dead? Both victims?

He got back to the locked gate at the dock and looked around before punching in the code. This is ridiculous, he thought. He was getting paranoid. Everything was quiet. Passing through the gate, he walked out to the J dock. Wind Dancer, with the For Sale sign on the back rail, looked lonely. Jack still felt a tinge of guilt about leaving her. He walked between the two boats and stepped onto Left Behind, *his* boat. Still took some getting used to.

Down below, he looked for a place to stash the USB drive. He spied a tissue box on the shelf next to the table and placed the white thumb drive in the box. Probably not a great spot, but he had trouble thinking like a thief. It would have to do for now.

Taking off his clothes, he lay down on the spacious berth up front. Let the night shift work on it, he thought, trying to shut down his racing mind and go to sleep. Let the night shift handle it.

SIXTEEN

"I need to talk to you about something, but I'm not sure where to start," said Jack. He and Chuck Thompson were sitting at a table on the deck at Ray's. "But first I need your promise that you won't tell anyone."

Chuck had always been as much a friend as a boss, and it had been that way since they first met. He and his wife Kay treated Jack as family, often having him over for dinner. Jack had grown close to the Thompsons, close enough that their two kids called him Uncle Jack.

"This sounds serious. Are you in some kind of trouble, Jack?" Chuck had a worried frown on his face.

"No, not that I know of. I'm just in over my head on something, and I need some advice and guidance."

Chuck laughed. "You must be desperate, is all I can say." Seeing the serious look on Jack's face, Chuck adopted a tone to match. "But you know you can trust me. And I'll help you any way I can."

Jack hesitated and plunged in. "Remember a few weeks ago you mentioned that Richard Melton had ruffled some feathers at corporate about Clearart? You pretty much told me to pass along the message to him to drop it." He watched Chuck for a reaction.

Chuck sat there, expressionless at first. Recognition flashed across his face. "Yes, I remember. He seemed to think there was a problem with Clearart."

"Well, there *is* a problem with Clearart. Richard put together the hard data to prove it."

For some reason, he decided to leave Molly out of it. He still wasn't sure about trusting the man across the table from him.

Chuck looked skeptical, but willing to listen.

Over a few beers, Jack proceeded to tell Chuck everything he knew about Clearart and Richard's discoveries. He detailed the numbers regarding the mortality rate involving Clearart from the new plant in Mexico. The only things he left out were his theory about Richard's murder and Molly's involvement. When he finished his story, he could see that his boss was visibly disturbed.

"And you have the facts to back this up?" Chuck asked.

"Absolutely. Pharmacists are pretty obsessive, and Richard was no exception. He was meticulous. We have a list of patient IDs with dates and the Clearart lot number associated with each. There's no doubt the mortality rates for Rivers Community patients getting Clearart produced in ACM's new plant are higher."

"We?" Chuck had picked up on Jack's slip of the tongue.

Jack cursed himself, vowing to be more careful. "Sorry. I still include Richard."

Chuck nodded. He seemed satisfied with the explanation. "This is heavy stuff, Jack." He stroked his chin as he considered what Jack had told him.

"I know. Sorry for dumping this on you, but I didn't know who else I could trust."

"I still find it hard to believe that someone is deliberately covering up problems with Clearart." Chuck was clearly bothered by the thought. "I mean, that's criminal. That crosses the line."

Jack wanted to tell him that he thought Richard's death was related, but realized he didn't have any proof. Chuck was struggling as it was, and Jack didn't want to further complicate things.

"I understand. My reaction was the same. But the more I dig, the more I believe it. Pulling the rug out from under ACM on Clearart could cost them hundreds of millions of dollars. Who could be behind this?" Jack asked.

"I'm not convinced yet, but if this is true, then it has to be at the highest levels. Someone at ACM corporate. Someone with the power and authority to pull this off. This is a scary proposition."

Jack debated on whether or not to broach the subject of their employer. "What about HealthAmerica? Maybe they're involved, too?" he asked.

Silence hung over the table as Chuck processed Jack's comment.

"Hold on, Jack. First of all, I've yet to be convinced there really is a problem with Clearart. I haven't seen a shred of evidence. And now you're suggesting that HealthAmerica is involved? What would they have to gain? Nothing. I might be able to see where ACM has a lot to lose and conceivably they would go to great lengths to protect their baby. But HealthAmerica has no incentive, none."

"But you know how much we make off of Clearart treatments. That's a lot of money." Jack said.

"Yes, but we made a lot of money off open heart surgery before there was a Clearart. So if Clearart falters, we might take a short-term hit, but it would be quickly replaced by something else. That's the beauty of the hospital business—we make money any way you go. Sorry, I can't imagine anyone at HealthAmerica willing to take that kind of risk."

Jack let it drop. Chuck made a good point, and besides, there was no proof that HealthAmerica was involved.

"Okay, so what do we do with this?" Jack asked. "We just can't ignore it. The evidence is too compelling."

"I honestly don't know, Jack. You've got to give me time to process this. And you're going to have to show me something concrete. I can't say as I've ever faced anything like this."

"Fair enough. Let me get Richard's information together."

They finished their last beer, and Chuck excused himself. "I should be going. Kay is wrestling with a couple of hyperactive kids and probably needs some help by now. I'll sleep on all of this and get back to you in a couple of days, okay?"

"Thanks, Chuck. I appreciate your time. Tell Kay and the kids 'hello' for me."

Jack watched as his boss walked out. He wondered if he'd done the right thing by telling him. He sat there for a bit, pulled out his phone, and called Molly.

"Hey. You busy? I just got through talking to Chuck."

"What did he say?"

"I'm over at Ray's. Why don't you come over and have some dinner with me?"

She told him to give her ten minutes.

Fifteen minutes later, Jack looked up and saw Molly walking toward him.

"So, how did it go?" she asked.

"He was honestly surprised, I think. And bothered by what I told him. I kept to the basics, giving him some of the data that Richard had come up with. I didn't tell him you were involved, and I didn't mention anything about our suspicions relating to Richard's death. He wants time to think on it and wants to see the data. Said he'll get back to me within a few days. That was pretty much it."

"That sounds promising. At least he didn't tell you to drop it or that he didn't believe you."

"I still think Chuck's straight up. Guess we'll see."

They ordered something to eat, had one beer, and left. Ray's wasn't the same. Alex had already left for Indiana. Too many ghosts, Jack thought; for all of them. He knew Molly could feel it, too, and he realized that Alex wouldn't be back. He didn't blame her, doubting that he and Molly would return often.

He walked Molly home and went back to his boat, still not able to connect the pieces of the puzzle.

The next evening after work, Jack went over to Molly's so they could go online and get the information together to show Chuck. She was seated at her dining room table in front of her laptop. He stood behind her, looking over her shoulder. He could detect just the faintest smell of a delicate perfume. Whatever it was, it suited her.

Molly signed on to the hospital system using Richard's logon. After she logged in, she tapped on the keyboard and proceeded to pull up the mortality data.

"Shit. Look at this, Jack. I can't believe it." Molly pointed to the screen and shook her head.

He looked at the bar chart on the screen. "That's the chart for the peer group. Bring up the one for just Rivers Community Hospital."

"Damn it. That is the one for Rivers." Molly was exasperated.

"Can't be. Re-enter the query." Jack was struggling to make sense of what he was seeing on the screen.

Carefully, Molly entered the query again, making sure she specified only data for Rivers Community Hospital. In a few seconds, the same chart displayed.

Stunned, Jack looked at Molly, not saying a word, trying to get his head around what he was looking at on the screen. "This doesn't make sense, Molly."

They stared at the screen as if, by watching it, some explanation would be forthcoming. The section labeled 16592 was roughly the same size as the other one on the chart.

Molly clicked on the keyboard and opened another window. She brought up another bar chart.

Jack looked at it. One piece, labeled 16592, was considerably larger than the other. "Yeah, that's the right one. The section representing the Mexican plant is larger. What's going on?" Jack asked.

"This is the chart from Richard's data on my hard drive. The one we verified the other night."

Jack look confused. "I still don't understand."

Molly looked at him and shook her head. "Think about it, Jack."

Jack sat across the table and looked at her. He had a puzzled expression.

"The first chart is from the hospital system. The second one came from Richard's data," she said.

"Wait a minute. You're telling me that the second chart came from the hospital database, but now when you go back into that same database two days later it has somehow changed?"

Molly nodded. "Exactly."

Jack shook his head. "So you're telling me that someone changed the data on the hospital computer system?"

"How else could that have happened, Jack?"

"Molly, maybe you copied the wrong file or something."

"Don't you think I thought of that? I used the same query that pointed to the same database! I double-checked the query to make sure it hadn't been changed. Somebody changed the database."

"Okay, okay. Calm down. So how do you prove it?"

Molly looked down. "Don't know," she said. "Everything is electronic now. When the bag is received by the pharmacy, they scan the bar code label on the bag to show it's received in inventory. Later, before it's sent up to the unit, pharmacy scans the bar code label on the bag, showing it going out to the floor. The unit scans it when it's received and scans it again when they hang it, along with the patient ID. Not like the old days, when there were manual logs that you could go back and reconcile. The whole trail is electronic."

Finally, Molly said what both of them were thinking. "They've changed the data, Jack. Somehow, they've changed it."

He still couldn't believe what he was seeing. But there was no other explanation. "How the hell could that happen? Somebody at the hospital went in and changed the data?"

"Maybe, but unlikely. Think about it. Since the acquisition by HealthAmerica, all of the applications at the hospital have been gradually converted to HealthAmerica's computer system. All of the hospital computers are linked together with corporate. They're controlled by the HealthAmerica data center in Atlanta. My bet is that the data was changed at corporate. Either changed or the query now points to a bogus database. Either way, this leads to HealthAmerica corporate," she said.

It was dawning on Jack now. "So, an electronic version of maintaining two sets of books."

"What does that mean?" she asked.

"One of the oldest ruses in accounting. If you're hiding something, you maintain two separate sets of accounting records, or books. Criminals have done this forever. If the auditors come in, they get to see the sanitized version. Only the crooks have access to the unabridged version."

Molly understood the parallels. "Make up a bogus database and substitute it for the real one. Bury the real one where only they, whoever they are, can get to it. Anyone else sees the sanitized version, as you call it."

"You got it." Jack had to admit, it was clever. Now if he and Molly took the data to someone, when they looked at the data on the computer, nothing was out of line.

"So how do you expose that scam?"

Jack explained that in the old days, as he called them, you would take the set of books you were auditing and trace everything back to the original source documents, usually manual records. Time-consuming, but eventually revealing. Since it was impractical to go back and recreate bogus source documents, one would eventually uncover the discrepancies between the two and the scam unravels.

In today's world, that was becoming increasingly more difficult. Since most of the source documents were now also electronic, it was much easier to manipulate and falsify data. Before, one would go back to each patient's paper medical record and verify the data. Now, since medical records were electronic, one was just going back to another electronic record that could just as easily be altered; much more difficult to trace back.

"So we're screwed?" She was angry and frustrated that someone had outsmarted them.

"Wait a minute, Molly. Why did they change the data?" Jack asked. "Think about it. As far as the bad guys knew, only Richard had the data. They steal his computer, kill Richard, end of story. No loose ends, right?"

Molly nodded.

"So why create a bogus database? That would be a lot of effort to do that. Why bother?" Jack continued.

"Insurance?" Molly guessed. "Just in case the data got out?"

"Not necessary. You've eliminated the person who figured it out. You have his computer with the data on it. There's no evidence anyone else—"

They looked at each other, the horrible thought registering simultaneously. Chuck. Jack had told Chuck about the data. Yesterday.

Jack banged his forehead with the heel of his hand. "Damn. I'm so stupid."

She reached out and put her hand over his. "Don't, Jack. We both agreed. He was our best shot. How were we to know?"

They sat there for another minute, still disbelieving what they were seeing on the computer and wondering what to do now. Realizing it was no use hoping, Molly signed off the hospital computer system. Both their minds were racing, trying to figure out how to proceed.

"Well, now we know for certain that someone is trying to cover this up. Richard was on to something, no doubt about it now." Frustration was still showing in Jack's voice. "We've just got to shift to Plan B."

"What's Plan B?" Molly asked.

"Not sure. But obviously we have to do something different." Jack got up and went into the kitchen for two more beers.

For another couple of hours, they sat there spinning different scenarios. They still didn't know who was behind this, but concluded it didn't matter at this point. Somebody was covering up the Clearart problem, and it needed to be exposed. They had copies of the real data and, given the resources and access, the truth could be discovered based on what they had. Nobody could go back and change every single piece of source data. At least Jack didn't think so.

What was now obvious was that someone pretty high up in HealthAmerica was in on the cover-up. This went beyond Rivers Community Hospital. ACM couldn't change data on the hospital's computer system.

Jack yawned and glanced at his watch. One o'clock. He didn't realize how late it was. "I think we've kicked it around enough for tonight. We both have to work tomorrow. Let's sleep on it and take a fresh look tomorrow night."

She walked him to the door and gave him a big hug after she opened it. "Don't worry. We'll figure it out." She stood back and smiled. "Hey, we're pretty sharp, right?"

Her smile was infectious. Jack found himself smiling back, in spite of the disappointing evening. "Yes, we are. Sweet dreams."

He heard her latch the door as he walked toward the elevator. Nothing they could do about it tonight. Get a good night's sleep; let the night shift work on it.

When he got down to the lobby, he walked out into the parking lot and turned left toward the marina. There was a slight breeze blowing off the river. It didn't help much; the air was still humid. There were a few cars still in Ray's parking lot, cars belonging to stragglers still out on the deck or cars abandoned for the evening by their inebriated owners.

He could see the lights of the marina ahead. When he got closer to the locked gate at the docks, he had the strange feeling that someone was watching him. He stopped and turned around to look behind him. Seeing no one, he slowly shifted his gaze to each side. A gray tabby cat crouched beneath the shadows of a palm tree, intently watching something that Jack couldn't see. There was no one visible in any direction. Everything was quiet, other than the ubiquitous clanging of the rigging in the masts of the sailboats in the marina.

Shrugging it off to nerves and being tired, he punched in the code on the gate and let himself in. He eased the gate shut not to disturb anyone sleeping. As he walked down the docks to his boat, the sense of someone watching still nagged at him. Too wired to go to sleep, he sat in the cockpit of his boat, facing the marina buildings.

He stared intently, scanning the walkway that ran along the seawall for any sign of a person. There. Somebody walked slowly down the sidewalk toward the locked gate that Jack had just entered. It was an average sized man wearing shorts, a tropical print shirt and a baseball cap of some type. That only described about forty percent of the population in Fort Myers, Jack thought.

The man walked up to the gate, looked to each side, then punched in the access code. The gate opened, and he walked through, careful to shut the gate with as little noise as possible.

Jack tensed as he watched the man walk toward J dock. When he got to the intersection of the main dock and J dock, he looked up and waved at Jack as he continued on to what Jack calculated was L dock, two docks over. Jack had to stand and crane his head to see where the man headed. He watched as the stranger stepped aboard a large powerboat. He opened the cabin door and flipped on lights as a familiar owner coming home for the evening.

Jack took a deep breath and sat back down. Damn. He needed to relax. He was getting paranoid, which wasn't good. After his heart rate slowed and he calmed down, he unlocked the cabin door and went down below. He shook the tissue box on the side of the cabin and heard the USB drive rattle inside. Satisfied that all was well, he shed his clothes and turned out the lights.

SEVENTEEN

Jack sat at his desk staring at the telephone message in his hand. Chuck had called earlier. Jack was in a meeting, so Chuck called Barb and asked her to tell Jack to call him ASAP. It was impossible to avoid Chuck forever. Sooner or later Jack would have to call him. Then what? How was he going to turn off what he started?

He was hurt that Chuck had betrayed him. He really thought that he could trust him. But he did want to hear what Chuck had come up with. Maybe it would help him figure out what steps to take next. Or steps not to take.

His gut told him to keep Chuck in play. Maybe he could use him somehow. It would arouse too much suspicion if Jack suddenly changed his mind about Clearart, since he'd been so insistent before.

Jack could imagine how it would sound. Oh, never mind, I was mistaken. There really was nothing to our discussion the other evening. Just forget about it. No, that wouldn't work.

He decided that he wanted to see Chuck in person. Maybe something about Chuck's demeanor would be of use. He called Mary, Chuck's assistant, and asked when he could have a few minutes with Chuck. She told him to come up around two forty-five and she would squeeze him in before Chuck's three o'clock meeting.

At quarter of three, Jack walked into Chuck's outer office. His door was open, and Mary nodded for him to go inside. He closed the door behind him and waited for Chuck to get off the phone. Chuck mouthed for him to sit down at the small conference table.

He hung up the phone and joined Jack at the table. "I swear. I spend half my time on the phone with corporate. There needs to be some kind of limit on that. Anyway, I've been thinking about our conversation the other night. It's been bothering me," Chuck said.

Jack watched his face closely for something, some kind of tell.

"This is a serious allegation," Chuck said, emphasizing the word allegation. "And I think we need to escalate it pretty far up and quickly."

"What did you have in mind?" Jack asked.

"I think you and I should take this to Vic. He needs to know, and he has the power to do something."

"Vic Chaney?" Jack was surprised.

"I know Vic. Remember, I used to work with him. Even though we don't travel in the same circles these days, I do have some history with him. And he has the clout to make things happen."

Jack was shaking his head. "I don't know. No offense, but Chaney doesn't have a particularly good reputation from what I've heard. Grapevine says he's ruthless. Why would he take the ball on this?"

Chuck hesitated a minute before answering. "Vic is ruthless, and he puts the company first, ahead of everything. Which is one of the reasons I want to get him involved.

Something this big could have a lot of fallout for HealthAmerica. If I know him, he'll go ballistic and be rattling cages before we finish the conversation."

"What if he has something to do with it? He's on ACM's board," Jack said in a soft voice.

"Come on, Jack. I told you before, HealthAmerica has nothing to gain. Vic Chaney is the Chief Executive Officer of a Fortune 500 company. He has more money than Citibank. And you honestly believe he would risk that for, what? For a drug company that's screwed up? No way." Chuck sat there glaring at him.

For a moment, Jack debated on telling Chuck about SA Ventures. "Sorry. Just trying to think of possibilities, that's all. I don't know, Chuck. I'm still not comfortable taking this to him."

"Jack." Chuck was choosing his words carefully now. "You've put me in a tenuous position on this. I have a fiduciary responsibility here. I guess what I'm saying is I'm not sure I can sit on it. The shit hits the fan and it comes out that I knew, well . . ."

The message was clear. Regardless of his previous commitment to not tell anyone, all bets were off.

Jack had created a monster, and it was developing a life of its own. He got up to leave. "I understand. But let me bring the data in tomorrow and go over it with you before you call. Just to cover the bases." He started to add that he didn't appear to have a choice, but decided to keep his mouth shut for once.

"Okay, that makes sense. Tell Mary to fit you in tomorrow afternoon."

Jack didn't comment. He got up and walked out of Chuck's office. He stopped at Mary's desk and made an appointment for the following day.

On his way back downstairs, he thought about calling Molly, but decided to wait until he saw her after work. He finished out the day uneventfully with the usual mix of meetings, telephone calls, and paperwork. He was working on budget numbers when Barb stuck her head in the door.

"See you tomorrow," she said.

Jack looked at his watch. Five thirty. The afternoon had flown by. "Okay. Have a good evening." An hour later, he had the budget numbers where he wanted for the time being. Logging out of his computer, he tidied up his desk and headed out the door.

Kevin was sitting on the back of his boat, beer in hand, when Jack walked out the J dock.

"Hey, Kevin. You look comfortable—more so than me."

Kevin was sitting in the chair barefoot, wearing shorts and a tattered NY Jets jersey. "Another day in paradise. I've got another one here if you'd care to join me," Kevin said.

"No, thanks. I'm headed over to Molly's as soon as I change." Jack took his shoes off and stepped aboard Left Behind.

"The guy from the boatyard was here today. Changed the oil on your boat."

Jack had his back to Kevin and froze before unlocking the cabin door. He turned around. "What guy?"

"Some guy from Blue Water Boatyard." Blue Water Boatyard was one of the big full service boatyards out on Fort Myers Beach. They had done some work on Wind Dancer before. "Said you wanted the oil changed. Wanted to confirm it was your boat. According to him, wouldn't be the first time they had been given the wrong slip." Kevin saw the puzzled look on Jack's face and realized Jack was confused. He laughed. "Not that boat. Wind Dancer," he said, pointing to the Catalina.

For a minute, Jack was even more confused. Then he realized what Kevin was telling him and nodded. "You threw me for a minute. I thought you were telling me he had worked on this boat."

"Yeah, I could tell." Kevin laughed again. "No, he stopped at Wind Dancer and asked me was it Jack Davis's boat. I said it was. Of course, I didn't tell him that you were a tycoon and owned the boat next to it as well."

"Hopefully I can be back to one boat soon. I can't afford two."

Jack turned around and unlocked the cabin door, his hand shaking slightly. He went down inside the cabin and looked around. Nothing was out of order. Of course, he had no reason to think there would be, but after the news he just heard, he wasn't sure about anything. He went forward to his berth, picked up the tissue box, and looked inside. The white USB drive was still there.

After changing, he walked back up the steps to the cockpit. Kevin was still sitting on his boat.

Jack stepped out onto the dock and over into Wind Dancer's cockpit. "Guess I better check and make sure he didn't mess up anything. You know how boat mechanics are," he said, mostly for Kevin's benefit.

"I hear you. Probably a good idea."

Jack unlocked the padlock and removed the companionway boards. This was the first time in almost two weeks that he'd been inside Wind Dancer. Nothing appeared to be ransacked. It was hard to tell if anything was out of place. He'd moved Peter's things over here after he moved into Peter's boat. That way he would have the time to go through them. But he wasn't sure exactly where he had put things. At the time, he hadn't paid attention.

Going through the cabin, he looked carefully at everything, trying to remember what had been there and if anything was missing. This is hopeless, he thought. What would somebody be looking for? Whoever it was had to be thinking they were looking through Jack Davis's things. Think like they do, he told himself. That shed a different light on the situation. If I was looking through Jack's things, what would I be looking for? Data? Data relating to Clearart? Hardcopy data? Electronic data? Computer.

With a new sense of direction, he stepped back and looked at the cabin from a different perspective. Computer. Peter had a laptop, but Jack had left that on the other boat. In his spare time, he'd been going through and copying files, slowly cleaning it up. He was planning on giving it to a school. So there was no computer on board this boat. Mark that off the list.

What next? Electronic data. Jack remembered Peter had three or four USB drives. And a portable hard drive. The USB drives were still on the other boat. He'd determined that Peter had used the portable hard drive for backup, so Jack had brought it over to this boat. Where had he put it? Think. On the shelf next to the chart table. Jack looked. It was gone. Someone had moved everything together so it would appear nothing was missing. But he was sure he'd put it there when he'd moved Peter's things over to this boat. There was no need to look any further.

He climbed up out of Wind Dancer's cabin.

"Everything all right?" Kevin asked.

"Fine, they didn't make too much of a mess."

"Anytime you need me to babysit somebody like that, let me know ahead of time. I'll be happy to check up on them."

"Thanks, Kevin. I'll keep that in mind."

Jack decided to go back on board Left Behind and grab the USB drive to take with him. Though he doubted anyone would have the nerve to come back tonight, he wasn't going to take any chances.

"You won't believe what happened," Jack said as Molly opened the door to her condo and let him in. "The bastards broke into my boat and stole a hard drive."

"What? Broke into your boat? What hard drive?" Molly was shaking her head as Jack paced the floor of her condo. "Calm down and start over. Slowly, please."

She sat on the sofa as he told her what had happened at the yacht basin, starting with Kevin's remarks as he walked up to his boat. She was shaking her head as he talked. Midway through the story, she got up and went to the kitchen for a couple of beers.

"Don't stop, I'm listening," she said as she hurried back and handed Jack a beer.

By now, he was sitting, but still agitated. He finished telling her the story, only stopping for a few sips of beer.

Jack suddenly remembered he hadn't told her about the rest of his day. "Oh, and there's more. This was a hell of a day. I forgot to tell you what else happened."

"What else? Wasn't that enough?" Molly shook her head.

He told her about his conversation with Chuck Thompson.

When he was done, she looked at him and said, "Anything else today?" She told him to open a bottle of Chianti and sit down at the dining room table.

He could hear her in the kitchen, but when he offered to help, she just told him to stay put. The smell of something good emanated from the kitchen. In a few minutes, she walked out carrying a pan of homemade lasagna and set it on the table. It smelled wonderful. She reappeared with garlic bread sticks and a salad before sitting down.

"I'd forgotten what a good cook you are. This looks wonderful," Jack said as she put a serving of lasagna on his plate first, then hers. He sprinkled some freshly grated Parmesan cheese on their lasagna. With the first forkful, he closed his eyes and savored the taste.

"This is really good, Molly. Where did an Irish girl learn to cook Italian like this?"

"My dad was Irish, but my mom was Italian. I think that's why he married her, because she was such a great cook."

"I'm impressed. This is delicious."

"Glad you like it."

They enjoyed the meal and most of the wine. It was a relaxing end to a stressful day, especially for Jack. Molly told stories about growing up in Boston. Jack didn't know whether it was the wine or what. She usually didn't say too much about Boston. But he was glad she was sharing with him, and it helped get his mind off the events of the day.

After dinner, he insisted that Molly stay put while he cleaned up the kitchen. After a meal like that, it was the least he could do. When he was done, he brought the last glass of Chianti out with him to Molly, where she was sitting on the balcony.

"Thanks for cleaning up," she said.

"Thank you for cooking such a tasty meal. What other secret talents are you hiding from me?" he asked.

She smiled at him, her green eyes sparkling. She ignored his question. "I'm glad you enjoyed it. It was my mother's recipe. I haven't cooked it in quite a while."

"Well, she would be proud. It was wonderful. Any time you want to cook that again, just let me know."

They sat out on the balcony, sharing the glass of wine and discussing what to do next. Whoever was behind this knew that Jack had a copy of the Clearart files. Once they figured out the files weren't on the hard drive they had taken from Jack's boat, they would be back. Maybe it was time to get Budzinski involved.

They decided to go in and get on the hospital computer again, take another look at the data and see if there was something else. Inside at the table, Molly logged on to the hospital system using Richard's ID and password.

ACCESS DENIED.

"Damn," Molly said, as she carefully typed it in again. She figured she mistyped something in her hurry to log in.

ACCESS DENIED.

She looked at Jack. "Now we can't even log onto the hospital with Richard's ID anymore. They've blocked it."

Jack wasn't surprised. Even if no one was trying to deliberately throw obstacles in their way, this was bound to happen. Sooner or later, Richard's ID would be disabled. He was surprised it took this long. Although Molly and Jack had hospital sign-ons, theirs were much more restricted than Richard's. Jack had no access to clinical information, and Molly had access limited to patients on her unit. They were back to the information they had on Richard's USB drive.

"You still have your copy of Richard's USB drive here?" Jack asked.

"In my bathroom. Why?"

"Just thinking. Whoever took the hard drive off the boat will be back when they discover it has nothing about Clearart on it. Your condo is a lot more secure than my boat. Next time, they'll probably get the right boat, but not a lot I can do about that."

As long as they had a copy of the information, they were fine. It was late, and they decided to call it a night. Not much else they could do anyway. Molly let Jack out.

When he got to the lobby, he looked around before stepping outside. A car was turning into the condo driveway, most likely a resident. An older couple was out walking a little white dog. The dog, some sort of Peek-a-something, was straining at the leash. When he opened the lobby door, Jack could hear it yapping. No one else was on the street.

Jack walked back to his boat a little faster than usual, carefully observing his surroundings on the way. Kevin was in for the night, his boat dark. Jack opened the door to his boat and looked around. Everything was just as he left it.

As he lay on the bed, something was nagging at him. He couldn't quite put his finger on it. Something about today had triggered a question in his mind. A piece of the puzzle was missing. It was right in front of him, and he couldn't see it. It was like night vision. If he stared at something in low light, it was harder to see. He had to keep his eyes moving and look to the side.

EIGHTEEN

Jack took the white thumb drive to his office. It would be safer there. He opened his top desk drawer and saw several other devices just like the one in his hand. He took a dark blue USB drive out of his drawer. After plugging it into the port on his computer, he verified that it didn't have anything important on it. He plugged the white drive into another port and proceeded to copy the file labeled 16592 from it to the blue drive. This file was the list of patients who had received Clearart from the Mexican plant, complete with patient ID's and dates.

He looked through several other files on the white drive before finding the one he wanted. This file was labeled 21734. After he copied that over to the blue drive, he removed the white one and put it in his desk drawer. He spent the next hour carefully transposing ten patient ID numbers between the two files. When he was done, he erased the file labeled 21734 off the blue drive. The file labeled 16592 now had ten patient IDs on it who had received Clearart from the other plant, plant 21734. He put the blue USB drive into his pocket.

An hour before he was supposed to meet with Chuck, Mary called and rescheduled. Something had come up, and

Chuck wanted to meet with Jack day after tomorrow. Just as well, Jack thought. He had plenty to do, and the longer Chuck waited to include Vic Chaney, the better.

Late that afternoon, when he was getting ready to leave, he opened the desk drawer and decided to take the white USB drive. Although he thought his office was safe, he felt more comfortable having it with him.

When he got to the marina, Kevin was washing down the deck of his trawler.

"You can start on mine when you're finished," Jack shouted at him.

Kevin turned off the hose. "What?"

"I said you could start on mine when you're done with yours."

Kevin laughed. "Which one? Now you've got two to keep clean. I'm just trying to get mine ready for a little trip. Going down to Naples in the morning. A good friend of mine from Jersey is there, and I'm going to spend the week with him and his wife. Think you can manage J dock without me?" Kevin and Jack were the only live-aboards on J dock.

"I suppose, for a week. Hope you have a good time," Jack said. Naples was only a couple of hours south of Fort Myers by water.

He walked down below and changed clothes. Back in the cabin, he looked at the two USB drives on the counter. Might as well put it in the same spot. He knew they would be back to his boat, and he wanted them to find something—something that appeared to be the real thing. He dropped the blue drive into the tissue box.

His laptop was on the table next to Peter's. Jack's computer was a newer, more powerful one than Peter's. He thought about it and decided to back up everything on Peter's computer to a portable hard drive he had. This would give him a chance to finish going through Peter's information later.

When he finished, he put the portable hard drive, the white thumb drive, and his laptop in an Earth Fare shopping bag. His phone vibrated in his pocket. He pulled it out and saw it was Molly. As soon as he pressed Answer, Molly started talking.

"Jack. The hard disk on my computer crashed. And every single one of the USB drives I had is gone, including Richard's." Molly was angry and afraid. "They broke into my condo, Jack. While I was at work."

"Hang on. I was just leaving the marina. I'll be there in ten minutes." He clicked the phone off and grabbed the shopping bag.

He walked as fast as he could over to her condo. No need to run. They were long gone by now. He got off the elevator and walked down the hall to her door. The door had no sign of forced entry. As soon as he knocked, Molly opened it.

Walking into the living room, she pointed at her laptop. "They didn't steal the damn thing. They just wiped out the hard drive. I turned it on and got that fucking blue screen. It was working fine last night. Then I looked for the USB drive. It was gone, along with a couple of others I had."

"Anything else missing?" he asked.

"Nope. Not a thing."

"Did you call anybody, the police, condo manager?"

"No. What the hell was I going to tell them? Somebody broke into my condo, trashed my hard disk, and took a couple of USB drives? That would get a lot of sympathy!"

Molly was pissed. Someone had entered her place, snooped around, and stolen something.

Jack wondered how they got in. Not that it mattered; what was done was done. They had gotten away with it, and there was nothing Molly could do. These people were anxious, and they were good. He wondered how long it would be before they got into his boat, the right one this time, and did the same thing. Not long, he figured.

"So much for my theory that your place was safe," he said. "Now I'm not so sure about any place." He told Molly about leaving the white USB drive in his desk, but deciding at the last minute to bring it with him. He was glad he did.

She finally noticed the shopping bag. "What's that? Dinner?"

He laughed and said, "Unfortunately not." He showed her the contents and told Molly what he had done earlier. He held up the white thumb drive. "We've got to figure out a secure place for this thing. Do you have a safe deposit box?"

"Oh sure, that's where I keep all of my gold and jewels." Molly rolled her eyes.

"Okay, smart ass. Just checking. Tomorrow I'll go down to the bank and rent one. That's the best place I can think of, given they've hit my place and yours." Then it dawned on Jack. "Wait a minute. How the hell did they know you were involved? Why would they come to your place?"

"You didn't tell Chuck?" Molly was worried again.

"No, I never mentioned your name at all. Not to anyone." Jack was puzzled. Other than being friends with Richard, why would they target Molly? Something didn't make sense.

Molly hit her forehead with her palm. "We're so stupid. Think about it. We've been signing onto the hospital computer using Richard's ID."

"Yeah, so what?" Jack still didn't understand.

"Every time we did that, we used my computer. Here in my condo. We might as well have put a neon sign over the door. A fifth grader could have tracked it back to here."

Jack just shook his head. "That was dumb, wasn't it?"

It was obvious to the bad guys that Molly and Jack were working together on the Clearart problem. They had to be careful. The only thing they had left was the single white USB drive sitting in the shopping bag on Molly's table. Not many options left. Of course, they would soon have the blue drive on Jack's boat, but it was a decoy.

He wanted to reassure Molly, but he didn't know who these people were. They were willing to do whatever it took to protect Clearart. Molly was just the custodian of the USB drive and not a threat, but tell that to Richard and Manny.

What to do now? It sounded like Chuck was going to take this to Vic Chaney whether they wanted to or not, so might as well ride along. Maybe they could learn something.

They again discussed taking this to Lieutenant Budzinski with the Fort Myers Police Department. Things were escalating, but Jack wasn't convinced. At some point, but not yet. He felt like the longer they could control things, the better off they were. Once they brought in the police, he and Molly would be out of the loop. His biggest fear was the bad guys getting away, and he was determined not to let that happen.

There was nothing they could do now. He insisted on sleeping on Molly's couch, but she tried to convince him she would be fine. She was in a secure building and they got what they came for.

"Right. A real secure building," he said. "And we don't know they won't be back."

She didn't argue and brought him sheets and a blanket. "Thanks for staying," she said as she leaned down and gave him a peck on the cheek. "Let me know if you need anything."

"I'll be fine. Thanks. Night." He watched as she went to her bedroom. He stripped down to his boxers, turned off the light and reached down to make sure the shopping bag was next to him before he fell asleep.

The next morning, he woke before Molly, slipped out and went back to the boat for his run. Everything in the cabin was just as he left it. He was almost disappointed, but he knew that sooner or later they would be back.

He changed clothes, but was a little nervous about leaving the bag and its contents in the boat while he ran. There was movement outside on the dock. He poked his head out the cabin door and saw Kevin busy on his boat.

"Hey, Kevin, when are you leaving?"

"In an hour or so. Why?" Kevin stopped what he was doing.

"Just checking. I was headed out for my run and wanted to say goodbye if you were leaving now."

"I've still got a few things to do around here first, so I'll be here when you get back." Kevin went back to washing the deck down on his boat.

Jack grabbed his running shoes and went topside to put them on. The boat would be fine with Kevin outside puttering about.

It was already warm at seven o'clock. The usual breeze was blowing, which made it tolerable, but it was going to be hot today. He went up to the main dock and stretched. When he was done, he set out on his usual route going south along the river past the Edison home, then down McGregor Boulevard and back.

Running was a good chance to think, to process what the night shift had deposited in the inbox of his conscious. So far, he and Molly had been reacting. They needed to start thinking ahead, anticipating ACM's next moves; think like their opponent, rather than just wait and see what came at them.

He knew they would break into his boat and take the computer and the USB drive. What next? It occurred to Jack they would check his office as well. Obviously, they didn't have to break in to infiltrate his computer, since it was hooked up to the hospital network. But they would have to check for offline copies of the data file, like USB drives. Would they sit back and wait for Molly or Jack to make a move? Or would they think they had gotten all the data? That would be logical, but risky. How would ACM know they had all of the copies of the data? They couldn't be sure.

This brought him back to the question of why they killed Richard. From a purely objective perspective, that seemed excessive. Again, why not just sabotage the data or retrieve any copies? Manny he could better understand. In his position, he probably knew too much. Maybe Manny talked to Richard again? He and Molly were missing a piece of the puzzle. There was something they were overlooking.

Before he knew it, he was back at the yacht basin. He quit running and walked another couple of blocks past the main dock to cool down before going back to the boat.

Kevin was still tidying up on his boat when he got back out to J dock. Jack filled his water bottle from the filtered faucet in his sink and walked back out to chat with Kevin.

They talked for a few minutes before Kevin left. Jack helped him with the lines, and then watched the trawler move slowly out of the slip and toward the river.

Jack took his shower and got ready for work. He put his laptop, the portable hard drive, and the white USB drive in his backpack that he used to carry things to and from the office. Toting a shopping bag to work might look a little too obvious.

When he got to work, he opened his desk drawer for a pencil. He got one, closed the drawer, then opened it again. The USB drives in his drawer were gone. He turned on his computer monitor, expecting a blank blue screen. The main hospital page was there, as usual. He logged on and everything worked fine. Then he realized they had access to his computer through the hospital system, so they knew what was on it. There was no need to erase the disk on his computer.

He reached down and took the white USB drive out of his backpack and stuck it in his pocket. He had several meetings this morning, and he was taking no chances leaving it in his office. As soon as his meetings were done, he was putting it in a safe deposit box.

At lunch, he told Barb that he needed to go to the bank and would be back in an hour or so. The Southwest Florida Bank was as good a spot as any. It was close and between the hospital and the marina. Jack went in and rented the smallest safe deposit box they offered. The bank employee had him sign the log and led him into the vault. She showed him where his box was located along the left wall. Asking for his key, she then inserted her key alongside his and opened the door.

Jack removed the box and walked to the table in the middle of the vault. Although she offered the use of a small room for privacy, he told her that he simply wanted to place something in the box and didn't require use of the room. He placed the white thumb drive into the box, finding it silly that even the small safe deposit box seemed much too large for the device. Once again, he noticed the number written on the drive and wondered if it was significant. He put the box back into the opening and locked the door, removing his key. He followed the bank representative out of the vault, thanking her for her assistance.

On the way back to the hospital, he was relieved to have the file in a safe spot. He wondered how long it would be before they broke into his boat now that Kevin was gone.

As soon as Jack got home from work, he opened his cabin door and looked around. Everything looked in place. He dropped his backpack on the settee. After changing, he came back out and checked the tissue box. When he shook it, not a sound came from the box. He looked inside and saw nothing but tissue. A smile crossed his face. With Kevin gone all day, they didn't waste any time in searching his boat. He powered up Peter's laptop, knowing what he would find. Sure enough, the blue screen came up and the computer wouldn't boot. The hard drive had been erased.

The next afternoon at work, Jack went upstairs for his budget meeting with Chuck. He did his best to look anxious and dejected when he walked into Chuck's office.

"What's the matter? You look upset?" Chuck said.

"I am. The data that Richard had put together on Cleartart. It's gone. I had it on my laptop, and my hard drive crashed."

"Damn." Chuck looked upset now. "Didn't you have a backup?"

Jack held his hands outstretched with palms up. "No. I know better, but I didn't."

"There's not a copy anywhere else, like on your computer here at work or something?"

"No, that was it. Richard may have had a copy, but if he did, I didn't know about it."

"So now we have no proof at all?"

Jack noticed *you* had become *we*. "Just Richard's comments."

"Well, we can't take that to Chaney, if that's all we have. No offense to Richard, but I know Chaney, and the first thing he'll ask for is proof. And what I'm hearing is that we have none."

Jack could see that Chuck was assessing his exposure now that the evidence was gone. Or was it relief that the problem had solved itself? Either way, Chuck had made his decision.

"I don't see any need to bother Vic with this. All we can hope for is that if there is a problem, ACM is working on it. Nothing we can do now. Let me know if you find that file, but I think we can consider it closed. You agree?"

Jack nodded. "Sorry, Chuck. I'm as disappointed as you are."

Chuck shrugged. "Out of our hands. Probably a blessing in disguise if you think about it. At least we can take that one off our list." Chuck moved on to the budget issues. For different reasons they were both relieved they didn't have to see Vic Chaney.

Jack called Molly as he was getting ready to leave the office.

"So, ready to cook me dinner again tonight?"

"No. But I'll let you take me to Winston's. Your treat. Shall I just meet you there?" Winston's was an upscale restaurant downtown on Bay Street, one of the best in Fort Myers as well as one of the most expensive.

"I was thinking more like Ray's if I can't persuade you to cook." Jack couldn't resist teasing her.

"Nope. Winston's or you eat alone. I'm tired of eating at Ray's, and I deserve something better with all that's happened in the past few weeks."

Jack knew she was grinning as she said it. "Well, who made you princess? A meal there would pay for my slip for a month." As soon as the words left his mouth, he knew he'd walked into a trap.

"Wrong answer. You no longer have to pay for a slip, my dear. So, what time do I meet you there?" She had him cornered and he knew it.

All he could do was laugh. "Guess I walked into that one, didn't I?" He looked at his watch. It was six fifteen. "Meet you there in thirty. I get to order for you."

He hung up before she could answer. Of course he was teasing; not about the price. Winston's would set him back a hundred and a half with wine. But it was a nice place. White tablecloths, candlelight, private and romantic. The food was excellent. They had the best lobster bisque he'd ever tasted.

He walked straight to the restaurant from the hospital. When he entered the restaurant, an attractive young hostess with long brown hair and short black dress greeted him. She correctly guessed that he was there with Ms. Byrne. He nodded to confirm, and she took him to a quiet table for two tucked away in the far front corner of the restaurant where Molly was already sitting.

She had on a blue and yellow print sundress with thin straps across her shoulders. Though Jack had on khakis and a yellow golf shirt, he felt underdressed as he approached the table. On impulse, he walked over to her side of the table and gave her a peck on the cheek before he sat down.

"What was that for? You either missed me or you think I'm going to go halves with you if you butter me up." She smiled as she said it.

"Chalk it up to missing you. I surrender on the latter part." He held up his hands as he looked on the table for a wine list.

"I already ordered a bottle of Cakebread Chardonnay. I figured you would approve."

"Good taste. What can I say?"

About that time the server, a young man who introduced himself as Keith, arrived with the wine.

"Good timing. At least I got here soon enough to get my share, thank goodness," Jack said.

They both laughed at that. Keith poured a taste in Molly's glass and she pronounced it drinkable, so he poured them each a modest glass. Good thing he didn't pour it for Jack to taste or his tip would have been drastically reduced. This guy may have a future, Jack thought.

They toasted each other and relaxed a while before ordering. Talking low, even though no one was seated around them, Jack told Molly about his discovery on the boat yesterday after work. She asked about the white thumb drive, and he assured her it was secure in a safe deposit box only a block away. He told her about the meeting with Chuck earlier and how he seemed relieved that he didn't have to involve Chaney.

Keith appeared and took their order. Molly selected the lobster bisque and a salad for each of them. Jack insisted that he would have ordered steak, but had no choice in the ordering of the wine and couldn't afford a bottle of red wine in addition to what they had. Keith looked momentarily confused until Molly proceeded to tell him that Jack was full of it and to ignore him. For an entrée, Molly ordered the crabmeat stuffed grouper and told Keith that Jack would be having the seared scallops. Keith appeared flustered, and seemed glad to take their menus and leave them alone.

"How did you know I wanted the scallops?" Jack asked.

"I didn't," she replied. "So are you telling me you didn't want scallops?"

"No, matter of fact, that *is* what I wanted. The grouper was a close second, though."

"Well, if you're nice, I might share."

After Keith brought the lobster bisque, Molly asked Jack about growing up in Jacksonville. He told her about his childhood, remembering things he'd thought long since forgotten. She laughed as he related stories of getting into trouble at an early age. He couldn't explain it, but he loved hearing Molly laugh. Each time it came with such a beautiful smile. The combination was intoxicating.

After a wonderful dinner and bottle of wine, they had no room for dessert and decided on coffee to finish the meal. As they sipped their coffee, Jack realized they hadn't mentioned Clearart or Advanced Cardiac Meds a single time during dinner. He wasn't going to break the spell now.

Keith brought the check after they waved off more coffee. When Jack opened it, he expressed shock and horror at the total, which only caused Molly to start laughing again. He could have sat there all night with that kind of reaction.

When they left Winston's, he insisted on walking Molly home. It wasn't that far, but Jack was worried about her walking home alone. And, truth be known, he just didn't want the evening to end.

They got to her lobby, and Molly stopped and turned to face him, signaling an end to the evening. She could see the disappointment in his face even though he tried his best not to show it. "It was a wonderful evening. Thank you so much. I really needed that." Molly reached out to hug him.

He moved closer and put his arms around her, catching the scent of her hair and a faint trace of perfume. "It was nice. I enjoyed it a lot." He started to add even if he had to pay, but he didn't want to spoil the moment.

She held him tightly and for a moment longer than usual. He liked the feel of her next to him and thought about the night they had spent together.

As if reading his mind, she pulled away, still holding his hand. "I should probably get upstairs before . . ."

"You sure?"

She hesitated, then kissed him on the cheek and pulled away. "I'm sorry."

He nodded. "At least let me go upstairs with you and make sure your condo is okay." He held up his hands. "Nothing else."

She consented, and they rode up to the eighth floor in awkward silence. When they got to her condo, she unlocked the door and Jack went in first. Everything looked normal and nothing had been disturbed.

At her door, he took her hand and squeezed it.

"Night, Molly." It was all he could say as he turned and walked toward the elevator. He listened to make sure she locked the deadbolt, but didn't turn around.

On his way back to the boat, he saw a homeless man shuffling along the sidewalk coming toward him. He was stooped with a scraggly beard, wearing shorts and a torn, faded t-shirt. Both were dirty with holes and looked as if they hadn't been washed in months. The man was dragging his left foot. With great effort, he sat at the base of the streetlight.

Jack tensed. He thought about what happened to Richard, and looked around to see if anyone else was nearby. He saw Hank, the marina security guard, not too far away, and another couple out walking. He relaxed, took a breath, and realized the haggard man wasn't a threat.

He felt sorry for him. Most people would walk past someone like that and try not to look at them. Jack reached into his pocket and pulled out a few bills, three ones, a five, and a twenty. He peeled the five and three ones off and stuck the twenty back into his pocket. With a wary eye, the man noticed Jack coming toward him and cocked his head.

When he got closer, Jack held out the corner of the five so the man could see it.

"How you doing?"

The man merely grunted, but kept looking at the money.

"Thought you might need a helping hand, get yourself a little something to eat," Jack said as he handed the man the eight dollars.

The man looked up at Jack and reached out to take the money.

Jack couldn't help but be shocked by the man's eyes. They were blue-gray, cold and clear, inconsistent with the rest of the picture.

The man took the money and mumbled thanks as he stuffed the bills into his shorts. He held his head down and refused to look at Jack again.

Maybe he was embarrassed, Jack thought. He'd gotten that reaction before when he'd given a homeless person money. "You take care of yourself out here, okay?" Jack said as he walked on toward the gate to the marina. When he got to the gate, he turned to look. The homeless man was back on his feet, shuffling along the direction Jack had come from.

NINETEEN

The middle-aged man wearing a plain ball cap took the elevator to the seventh floor of Palm View condos. He was average height and build. His khaki shorts and floral print shirt were consistent with thousands of men his age in Fort Myers. He never wore clothes with logos and always picked neutral colors, nothing too bright or splashy. His clothes came from Walmart or the thrift store and he always paid cash.

There was nothing remarkable about his features. The contact lenses were a different color than his eyes. Since he'd been in Fort Myers, his hair was dark brown, cut short but not too short. He had no scars nor tattoos showing, no beard or mustache. He wasn't unattractive, but at the same time not particularly handsome either. He was the basic everyman who blended in with the masses. That was a big part of the reason he'd been so successful.

He unlocked the door to the rented condo after nonchalantly looking each way to see if anyone was in the hall. After locking the door, he unbuttoned the shirt and took off his prosthesis that gave the appearance of a slight paunch. Coupled with an almost imperceptible stoop and a deliberate shuffling walk, it made him look ten years older than he actually was.

His name was Robert Smith. At least that's what the Kansas driver's license said. Smith was the most common surname in the United States by a large margin. Robert was the third most common given name for males, although there wasn't a lot of difference between the top three.

He'd rented the condo for ninety days under the guise of house hunting related to a job change. Payment had been made in advance and was made through a shell corporation set up in Delaware. As soon as the check had cleared, the corporation and bank account had been closed without a trace.

Smith had wanted to keep a close eye on the nurse and the accountant for a few weeks until he made certain they were out of play. Although he'd cleared the hard drives on each of their computers and had the thumb drives in his possession, something still bothered him. One of the thumb drives he'd taken from the woman's condo had patient information on it. The hard drive he'd taken off the small sailboat had nothing on it relating to Clearart. When he discovered his mistake, he went back and took the thumb drive off the other sailboat. It had patient information on it, but something didn't seem right.

In the many years he'd been doing this work, he'd learned to trust his instinct. Although he didn't have any proof, his gut told him something was going on. So, he decided to stay in the rented condo in her building for a few more weeks.

Florida was an easy state to hang out in for a stranger, especially south Florida. The influx of visitors from all areas of the country made it easy to fit in. Faces changed constantly and renting a condo was the norm here. With the real estate market as depressed as it was, the owners were glad to get a rental for ninety days. Though he was willing to pay their asking price, he negotiated a slight discount to reinforce the appearance of it being legitimate. This condo was perfect. The complex had no doorman and depended on the locked front door at night, with only residents having a key. Only the penthouse had a separate key for the elevator. Every other floor was accessible to anyone once they got in the front door.

He'd watched the two carefully for the past week. On the surface, nothing seemed amiss. His contact in the data center in Atlanta for HealthAmerica had assured him there were no more queries from either of them relating to Clearart. He'd even offered to give him online access so he could monitor it himself, but Mr. Smith wanted no part of that. Too much of a trail. As long as he had the pictures of the HealthAmerica employee in Atlanta, that was all he needed. He would give him anything he wanted anytime as long as those pictures were kept under wraps. Mr. Smith didn't abuse his power and used it judiciously, knowing that by doing so he had a friend for life. Over time, he'd accumulated a large stable of such friends.

Something didn't seem right with the two subjects in Fort Myers. They carried on what appeared to be their normal routine. Occasionally they would meet upstairs in her condo, sometimes at his boat. Between, they could be found at Ray's, an easy place to blend in when needed. As far as he knew, they didn't have a copy of the information that Garcia had sent to Melton. But Smith had not yet been able to find it.

What troubled him were the accountant's frequent trips to the bank. That seemed out of place. There was an ATM outside the bank, but the man never used it. He knew the hospital required direct deposit for its employees. He'd found that out from inquiring with them about a job. So why was the man going into the bank? The stranger was reluctant to follow him into the bank; too many cameras and too many observant people.

He decided to place her condo under audio surveillance. They seemed to meet there more often than his boat. Access was certainly easier, and he could monitor any conversation unnoticed in his unit. That morning after she left for work he placed two tiny bugs in her condo. He put one in the lamp over the dining room and one outside in the light on the balcony. He thought about putting one in her bedroom, but based on his observations, the two weren't intimate, and he decided that would be unnecessary.

The next few days were uneventful for Jack and Molly. Molly tried to gather information on current patients taking Clearart from the Mexican plant. She kept everything by hand, being careful to not use the computer in her office for anything other than routine things she normally did. She thought about using one of the computers at the nursing station, but decided it was too risky. The computer at each patient's bedside was a possibility, but she would have to log on using her ID. That might attract attention if anyone was watching electronically, so she vetoed that as well.

Everything would be strictly handwritten. When she went into a patient's room, she would determine if the bag hanging was from 16592. If it was, she made a handwritten note. Once a day, in her office, she would pull up the census list and make a note of the patient's ID number. Looking at the list of patients on her unit was something she'd always done and therefore wouldn't arouse any suspicion.

The hard part was determining if a patient died after he left the hospital. She was afraid to go into the hospital database. They thought about checking the obituaries in the local paper, but some of the patients were from out of town and wouldn't show up if they had died after leaving Fort Myers.

She thought about going to her friend in Medical Records, but was afraid that might draw too much attention. Finally she decided she'd call the cardiology group periodically, claiming to check on how their patients were doing under the guise of a quality of service follow-up. Since there was only one large cardiology group in town, every patient came through them even if they were from somewhere else. She was careful to keep her requests vague enough to avoid suspicion. Since she was one of the nurse managers on the unit, it would appear legitimate.

She would take the list home and, when she saw Jack, they would enter the information on his computer. Once every few days, he would back up the information on another thumb drive and swap it with one in the safe deposit box. But he never took the white one out of the bank. They were beginning to think they were working unnoticed while compiling the additional data.

That evening they were meeting at Molly's condo to go through the data. Sitting at her dining room table, she organized the information. She ran the same analysis that Richard had originally used. When she'd finished, she clicked the mouse to display the familiar bar chart.

Jack was looking over her shoulders. "Damn. The percentages are even higher than Richard's original data." The data still showed a higher mortality rate for Clearart from Mexico.

"Not surprising. Look at the absolute numbers." She clicked the mouse again. ACM was shipping more drugs from the plant in Mexico, so the number of deaths was also climbing.

Molly thought for a moment. "We're barking up the wrong tree, Jack."

He cocked his head and looked at her. "What do you mean?"

"We've got a bunch of data on old people with health problems that died. It happens they received Clearart from a specific plant. So what? That doesn't prove anything."

Jack got up and paced. He thought better while he was doing that. She was right. At the end of the day, they didn't have anything. What was the term? Circumstantial. This was why it was such a perfect scam and almost undetectable. The data they had didn't amount to much. They were missing something. Richard would have seen what he and Molly had just figured out. There had to be more.

"What would prove that there was a problem with the Clearart?" he asked.

"I don't know. Maybe a patient who was getting the bogus drug?"

"No. That would be better, but that would still not prove anything in itself. What would be the ultimate proof?"

She thought for a minute, then grinned. "A bag of the bogus Clearart itself?"

"Exactly."

"Well, why didn't you just say so. We can walk down to the hospital, go up to the pharmacy window and ask them to please give us a bag of Clearart that costs, what, in the neighborhood of $10,000?"

"You know, you can be such a smart ass sometimes."

"That's why you love me." Molly smiled.

He shook his head. "Seriously, how do we go about getting our hands on some of it?"

She frowned. "Not easy. That stuff is controlled as tight as gold bars at Fort Knox."

"Could you swap something else for it, like saline or something like that?"

"Are you crazy? You want me to swap a prescribed medicine out and give a patient a placebo? Besides losing my license, I could spend ten or fifteen years in prison. That's gross medical malpractice." She was furious at even the thought.

He started to say giving the patient a harmless placebo would be better than a tainted drug, but decided to declare a truce instead. "Sorry, just thinking out loud, okay? We've got to figure out a way to get our hands on it."

"I think we need to go see Budzinski," Molly said. "Couldn't he just like subpoena some of it or something?"

"Maybe, but he would have to have some good reason to convince a judge to authorize that. And we don't have a good reason at this point. By the time we showed him the data and he shared it with others, ACM would be shipping the good stuff. Where would that leave us, besides looking like fools and unemployed?"

She shook her head and exhaled. "I don't know, Jack. I feel like I'm way over my head here. We both are." She looked up at him.

He sat back down next to her. "So a bag of Clearart doesn't really buy us anything. We have an exact copy of everything that was on Richard's thumb drive, right?"

"Sure, it's in a separate folder on your hard drive. Why?"

"I think Richard left us more. We quit looking too early. Richard was too smart not to have figured out what we just did. Which means there has to be something else. Pull up that folder."

Molly clicked the mouse a couple of times and displayed the folder with the copy of all the contents from Richard's thumb drive. They scanned the list of included folders and file names, clicking on several only to find they were notes or just iterations of data he'd collected. They read Richard's note again.

"He says he knows who's behind it. He has proof, and it's in a safe place," she said.

"We haven't found it yet. What's in the folder labeled Backup?" he asked.

"His backup of the data."

"Are you sure?"

"No." She double-clicked on the folder. There were twenty or thirty files listed. All were named Clearart Backup followed by a series of numbers representing the year, month, and day. "Looks like backup files by date."

Jack started to get her to move on to the next folder when he noticed something unusual about the date on one file in the middle of the group. "Wait a minute. Click on the file that ends in 0431."

"Why that—" Molly caught herself and looked up at Jack. They both smiled as she turned back and double-clicked on the file.

It was another note from Richard.

> I have a storage unit, not rented in my name, which is paid for a year in advance. The number is written on the thumb drive. Two people know where it is and know the combination. The proof is inside.

"So we don't have the proof yet, but do you have a clue what he's talking about?" Molly asked.

Jack shook his head. "I was hoping you did."

They looked back at the screen and read the note again.

"I never knew Richard had a storage unit. Did you?" Jack asked her.

"No. I never heard him mention it."

"I think we're the two people he is referring to. And he left the thumb drive with Barb."

"Agreed. But how in the hell are we supposed to know where the storage unit is?"

"Good question. This makes no sense at all. I feel like we're so close, but so far."

Neither had a clue as to what Richard was talking about. They realized it was getting late, and both of them were tired. Molly suggested they sleep on it and maybe something would come to them. Richard's message was their only chance. If only they could decrypt it.

Jack backed up the file to the USB drive, turned the computer off, and put everything in his backpack. They agreed to muddle it around some and touch base again tomorrow evening.

They talked about the upcoming weekend. Tomorrow was Thursday. He and Molly had already discussed taking the sailboat up to Useppa this weekend. He wanted to leave

Friday afternoon and stay two nights, but Molly had a meeting late Friday that she couldn't change. They decided to leave before lunch on Saturday.

"I'll bring the wine," she offered.

"Sounds good," he said.

The meals were decided and Jack had his shopping list.

Molly yawned. "Sorry, Jack. I'm beat. And I have a six o'clock in the morning."

It was midnight already. Jack packed his stuff, and she walked him to the door.

"I'm looking forward to this weekend," she said as she hugged him goodnight.

"Me, too. It'll do us good to get away."

Downstairs in the seventh floor condo, Mr. Smith took off his headphones and stroked his chin. He was gratified his hunch was correct, but now he had a major problem on his hands. He clicked on the computer in front of them and brought up the file the two had just referenced. In a few seconds, he was reading the same note they did.

Shit, he thought. The two people were obviously the pair upstairs. But they didn't know what Melton was talking about either. A storage unit, God knows where, rented in an unknown fictitious name with an unspecified combination. Mr. Smith had to admit that was pretty clever. He'd underestimated Melton. There had to be dozens of such facilities in Southwest Florida. It would be like finding a needle in a haystack. Even the number of the storage unit wasn't in the memo. It was written on the thumb drive itself, which wasn't in his possession.

At least he could cross off the files in the safe deposit box. As the couple had surmised, the data was of limited value. And a bag of Clearart would be of little value. More disturbing was what Melton had stashed away. It had to be the information Garcia sent him. Smith had to find the storage unit. The easiest way would be to let the couple lead him to it. And he knew exactly where to find them Saturday evening.

The next afternoon, Jack went home and changed. Taking his computer with him, he walked over to Molly's condo.

Molly pulled out the list of storage places in Southwest Florida and they started going through the names. Nothing clicked. After a few beers, they got sillier as they started giving outlandish reasons for their choices. Bayfront Storage was a candidate because Bayfront had eight letters and Richard's birthday was in August, the eighth month. The reasons got more obscure as they worked their way through the list. Halfway through the list, Jack got serious all of a sudden.

"Go back to the *B*s," he said.

Still laughing, Molly saw that something had triggered a thought with Jack. She quit laughing and went back to the page with the *B*s.

"Read them to me again. Just the *B*s."

She obliged, and when she got to the end, Jack said, "That's it. Burns Climate Controlled Storage."

"I don't follow."

"Burns. A play on your last name, get it? That's why you have to read it out loud. Looking at it doesn't work. But it sounds exactly like your name. The double meaning. That's so Richard." Jack was excited. "Where is it?"

Molly read it out loud again. "Well, Einstein, I think you may be right." She looked at the address. "Summerlin Road."

"Perfect. Not too far from his house."

Molly put the list down. Jack was right. That had to be the one. It was the only one that made sense, looking at it from Richard's point of view.

"Okay, genius. Maybe it is the place. Then what's the combination?" she asked.

"Do I have to do all the work? I was hoping you could contribute something here."

Molly flipped him a finger. He was stifling a laugh as he got up to get another beer. They bounced around a few ideas on the combination. Both agreed it wouldn't be as obvious as Richard's birthday or even one of theirs. Jack suggested maybe the plant number, but again they decided that would be too easy.

Molly put a frozen pizza in the oven for dinner and opened a bottle of Chianti. She poured them each a glass, and they walked out onto the balcony. Leaning on the railing, they watched the lights of the boats move up and down the river. The last full moon of the month was high in the sky, following the sun that had set not too long ago. The moonlight reflecting off the river was magical.

They continued to debate possible combinations for Richard's note. Jack suggested Molly's birthday, since it would fit with the name of the storage facility. It was plausible, but neither felt like that was it. They thought about the registration numbers on Richard's boat. Again, while possible, it didn't seem right.

When the pizza was ready, they went back inside to eat. She prepared a small salad, and they sat at the dining room table to have dinner. They were starting to get frustrated by their lack of progress. Without the combination, they had nothing.

At last Molly figured it out. "The date we started at Rivers Hospital. That's got to be it. It's an important date to all of us. It was the same code he used on the other file. Plus, it's not something anyone would easily figure out."

"April 11, 2008," Jack said. The more he thought about it, the more he agreed. Again, it was something Richard would do. That was the key. It felt right.

"What was the number written on the thumb drive? Richard said that was the storage unit number," he said.

"I'm not sure. I thought you knew it?"

"Damn. I don't remember it either. I should've gone to the bank today, but I figured you'd remember it. I'll get it tomorrow."

They thought about going to the storage facility tonight to look around even though they didn't have the unit number. But it was late. At this hour, the gates were probably locked. There had to be a key or combination for the gate, and it was doubtful the combination for access to the unit was the same. Rather than bumbling around and drawing attention, they decided to wait until the next day.

Mr. Smith took off his headphones and massaged his cheeks. He'd been listening to them all evening. Although it was recorded, he preferred listening in real time, using the recording for backup. He had the place and the combination. Now all he needed was the unit number.

He played the last part of the conversation back. Davis was going to the bank tomorrow to get the unit number.

Smith switched the monitor off and decided to get some sleep. The next few days were going to be busy.

TWENTY

The next morning, Jack was anxious to go to the bank and get the storage unit number off the thumb drive. He'd hoped they could go out at lunch and check it out, but Molly was tied up and unable to leave the hospital. They decided to leave work early and go that afternoon.

At lunch, Jack walked over to the bank to get the number. He pulled the safe deposit box out, opened it, and read the number written on the white drive. C157. He closed the box, put it back into the wall, and removed his key.

On the way back to the hospital his eyes darted from one person to the other on the busy sidewalk, trying to determine if he was being watched. He had no idea what to look for and soon gave up.

Around four, Jack met Molly downstairs in the lobby of the hospital and they walked over to the yacht basin.

"What do you think's in there?" Molly asked.

"I don't know. But we'll soon find out."

Jack was busy negotiating traffic on Cleveland Avenue as he headed south. A couple of miles later they turned right on Colonial Boulevard. In two blocks, they were sitting at the traffic light to turn left onto Summerlin Road.

"It feels kind of creepy going into Richard's storage unit, doesn't it?" Molly said.

Jack had been thinking the same thing. Though Richard was never far from their minds, he'd been respectfully relegated to the back. He was gone. They understood that, and nothing they could do would bring him back. But they both wanted to see justice done and wouldn't rest until somebody paid the price.

"Part of me is dreading the prospect of finding nothing. Then what?" Jack asked.

He was always thinking ahead. That was one of the things Molly liked about him. She reached over and put her hand over his for a moment. "One step at a time, Jack."

They saw the sign for Burns Climate Controlled Storage and turned left through the open gate.

Three cars behind them, a silver Ford Taurus turned right into the shopping center parking lot across the street. He had been waiting for them at the marina. The driver pulled into a parking spot facing the storage facility.

The storage facility had a muted red metal roof and was enclosed by a tastefully done dark brown aluminum fence. The access road inside the fence paralleled Summerlin with the storage units perpendicular to the road. Jack slowed as they entered the parking area and turned right on the access road past the office.

Molly spotted the sign on the first row of storage units. Above the sign was a large A on the building. The sign pointed left down the first driveway for Units 1-50. The next building was marked B with a sign for Units 51-150.

When they got to the third driveway they saw the sign for Units 151-250 underneath a large C on the building.

"Turn here," Molly said.

Jack turned down the driveway and drove slowly between the two buildings, looking at the numbers on each door. Odd numbers on the left, even on the right. Most of the doors had keyed locks through the hasps. Molly pointed to the left. Jack pulled over and parked in front of the steel door marked C157. A combination lock was threaded through the hasp.

They got out and looked around. No one else was in the area. Even though Richard had given them permission, sort of, they still felt like they were breaking and entering. They were glad no other people were around.

It was a brass MasterLock with a four digit dial on the bottom. They had been expecting a combination lock with a round dial, like a gym locker. The combination for April 11, 2008 would be a simple translation to Left 04, Right 11 and Left 08. But with only four digits to work with, which were the correct four? And that was assuming the date was the combination. What if it wasn't?

"Good thing this isn't one of those electronic locks that only gives you three tries," Molly said.

Jack noticed the camera mounted on the corner of the building. It was pointed down the driveway toward them.

"Yes, but we probably won't have all day to try. Don't look up, but there's a camera on the corner of the building pointed our way. Remember, we don't even know what name Richard used to rent this damn place." Jack tried to look as casual as possible.

Molly grabbed the lock. "Let's try the month and day first." First she spun all of the dials to clear it. She entered 0411 and pulled on the lock.

"Damn." It didn't open.

"Got to be the month and year. Try that."

Molly spun the dials again. She carefully entered 0408 and pulled down on the lock. Once again the lock remained closed. She tried the month and day again, but with the same result. Maybe they hadn't figured out the combination after all. Jack could tell she was getting frustrated.

After several more tries, Jack noticed a man walking down the lane toward them. He was wearing some kind of monogrammed shirt. As he got closer, Jack could see the monogram was the same logo as on the sign out front. He turned and whispered to Molly, "We have company. Looks like the manager of this place was watching the security cameras."

She glanced out of the corner of her eye and saw the man about thirty yards away and closing. She was running out of ideas. One more try before they had to explain what they were doing. She entered a four digit number and pulled down on the lock. It opened. Quickly, she removed the lock and held it up, almost as a trophy for the manager who was now only yards away.

"Sweetheart, you're such a ditz," Jack said, a little louder than necessary. "I told you it was upside-down. You never listen to a thing I say." He turned and smiled at the manager, shaking his head to emphasize the point.

Seeing the look the woman gave her boyfriend, the manager apparently decided to just nod and keep walking. However, he couldn't resist giving the male a little head shake and a *I feel your pain look*, one guy to another. This, of course, made Jack stifle a laugh, which in turn pissed Molly off even more.

"You're such a pig," she said under her breath.

Jack waited till the manager was around the corner and out of hearing distance. "Just going with the flow." He lowered his voice a notch. "What did you do? What number did you use?"

"Richard was a geek, remember? He always put dates in a year, month and day format. Used to drive us crazy. So the format was 080411."

"Okay, so how did you know which four numbers to use? I watched you. You only had time to enter it once."

"Duh. Now who's the ditz? We had already used 0411. That was the first combination we tried. So it had to be 0804."

"Not bad. That's pretty good for a ditz." Jack was laughing as Molly punched him on the arm.

She pulled the door open, and together they looked inside the storage unit, as if expecting something to come out after them. As their eyes adjusted to the dark, they saw something in the back of the room. Jack reached inside the door and felt around for a light switch. Locating it, he switched it on. A fluorescent fixture above blinked and came on, illuminating the small room. There was a briefcase on the floor. Nothing else was in the unit.

They walked inside, and Jack opened it. Inside was a FedEx envelope. Molly wiped the tear off her cheek, reached in, and picked it up.

Her hand was shaking slightly as she opened it and took the papers out. Another tear rolled down her cheek as she recognized Richard's boarding school penmanship. Jack put his hands on her shoulders as they read Richard's letter. It was dated the day he was killed.

> My Dearest Friends,
>
> If you are reading this, then I am most certainly not able to be with you. I apologize for the cryptic nature of my communication, but as you have probably surmised by now, it was entirely necessary.
>
> I decided to put the proof here. I suspect electronic means such as emails, etc. have been compromised. I could not be sure about the thumb drive I left for Jack and did not want to risk putting everything on it.
>
> My friend, Manny Garcia, sent this to me. It contains everything you need to nail the bastards. It cost him his life.

Molly looked up at Jack when they had finished reading the letter. There were several other pages behind Richard's letter. She pulled them out and held the first page up. It was a fax copy of what appeared to be a legal document, a copy of a document that described a joint venture between Advanced Cardiac Meds, Ltd. and Dos Amigos, S.A. for a manufacturing facility in Mexico.

The second page was a copy of the ownership structure of Dos Amigos, S.A. It listed only one owner, a corporation based in the Bahamas, SA Ventures, Ltd.

"So not only is Chaney invested in ACM, he's behind the plant in Mexico as well."

They flipped through the other documents, skimming them as the final pieces of the puzzle fell into place.

"Richard was right all along. The Mexican Clearart is nothing but a placebo," said Molly. "It's all about the money. Richard and Manny were killed because of it."

"And Peter, along with countless others, who received a drug that was supposed to help them.

"The smoking gun," Jack said. "Now we have something to take to Budzinski."

He pulled out his phone and called Budzinski. The message said that he was out of the office until Monday.

"What do we do with this in the meantime?" Molly asked.

Jack looked at his watch. The bank was already closed, so it was too late to put it in the safe deposit box. That would have to wait until Monday.

"We leave it right here. It's much safer here than anywhere else. Monday we can move it to the safe deposit box. Or we can bring Budzinski here."

Molly asked for Jack's cell phone. He handed her the iPhone, and she took pictures of the letter and each document.

"Just in case," she said. "With all the strange things that have been happening, I don't want to take any chances."

"Good idea."

They locked the storage unit back up and drove home to the marina. On the way, they discussed the value of what they had. Certainly it would paint ACM in a bad way, pointing out they were deliberately covering up bogus medicine. And it also showed a connection between HealthAmerica and ACM. But they still had to tie it to Richard's death. That was going to be harder to prove.

* * *

Across Summerlin Road from Burns Climate Controlled Storage, Smith was sitting at a table on the sidewalk in front of an ice cream shop, eating ice cream and appearing to read the local newspaper while watching the storage unit. After the pair stopped and he knew the right unit, he parked and walked over to the shop to wait for them to leave. He also wanted to see if they took anything out.

He had on his trademark ball cap, tropical shirt, and shorts. If anyone had noticed, he would appear to be another middle-aged tourist in Fort Myers taking a break in the shade.

The ice cream had been refreshing, but he was more interested in watching the pair. He'd debated whether or not to follow them into the facility. But since it was daylight and he knew the storage facility was heavily monitored by video cameras, he decided to watch from across the street.

As soon as they left, he would go inside and see what was in the unit. He was betting they would leave it in the storage unit, thinking it would be safe there. If they had removed whatever it was, then he would simply have to retrieve it tonight.

After a short period of time, he watched as they got back into the car. They didn't appear to have anything with them. He saw them leave the facility and make a right turn on Summerlin Road. Smith tidied up his table and went to his car.

He drove across the street and pulled up in front of the unit marked C157. Unlike the two who had just been here, he'd assumed a four digit combination. He'd already listed the logical possibilities based on the calendar date he'd heard them say in her condo. Since he was ex-military, the year-month combination wasn't unusual to him. He slipped on thin latex gloves and opened the unit on the second combination he tried. He looked inside the briefcase and removed the FedEx envelope, quickly looking at the contents.

He put everything in his folded newspaper and left the unit, careful to keep his ball cap pulled down over his face and the newspaper out of camera view. Another license plate adorned the Taurus specifically for this trip. A video of it would be a helpful diversion. Although Smith had the information he was looking for, the pair would have to be dealt with. Now they knew too much.

TWENTY-ONE

Jack was sitting under the bimini on Left Behind when he saw Molly wearing her floppy hat and walking down the dock swinging a day bag. The green straps of her bikini top were visible underneath the flimsy tan cover-up she was wearing, as was the outline of her bikini bottom.

The cover-up barely reached her thigh, showing off her nice legs. This was starting to be torture.

"Hey, sailor," she said.

"Hey, gorgeous, want to go for a boat ride?"

Molly flashed him a big smile as he took her bag and helped her aboard. She gave him a peck on the cheek and took the bag down below to stow it.

He watched her from behind as she disappeared down the steps to the cabin. He started the diesel, and a few minutes later Molly reappeared topside. She had a tube of sunscreen in her hands and took off her cover-up.

"Would you please put some of this on my back?" she asked, handing him the tube. "I put it everywhere else before I left the condo."

Jack inhaled and squirted some sunscreen onto his right hand. He started with her shoulders, rubbing the lotion in, and slowly worked his way down her back. He put his hand underneath the string for her top. The feel of her skin beneath his hand was almost more than he could bear. Cautiously, he ran the tips of his fingers under the top edge of her bikini bottom and felt her skin ripple when he did. He wanted to linger a while, but handed her the tube back and said, "Done."

"Want me to put some on your back?" she asked.

With brown hair and skin that tanned easily, Jack didn't need it. But he wasn't going to pass up her offer.

He took off his shirt and turned his back to her. He felt her soft hands start at his shoulders, rubbing the lotion in. God, that feels good, he thought, as she moved slowly down his back. When she got to his waist, she returned his gesture. He could feel her slender fingers underneath the edge of his swim trunks making sure to cover that in-between area.

"Okay. You should be good for the trip." She put her cover-up back on, but didn't bother to button it.

He decided to leave his shirt off and get some sun on the way up. "Thanks." It was all he could say. "Ready to shove off?"

There was a steady breeze blowing out of the south. He checked the gauges to make sure everything was normal. Molly went forward to handle the lines up front and the dinghy.

Satisfied that everything was in order, Jack went to the middle of the boat and removed the spring lines. Moving back to the cockpit, he removed the stern lines and hung them over the hooks on the pilings. Molly looked back at him and he nodded, giving her the go-ahead to remove the bow lines. He engaged the prop and eased the throttle forward. Left Behind started ahead, leaving the slip.

Once Jack cleared the slip and turned left, Molly walked the dinghy back along the starboard rail and tied it off at the stern, the dinghy free to trail behind them. She sat next to Jack as they motored out of the marina the short distance to the main channel in the river.

At the river Jack advanced the throttle to a comfortable cruising speed and turned west, heading toward the Gulf of Mexico. Although the river was broad at this point, it wasn't that deep. Only a boat with a shallow draft and manned by someone who knew the river would stray out of the clearly marked channel. In a boat the size of Left Behind, drawing slightly over four feet, Jack wouldn't tempt fate. He followed the channel closely.

They passed under the Caloosahatchee Bridge with not a lot of room to spare. There were two more bridges they had to pass under. All three listed clearance at fifty-five feet and Left Behind needed fifty-four feet. In reality, it was not as close as it seemed, since clearances on nautical charts were listed above the Mean High Water mark, which was an average of the high water marks over a given period of time.

As they passed Molly's condo, Robert Smith was sitting on the balcony of his seventh-floor unit watching them through his binoculars. He knew what their plans were, so there was no need to follow them this time. After they passed out of sight, he looked at his watch. There was still a lot to do before he left this afternoon. He went back inside the condo to prepare.

Before long, they had passed under the Cape Coral Bridge which connected the City of Fort Myers to the relatively new City of Cape Coral. After they passed Shell Point, there was a fork in the waterway. The channel to the left, the continuation of the Okeechobee Waterway, led out under the Sanibel Bridge and to the Gulf. The Intracoastal Waterway was on the right, leading through a narrow and treacherous stretch referred to as the "Miserable Mile." The cross currents coming through here could be strong. That was particularly problematic in a sailboat that moved along at a modest six or seven knots, roughly eight miles an hour. On more than one occasion, Jack had gone through here in Wind Dancer at a forty-five degree angle to the direction of the channel to compensate for the four knot current. Today, however, the gods were smiling on them, and they made it through without a problem.

They headed north up through Pine Island Sound. He was thinking about their last trip through here with Richard. He smiled as he thought about how much fun they had together. The three of them had been like family, and it was strange to be without the third person now. Even stranger was the realization that he would never be with them again.

It was also a much different trip in a sailboat instead of a power boat, like the difference between winding down a two-lane country road in a convertible versus cruising up the interstate at seventy miles an hour with the windows up and the air conditioning on.

Just off the Intracoastal next to the small channel going into Useppa Island was a nice anchoring spot, a popular layover for people traveling the Intracoastal. It was directly across from Cabbage Key and well protected from all but a westerly breeze.

They got there around three. Jack couldn't believe the anchorage was crowded, with six boats already there. All were flying the flag of a Great Lakes sailing club. The only good spots left were out by the Intracoastal or up close to Useppa. There was too much boat traffic next to the Waterway, so he opted for a spot closer to Useppa than he normally liked to be.

Jack guided Left Behind upwind to where he wanted to anchor. He reversed the prop to stop the boat. When the boat stopped all forward motion, Jack put the prop in neutral. Molly let the anchor down and signaled to him when it hit bottom. The boat started drifting backward as she watched how much anchor line payed out. When it got to where she wanted, she tied off the line on one of the bow cleats and locked the anchor winch. Once again, she signaled to Jack, who put the prop in reverse and revved the engine. The boat was straining against the anchor line, but not moving, indicating the anchor was properly set. He reduced the engine speed to idle and put the prop back in neutral. When he pushed the Stop switch, the diesel shut down and everything was quiet. He reached over and switched the ignition off.

Molly walked back to the cockpit while Jack was below getting the traditional cold beers out to signal the end of the day's boating. He came back up, handed Molly a beer, and sat opposite her. She toasted him and he knew she was thinking about Richard.

"I got us a couple of nice New York Strips for dinner. Thought we could grill them." He knew Molly didn't eat a lot of beef, but a good steak on a charcoal grill on a boat was hard to turn down.

"Sounds good. I haven't had a steak in a while. I'll make us a salad when you start cooking."

They relaxed while they finished their beer and, when they were done, Molly suggested a quick swim before dinner. He watched as she took off the cover-up, giving him an unobstructed view of the skimpy green bikini that fit her so well. Jack was admiring her figure when she asked if he were joining her. He took the last swallow from the bottle and stood to check his pockets.

He followed her down to the swim platform on the back of the boat, watching her cute little rear and remembering the glance of it uncovered. She bent over and unhooked the swim ladder, pushing it over the side. It splashed as the bottom rungs disappeared under the water.

The water was pleasant; refreshing, not cold at all. It was clear, though the bottom was muddy and he couldn't see it. It was hot enough that the water felt good. They swam around the boat and treaded water behind it as they cooled off.

"Are you getting hungry?" Jack asked.

"That must mean you are." She laughed. "Sure, I was about ready to get out anyway." She swam over to the ladder and climbed out of the water.

Jack watched as she took the deck shower out and rinsed off. She looked even better wet, he thought. *Damn, got to quit looking at her that way. It's driving me crazy.*

He dove underwater and swam over to the ladder, surfacing at the last minute. Molly had already walked up into the cockpit for a towel. He climbed up and quickly rinsed off. She handed him a towel as he climbed the few steps up into the cockpit.

He toweled dry and sat down. After they dried off, he got up and walked past her on the way down below to get something to drink. Something about a cold beer on a boat on a hot day; it was a great combination.

"Want anything besides a beer?" he asked.

"A glass of water, thanks." Molly grinned, but Jack gave it no further thought.

In a few minutes, he came back up with two beers and a glass of ice water. Molly took the glass of water and took a sip while Jack set the beers down on the cockpit table. Too quick for him to react, she grabbed the waistband of his swim trunks and dumped the entire glass of ice cold water down the front of his bathing suit. Jack yelled both from the quickness of the attack and the icy water on his crotch.

Molly was grinning from ear to ear as Jack danced around the cockpit, trying to get the remaining ice out of his trunks.

"Damn, that was cold. Oh, payback is going to be hell," Jack said when he could finally talk. "You just wait."

Molly was laughing so hard she had tears in her eyes. "It'll be worth it. You know, you should save some of those moves for the dance floor tonight over at Cabbage Key."

By now Jack was laughing almost as hard. When they both calmed down, he decided it was time to start the grill. Molly went below to prepare the salad. He couldn't help but notice she still wore only her bikini. No complaints from him.

As he was getting the grill ready, he noticed another boat coming toward them. It was a small sailboat with a little cuddy cabin and towing a dinghy behind. It was a Catalina 22. Jack waved at the man driving as he went past them and turned, looking for a spot to anchor. At a close but safe distance from Left Behind, the man stopped the boat and went up front to release the anchor. He was doing everything by himself, so Jack figured he was alone.

"Hey, like to come over and join us for a beer?" Jack shouted across the water at the stranger.

"Sure," the man answered. The man got into his dinghy and rowed the short distance over to Jack's boat.

Jack went down to the swim platform to greet the man as he pulled up. He tossed Jack the line, and Jack secured it to the swim ladder.

The barefoot stranger stepped up onto the swim platform and stuck out his hand. "Robert Smith." He was muscular, wearing swim trunks and a plain blue t-shirt. His brown hair was cut close, almost military-style.

"Jack Davis," he said as he shook his hand. He noticed Smith's eyes. There was something odd about them, but he didn't want to stare.

He followed Jack up the stern ladder to the cockpit. Molly was standing there, and Jack introduced them. He noticed that Molly had put her cover-up back on. Smith sat opposite them, and Molly handed him a cold beer.

"Many thanks. Nothing like a cold beer after a day on the water."

They toasted to that, and everyone took a swallow.

Jack had noticed the boat came from the south. "Where are you coming in from?" he asked.

"Naples. Got a little later start than I wanted. Headed up to Sarasota to see some friends. How 'bout you folks?"

Jack tried to place the accent. Maybe Midwest. Fairly neutral.

"We live in Fort Myers," Molly answered. "Just up for a weekend trip."

"That's nice. This is a pretty spot."

They chatted about the area and sailing. Smith admitted he was a novice sailor, but enjoyed it. Hoped to move up someday to a boat like theirs.

Jack had an uneasy feeling about the man. He couldn't put his finger on it, but something didn't ring true. And his eyes. They were the coolest blue-gray eyes he'd ever seen, like a hawk's eyes; observant, not missing a thing. Jack tried not to stare, but stole a glance every time he could.

Robert Smith finished his beer and stood. "I appreciate the hospitality, but I need to get back to my boat. I've got some things to do that I want to finish before dark. Nice to meet both of you."

He stuck out his hand to shake Molly's and Jack's. Jack followed him down to the swim platform and untied the painter for the dinghy. He stood and watched Smith row back to the Catalina.

He climbed back up to the cockpit where Molly was sitting. The boats were pointing south into the wind and current, so Jack couldn't see the Catalina from where he was sitting in the cockpit.

"What's the matter?" Molly asked. "You didn't care for him, did you?"

Jack hoped it hadn't been as obvious to their visitor. "No, he was alright. Something just didn't seem quite right with him. Can't put my finger on it. And his eyes; did you notice them?"

"My God, they were like ice. I'm not sure I've ever seen eyes that color."

"I've seen him somewhere before. I can't place it, but you don't forget eyes like that."

Molly got up to go below. "I'll go down and finish the salad while you start the grill."

He got charcoal and the chimney starter out of the aft locker. Setting the chimney in the stainless steel grill attached to the stern rail, he poured some briquettes in and lit the newspaper underneath the chimney.

After ten minutes, he dumped the white-edged charcoal out of the chimney into the bottom of the grill and placed the wire grid over the top. He placed the steaks on the grill and covered it.

By the time dinner was ready, the tide had changed and the boats in the anchorage had shifted and were now pointing west toward the Intracoastal. Sounds from the flotilla boats behind Jack carried effortlessly across the water. That group certainly was having a good time tonight. All of them were on board the largest boat of the group, and the drinks were flowing. Although Jack was facing Smith's boat, Smith wasn't topside. His dinghy was still there, but no sign of him.

Molly had opened a nice Terra Bella Cabernet Sauvignon for dinner. They ate at the cockpit table, enjoying the gentle breeze. The steaks were delicious and went well with the wine.

After dinner, they relaxed with a glass of wine. It was dark, and Cabbage Key was in full swing now. Music was blaring from across the water. They cleaned up, changed clothes in their respective cabins, and came back up topside. Jack looked over at the small boat close to Useppa. There was a dim light on in the cabin, but the occupant was nowhere to be seen.

Jack locked the cabin door and checked to make sure the anchor light was on. Satisfied everything was as it should be, they went down to the swim platform where Jack pulled the dinghy up close and handed the painter to Molly. He boarded first so he could go to the back and start the small motor. After he got it started, Molly pushed them back, and he drove them over to the small dinghy beach area at the Cabbage Key marina.

Smith sat in the cabin of the small sailboat checking his equipment one more time. The little parabolic mike had worked well. He just wanted to listen in on their conversation to see what their plans were for the evening. He'd been prepared to board Left Behind and deal with the two if needed, but since they were going over to Cabbage Key after dinner that was no longer necessary. It was less complicated this way. Simple was always better.

On the table before him was a tiny electronic device he intended to fasten to the propane line on the Island Packet. In the elapsed time set, the tiny device would puncture the line, letting the highly flammable gas escape. Since propane was heavier than air, it would settle in the bottom of the boat. After several minutes, the device would emit a spark, igniting the mixture in a fireball of death.

By the time it exploded, Smith would be safely anchored behind Sanibel Island, far enough away to avoid suspicion and questions. It would be almost impossible to find the device in the debris. A propane explosion in an enclosed cabin on a boat was almost always lethal to anyone in the cabin. Done this way, it would appear to be an accident, not unheard of in boating.

The problem was getting onboard the boat to plant it. By anchoring close by, he'd given himself a couple of options. He could row the dinghy over, but that would be more visible. With the way the other boats were positioned, they would have a clear view.

Since he was close, he decided to swim. Then he could go aboard, plant the device, and return to his own boat. The close proximity of boats on the opposite side of the Island Packet made that a little risky, but hopefully the people on the other boats would be too busy to notice.

Smith was wearing an ultra thin dull black wetsuit and black gloves. He'd smeared black camouflage makeup on his face so that nothing would reflect light. From experience, he knew that on a dark, moonless night like tonight, he would be almost impossible to see.

What he didn't realize is that he wouldn't be invisible to other creatures like Old Joe. Old Joe lived on the undeveloped southern end of Useppa Island, although Cayo Costa and Cabbage Key were also part of his domain. Tonight, however, he was on Useppa.

Old Joe was an American Alligator, *Alligator mississippiensis*, slightly over thirteen feet long and weighing more than a thousand pounds. It was true that alligators needed fresh water, but he'd learned to tolerate well the brackish water of the slough on the end of Useppa. The park ranger at Cayo Costa had seen him years ago, one of the few people who had, and christened him Old Joe.

When Smith entered the water, making a small splash not noticeable to the humans around, Joe turned toward the sound. With the alligator's night vision keen as an owl's, coupled with an incredible sense of hearing and smell, most prey in the water did not stand a chance. Joe slid into the water and made his way toward Smith to investigate.

For Smith, the boats were positioned perfectly, with the sterns angled toward Useppa. This allowed him to swim between the boats undetected.

It was a new moon, so little light reflected off the water. He didn't realize he was being stalked. When he was close to the Island Packet, he slowed, careful to be quiet. The Island

Packet was between him and the other boats, which was ideal. He would be able to easily board without being seen.

Smith thought he heard something in the water behind him, stopped and quietly treaded water. He didn't hear anything else, and assumed it was a fish jumping, probably a mullet.

Old Joe came a foot out of the water and struck the man at his waist. At a thousand pounds, his weight easily took them both underwater. Smith screamed, but only bubbles came out. Instinctively, Joe rolled under water with his prey to submerge and drown it.

In a matter of minutes the struggle was over. The twenty pairs of inch-long teeth on each jaw had done their job, coupled with two thousand pounds per square inch of pressure. Should anyone ever find the body, it would have been a tossup as to whether it was asphyxiation or massive trauma that was the cause of death.

On the deck of the lead flotilla boat eighty feet away, the members of the sailing club were laughing and talking. Nobody heard anything over the din of the music and the chatter onboard.

TWENTY-TWO

Around midnight, Jack and Molly arrived back at Left Behind. The band had been good, and they had danced more than usual. All evening she had encouraged him to repeat his ice-in-the-shorts dance. By the end of the evening, the crowd on the dance floor was cheering Jack on as he attempted to replicate it. Molly was hysterical.

They were still laughing as they pulled up to the swim platform on Left Behind. Unsteady, Molly got out first and held her hand out for Jack as he made his way to the front of the dinghy. The tide and breeze had shifted slightly, and the only boat behind them was Smith's. Lights from the other boats twinkled around them. On their boat, the anchor light gave the barest illumination of the cockpit. The cabin was dark with the exception of the glow coming from a small light in the galley. They could still hear the music from Cabbage Key as the band played their last set.

"Let's go for a swim," Molly said as she lifted her arms and took her shirt off.

"Are you crazy? There're sharks in the water up here. You realize that, don't you?" Jack kept watching as she slipped her shorts off and threw them up inside the cockpit.

Ignoring his comment, she put her hands on her hips, standing there in nothing but a bra and panties. "Just a quick one. Come on, don't be a wuss."

With his mind fuzzy from tequila and intoxicated by the sight of a scantily clad Molly in front of him, he could only say, "What the hell." Unbuttoning his shirt, he was surprised to see Molly reaching up to her bra and unhooking it, throwing it into the cockpit to join the rest of her clothes.

Watching his expression, she laughed and said, "What's the matter? Haven't you ever gone skinny-dipping? I thought you were a Florida boy." With that, she peeled her panties off and dove into the water.

Jack was in shock. Did Molly really just take off all of her clothes?

"Come on, wuss," she yelled at him from behind the boat.

All he could think was this is insane. He shed his clothes and joined her in the water. The cool water had a sobering effect on him.

"About time. I was beginning to think you were too shy to join me. So have you ever skinny-dipped before?" She was treading water and facing him only a couple of feet away.

Jack tried not to think about her naked body that close. "Of course." She had challenged him now. "Ocean, lakes, ponds, rivers, pools. You name it. As you said, I did grow up in Florida."

"All those places? I'm impressed."

"So where did a good Irish-Catholic girl from Boston go skinny-dipping? Or is this your first time?"

"What if I told you it was?" She watched him for a reaction.

"Bullshit. You're going to try to tell me that you've never skinny-dipped before? I don't believe it." He was trying to determine if she was serious or not.

"I'm actually pretty shy about taking my clothes off."

"Yeah, right. I could tell by how quick you did that a few minutes ago."

"I really am. I don't know what possessed me to do that. Just caught up in the moment." She started grinning. "It was that dance of yours. Drove me to it."

He couldn't help but smile as she started laughing.

"Wish I'd have known. I would have perfected that a long time ago." He splashed her and backed away.

"Hey, you got my hair wet." She was still laughing.

"You're swimming, for Pete's sake. Of course your hair is going to get wet. Don't blame me."

After a few more minutes, they swam over to the ladder.

"You first," she said.

He stared at her. "I don't think so. Go ahead, you first."

They had gotten a little uncomfortable with the thought of climbing up naked on the swim ladder with the other person watching.

"Okay, but you have to turn around."

He just shook his head and backed away from the ladder. He faced the other direction, but as soon as he heard her climbing up, he turned back around to look. The water glistened off her skin as he watched her climb up the ladder. As soon as she got up there, she turned around. My God, she had a beautiful body. She saw him staring at her.

"You rat!"

Grinning from ear to ear, he said, "I never promised I wouldn't look."

She was smiling and made no attempt to cover herself. "Well, Mr. Skinny-Dip, I hope you're enjoying the view. Your turn now." She crossed her arms over her breasts, stared straight at him, and waited.

He paddled around for a bit and realized she wasn't going to move. Without saying a word, he pulled himself up the ladder and stood on the small platform facing her, his arms down by his side.

"Satisfied?" he asked.

"Not completely," she said with a slight smile on her lips. She turned on the deck faucet and sprayed him with cold water.

"Geez, that's cold." He tried to cover himself, more from the chilling spray than modesty.

"Looks like you needed cooling down."

She then turned it on herself and rinsed off. She reached out to hand a towel to a shivering Jack. He grabbed it before she could react, looped it around behind her, and pulled on the towel to draw her close to him.

She didn't resist. When their bodies touched, he dropped the towel, not wanting anything in his hands but her. They kissed, a deep, passionate kiss expressing a long-repressed desire. He felt the curve of her body below her waist, and with his other hand ran his fingertips down her side. She shivered, and his legs got weak as her hands explored his body.

No words were required as he took her hand and led her to his cabin. When they got to his berth, she lay on her back as he admired a view he'd only dreamed about before now.

The first time was pure lust. Like a starving person at a banquet, they tried everything, if only for a mouthful. It didn't take long before they both were done, satisfied for the moment, but still hungry.

The next time was to savor, the urgency not quite as strong and their unselfish patience taking charge. They were determined to please each other, and they succeeded beyond their wildest dreams. Satiated and exhausted, they fell asleep in each other's arms.

The smell of fresh coffee awoke him the next morning. He reached over, but no one was there. Was that a dream last night?

He opened his eyes and could see through the hatch and portholes that it was light outside. There was the faint scent of something on the pillow—Molly. He sat up, his legs hanging over the end of the berth, and looked around. No evidence of anyone else, but then he remembered they were naked on the back of the boat.

He put on a t-shirt and shorts and stumbled out into the main cabin. Molly had turned the coffee pot on, and he could see her legs up in the cockpit. He poured himself a cup and climbed the steps to join her.

"Good morning," she said.

She was wearing one of his shirts, and Jack couldn't help but wonder if she had on anything else underneath. He shook the thought out of his head. Her cup of coffee was on the cockpit table.

"Good morning," he said. He took a sip of coffee and stood there, not sure what to do or say.

She patted the seat next to her.

He stumbled over, sat down, and turned to face her. "About last—"

She leaned over and kissed him, hard, on the mouth. He almost spilled his coffee as he reached up with his hand and put it on the back of her head, tangling it in her hair.

He kept it there, keeping her close, pulling back only enough to look into her eyes. "Glad to know last night wasn't a dream."

She smiled and shook her head. They sat that way for a few minutes, kissing and looking at each other.

"What have we done, Jack?" she said.

Thoughts were racing through his mind, and he didn't have an answer at first.

He grinned and said, "All I know is it was the best night of my life. Something I've wanted for a while, and no regrets. You?"

She nodded. "I feel the same, but I'm scared."

He took his hand off her head, but wrapped it around her fingers and held them tight. "Me, too. Don't want to screw up a great friendship."

"I need to take it slow."

He wrinkled his forehead, a little puzzled.

"But I wanted you to know how I felt. That's why I did that a few minutes ago."

His face relaxed. He smiled and took a sip of coffee. "Thanks. You can do that any time."

They sat back with their coffee, looked around, and realized the Great Lakes sailing club boats had already gone. With the exception of a trawler weighing anchor, their boat and the small sailboat next to them were the only ones left at this late hour.

He looked over at Smith's sailboat and noticed no sign of anyone on board. The anchor light was on, even though it was almost noon. The dinghy was still tied to the stern. That was odd, he thought.

Molly insisted on cooking breakfast for them. She got up to go below, and Jack realized she had nothing on underneath his shirt. He exhaled. Taking it slow wasn't going to be easy.

By the time they finished breakfast, it was almost noon.

"Why don't we take the dinghy over to Cayo Costa before we leave? Get a little beach time in?" he suggested.

"I was just thinking that. Great minds, right? Let me go down and put on my swimsuit."

He opened one of the side lockers and took out the beach umbrella, a couple of beach chairs, and a small cooler. By the time he'd finished loading the cooler with soda and water, no beer this early, Molly came up out of the cabin. She had her sheer cover-up on, the one she wore yesterday. Jack could see bits of black underneath and assumed she was wearing a black bikini today. She never wore any kind of bathing suit except for a bikini, and she must have owned a dozen or so. He wasn't complaining.

They loaded the dinghy and motored over to the dock at Cayo Costa, just across the waterway and past Cabbage Key. A few minutes later, they were on the Gulf side of the island setting up the umbrella and chairs. Molly pulled the cover-up over her head and tossed it onto her chair.

"Is that a new bathing suit? I don't remember it," he asked. It looked good on her.

She twirled around for him, modeling. "Just got it this week. Haven't had a chance to wear it yet. What do you think?"

"It looks really good on you."

"Thanks, glad you like it. Let's go for a dip," she said and walked toward the water.

Jack got up and took off his t-shirt. He followed, enjoying the view and hoping the water was cold. Not cold enough. They frolicked in the warm Gulf water for a while and, after a short walk on the beach, they sat under the umbrellas watching people coming in.

"Tell me about your ex," she said. "What was she like? Based on what little you've told me, I picture her as about six-four, two-hundred pounds, with horns, covered with tattoos."

He laughed. "I didn't realize you'd met her."

"C'mon, I don't believe that. There must have been something there at one time."

Their relationship had moved to a new level, he thought; not bad, but different. There was a new degree of familiarity present between them, yet they were a little tentative with each other as they explored the new boundaries.

"Where to start? Her name's Lisa. And yes, I thought she was the one. Of course, don't we all think that in the beginning? Blonde—"

"I knew it. Sorry, didn't mean to interrupt. I just figured you for the blondes. Go ahead."

"I had just finished college. Went to work for a big insurance company in Jacksonville. That was where we met. We started dating. The only thing I was serious about was my career. She accepted that, encouraged it in fact. Looking back, I think she was trying to hitch a ride. Not that I was a prize or anything, but I was busy climbing the ladder. First one to work, last one to leave. I don't think I took a day of vacation for the first five years I worked there. Moved right up the org chart. She liked that."

"So she was your trophy wife, huh?"

"I guess you could say that. She came from the right side of town, where I was trying to get to. I grew up on the wrong side of Jacksonville. That was one of the things that drove me. I figured if I worked hard enough, I could overcome that. Doesn't work that way, as I found out later. We had the nice house, his and hers BMWs, country club membership, the works. Only thing was I was miserable. Thought all that would make me happy, but it didn't. I started easing up a bit. She turned the screws tighter. Said she wanted to have a family. At least I was smart enough not to fall for that."

Molly put her hand on Jack's.

"She was spending money faster than we could make it. One day, I came home from work, told her I wanted to change jobs. Move to Montana. Take a much lower paying job, get off the treadmill. She went ballistic. The dark side came out. Screaming, throwing things, telling me I couldn't do that to her. She had stood by me and I owed her. The next day, she calmed down and told me I just needed a break. She had booked us a trip to the Virgin Islands, some pricey, upscale resort—naturally. Called my boss and sweet talked him into giving me the time off. I found out later she actually told him we wanted to start a family and I needed a vacation.

"It ended up being the most miserable week of my life. It was clear her only objective was to get me drunk enough to make love to her with no protection and get her pregnant. So I got to see the real Lisa. One minute sexy, coming on to me, the next screaming like a lunatic. That went on the entire week. We got home and I told her it was over. I had enough. Then she set out to destroy me. Hired some hotshot attorney in Jacksonville and tried to make me out as the crazy one. So I rolled. Basically let her have everything but my retirement and enough to buy a boat.

"As soon as the divorce was final, I bought Wind Dancer and started down the east coast of Florida. I wanted to stay in Florida, but get as far away from Jacksonville as possible. Along the way I managed to get a job at Rivers, sailed the boat around the coast of Florida up to Fort Myers, and here I am."

Molly patted his hand. "I'm sorry."

Jack shrugged. "One of life's lessons. An expensive one. Some of us have to learn the hard way." He looked into her eyes. He could see the kindness there. "So, no more blondes for me, contrary to your observation. Only redheads."

She liked that and smiled her approval. "I was just teasing you. You know I would never say anything to deliberately hurt your feelings. I had no idea."

"This session with Doctor Byrne wore me out."

"I didn't mean to pry," she said, still holding his hand.

"You didn't. Thanks for listening. I probably needed to unload some of that baggage. Just hope I didn't scare you away."

"Not a chance."

Around mid-afternoon, they got back to Left Behind. As they pulled up to the swim platform, Jack noticed the Catalina hadn't moved and the anchor light was still on. They rinsed off with fresh water on the swim platform before going up under the bimini to dry off.

Molly noticed him checking out the sailboat. "Why do you keep looking at that boat?"

"I haven't seen Smith since he came over for a beer yesterday afternoon. The companionway hatch is open and the anchor light's still on."

"Maybe he went over to Cayo Costa or Useppa and left it on by mistake."

"His dinghy's still there. Maybe he left the anchor light on by mistake, but why would he leave the boat open?"

Molly shrugged and said she was going below to clean up from breakfast.

"I think I'm going to ride over there and take a look. Just make sure everything is okay," Jack said.

"Probably not a bad idea before we leave. I'll go ahead and put everything away to get ready," she said as she disappeared down below.

Jack got into the dinghy, cranked it up, and went over to the Catalina. Pulling up alongside the boat, he put the motor in neutral and held on to the edge of the small sailboat.

"Hello? Anybody on board? Robert?" No answer. He shouted again, and again, no answer. He backed up the dinghy and went to the stern of the boat. The swim ladder was down in the water. Jack grabbed it and tied the dinghy to a cleat on the rail of the boat.

He climbed up into the cockpit, again announcing his presence. There was no answer and no sign of anybody on board. Slowly, he moved to the open companionway and looked below. There was some equipment scattered on the small table in the galley. An open, half-consumed bottle of water was on the table along with a bag of chips and a partially eaten can of something.

He eased down the stairs into the cabin. There was no one on board. A set of earbuds was on the table, hooked up to a small box the size of a deck of cards. Plugged into the box was a small parabolic dish. He wasn't sure, but it looked like some kind of listening device. He started to pick it up, but figured he probably shouldn't touch anything.

It hit him; where he had seen those eyes. Those were the eyes of the homeless man whom Jack had given money to a few nights ago at the marina. That was where he'd seen him. It was definitely the same eyes.

There was a cell phone on the table. Next to it was a set of car keys and a single key on a keychain labeled Palm View Condominiums. To hell with it, he thought. The guy was following us, and I intend to find out who he is. Jack reached over and grabbed the phone and the single key. He stuck them into his pocket and went back outside. He looked around, wondering where Smith was. He knew he didn't want to be there when he showed.

Jack got back to his boat and secured the dinghy. Going down to the cabin, Molly had just finished cleaning the galley.

"Well, anybody home?" she asked.

"No. Something weird there. It's like he left in a hurry and was expecting to come back. But I remember where I've seen him before." He told her about the encounter with the homeless man at the marina. Then he pulled the phone and key out of his pocket and laid it on the table.

"We've got to leave, Molly. Now."

"He has a place at Palm View? Was he following us? Why did you take his phone and key?"

"I don't know, but something's wrong. It sure looks like he's been following us. And it looked like he had some sort of listening equipment on board. I don't know if he has a place at Palm View or not, but if he wants his phone back, he'll call. My bet is he damn sure won't report it to the police. This guy's up to something, and I intend to find out what."

"How did he follow us?"

"Don't know, but I don't want to be anywhere near here when he gets back to his boat. We need to get back to Fort Myers where there're more people around."

"Maybe we should call Budzinski?"

"Maybe so."

It was almost dark when they got back to the marina. Jack wanted to talk to Kevin, but he wasn't back yet. He and Molly sat in the cockpit of Left Behind and discussed what to do.

"We need to turn this over to the police," Molly said.

In principle, Jack agreed. But he also knew that as soon as they brought the police into it, he and Molly would be cut out of the loop. He was determined to nail Chaney, and was afraid that any official investigation might end with Smith.

He was convinced that Chaney was pulling the strings and wanted to see him be painted with it. People like that got away with too much.

At the end, he convinced her to at least wait until they got the package Richard had left them and put it in the safe deposit box. And he'd conceded to take it to Walter Dobbs.

"It's late. I need to be going," Molly said.

"Excuse me? You're not going anywhere tonight. You think I'm letting you go back to that condo by yourself? No way."

Molly started to protest, and Jack continued. "Not with Smith out there somewhere. You've got your things here on the boat, just stay here tonight. We can go over in the morning, when it's daylight, and you can get ready for work."

She looked around the marina. "You think we're safe here?"

"Safer than your place." He pointed to the office. "We're behind a locked gate, we have a security guard and it'll be a lot harder to sneak up on us here. Don't forget, Smith had a Palm View keychain. We don't know if he's staying there or not, but I don't like the looks of it."

Molly seemed to think about it, and said, "You're right. Probably makes sense until we can figure things out."

Jack nodded, then grinned. "Besides, wouldn't it be nice to sleep together tonight? I wasn't that bad, was I?"

She smiled. "No complaints here. Maybe we'll get more sleep tonight."

Jack laughed. "Good chance. Don't think I can keep up last night's pace."

They went below and as Molly got ready for bed, Jack opened the small safe in the main salon and pulled out the black SIG 9mm pistol. He pulled the slide back and released it, chambering a round. He dropped the magazine, inserted another round, and then clicked it back into the pistol. Fourteen rounds should be sufficient.

TWENTY-THREE

Monday at lunch, Jack drove to the storage unit to get the documents and put them in the safe deposit box. He pulled into the facility and parked next to the door of C157. Dialing the combination on the padlock, he unlocked it and opened the door.

When he opened the briefcase, it was empty. Impossible. He looked in the pockets on the lid of the briefcase. No FedEx envelope. Nothing. The briefcase was empty.

He slammed it shut. Scanning the small room, there was no sign that anyone had been there or any sign of forced entry, yet the materials were gone. Shit. He kicked the briefcase in frustration.

Taking his phone out of his pocket, he pressed Molly's number.

"Hey, what's up?" she answered.

"It's gone, Molly. Somebody got into the storage unit and took everything."

Molly screamed into the phone. "What? What do you mean, gone?"

"I'm standing in the storage unit now. Everything we found here is gone. The briefcase is still here, but it's empty."

"Somebody broke into the storage unit over the weekend?" Molly was still trying to make sense of it.

"No, no signs of a break-in. The door was locked. Somebody knew everything."

"How?" It was an expression of disbelief. She wasn't expecting an answer.

After work, a dejected Jack walked home the few blocks to the yacht basin. All afternoon he'd been preoccupied with trying to figure out how someone had waltzed into the storage unit and stolen the evidence.

Walking out on the J dock toward his boat, he saw that Kevin's boat was back. He was out on the deck sitting in his usual spot with a beer in hand.

"Hey, Kevin. Glad you're back. How was your trip?"

"Good, thanks. Glad to be home. It was great to see Bud and Lizzie, but I didn't want to wear out my welcome. You know what they say about fish and company—after a few days they start to smell. Did I miss anything around here?"

"No, not that I know of. Molly and I went up to Cabbage Key this weekend, got in late yesterday afternoon."

"Cabbage Key, huh? Mike told me they found an abandoned boat up there. Suspicious circumstances." Mike was the marina manager, the source for any local news involving the boating community. "Come on over for a beer when you get changed. I'll fill you in."

Interesting, thought Jack, as he unlocked his boat and went down below to change. He wasn't in the mood to talk to Kevin; he was still thinking about the briefcase. By the time he got back up top, Kevin had pulled up another deck chair with a cold beer sitting in the arm.

Jack sat down and Kevin proceeded to tell him about an abandoned sailboat they found in the anchorage at Useppa across from Cabbage Key. The sailboat was a rental from Fort Myers Beach. The Marine Patrol, thinking it was odd that a small sailboat was still anchored there Monday morning, went aboard to see if there was a problem. According to Kevin, they found some interesting gear on the boat.

"What kind of gear?" Jack asked. He was trying to figure out if it was the boat next to him and Molly. It certainly sounded like it.

"Some kind of terrorist shit, is all Mike said."

"Terrorist shit? On a sailboat in Pine Island Sound? That's weird." Jack was worried now. That sounded like the stuff he saw on the boat.

"I don't know. Just telling you what Mike told me. Hey, there're some big Kahunas on Useppa." Kevin took another swig of his beer and belched.

"I guess so. Still sounds strange. Did he say what kind of boat it was?"

"A Catalina, like a 21, 22, something like that. I don't know much about sailboats."

Jack remembered the sailboat that had pulled up next to them and anchored Saturday night. It was a Catalina 22.

"If I'm not mistaken, that's the same boat that anchored next to us Saturday afternoon. And it was still there Sunday after lunch when we left," Jack said.

"Holy shit!" Kevin was impressed by Jack's apparent brush with mystery. "Did you see anything?"

"No—well, maybe. A man by himself pulled in late Saturday afternoon and anchored next to us. Close to Useppa, come to think of it. There was a flotilla of snowbirds already there who had taken the good spots, so we had to anchor next to the south end of Useppa. Anyway, we invited this guy over for a beer. He came over, had one beer, and that was the last we saw of him. Wait till I tell Molly."

"Maybe you should go tell Mike. You know, in case somebody wants to talk to you or something." Kevin looked at his watch. "Let's walk up to the office. We can catch Mike before he leaves."

Jack wasn't too interested in going to tell Mike. He was worried because he'd gone on the boat and had taken the cell phone and the key. Too late to undo that. This was an adventure for Kevin, and he wasn't going to be denied the opportunity to participate. They walked up to the office and went inside to find Mike. He was behind the counter getting ready to close up for the day.

"Gentlemen," he said. "What could I do for you? It better be quick. I'm two minutes away from closing." Mike was never one to mince words.

Before Jack could say anything, Kevin piped up. "You know that boat they found up at Useppa? Jack here knows all about it. He was up there this weekend."

Mike stopped what he was doing, clearly interested in this turn of events. "That so, Jack?"

"Well, yes, I was up there and saw the boat, I think. Kevin says it was a Catalina?"

"That's right."

"Well, a Catalina 22 pulled in late Saturday afternoon and anchored right next to us," Jack said.

"Us?" Mike look confused.

"Me and Molly, my friend."

Kevin interjected again. "You know, the hot redhead. Sorry, Jack, but she is." He turned back to Mike. "She comes down here a lot. I know you've seen her."

Mike just nodded.

Jack told him about seeing the man Saturday afternoon and inviting him over for a beer. He came over for one beer and went back to his boat. They didn't see him again. He told Mike the boat and dinghy were still there when they left on Sunday afternoon. He mentioned taking his dinghy over to see if anyone was there and no one was on board. He conveniently left out the part about going into the cabin.

"What's this Kevin is telling me about the guy being a terrorist?"

Mike looked at Kevin as if he were looking at a complete moron. "No, that's not what I said. I said I heard the Marine Patrol found some odd gear on board, equipment that might be used for surveillance and such. It wasn't the kind of gear you could get at Bass Pro Shop." He shook his head.

Kevin, properly admonished, kept quiet.

"If it's okay with you, Jack, I'll pass your name along to my buddy with the Marine Patrol. He may want to talk to you about it," Mike said.

"Sure, no problem. Did they think the guy was spying on someone at Useppa?"

"Not sure, but that's the only thing they could come up with that made sense."

"Guess we better let you get closed up. Have a good evening, Mike."

"You bet. Same to you guys." Mike went back to what he was doing behind the counter when they came in.

Walking back down the dock, Kevin turned to make sure they were out of earshot. "I'm telling you, Mike said the guy had all sorts of spy stuff on board. That's exactly the term he used. Spy stuff." Kevin's feelings had been hurt, and he wanted to vindicate himself with Jack.

"You know how cranky Mike is. Don't worry about it." Jack let him know all was well. "It's pretty weird for Fort Myers, you have to admit."

At six thirty, Jack walked over to Ray's to meet Molly.

"What are we going to do now?" Molly asked.

"Hell if I know. That was everything. We're back to square one."

He told Molly about the abandoned boat and his conversation with Kevin and Mike earlier.

"That's strange. Maybe it did relate to someone on Useppa," Molly said.

"I know. And according to Mike, the equipment on Smith's boat was some hi-tech surveillance stuff."

"Creepy. So he wasn't following us? Who was he watching?"

"Don't know," Jack said. "And I'm not yet convinced he wasn't following us. But, lot of big shots on Useppa. Maybe it was someone there, but who knows?"

The next morning at work, Jack's cell phone buzzed. He was at his desk and picked up the phone to see who was calling. The number didn't register, and he thought about not answering, but decided to anyway.

"Hello?"

"Jack Davis, please." The male voice on the other end was formal and professional sounding.

"Speaking."

"Mr. Davis, this is Special Agent Frank Carter with the Florida Department of Law Enforcement, Fort Myers office."

What was this about?

"Your name was given to me by Sergeant Tatum of the Florida Marine Patrol. He told me that you may have some knowledge relating to an investigation we're currently conducting. I was wondering if I could come by your office sometime today and discuss this with you."

Jack's initial response was you have the wrong person, but then he recalled Mike saying he would pass Jack's name along to his friend in the Marine Patrol.

"Uh, sure." Jack looked on the computer screen at his calendar for the day. "How about two thirty?"

"Two thirty would be great. I'll see you then."

The line was disconnected. How the hell does he know where I work? Mike. The call reminded Jack to call Budzinski with the Fort Myers Police Department. He reached for his phone, but decided to wait until he'd talked with Frank Carter from FDLE first.

Lunch came and went and, before he knew it, Barb walked in and laid a business card down on Jack's desk.

"He's here to see you. Says he has an appointment." She waited for instructions.

Jack looked at the card. Frank L. Carter, Special Agent, Florida Department of Law Enforcement. Listed below his name were a Fort Myers address and several telephone numbers.

"Thanks, Barb. Yes, send him in, please."

In a few minutes, a slender man in a gray suit, white shirt, and blue tie walked through Jack's door. He had short salt and pepper hair and moved with the grace of someone in good physical condition. Jack rose to shake his hand and offer him a seat. His handshake was firm and he looked straight at Jack.

Carter wasn't much for idle conversation. He explained that FDLE was conducting an investigation relating to an abandoned boat found Monday off Useppa Island. Jack's name had been supplied by the Florida Marine Patrol. The investigation had since been turned over to FDLE, which is why he was here in Jack's office.

Carter opened a notebook and started with the questions. "I understand that this past Saturday, you and a friend were anchored off Useppa Island? Could you tell me why you were there?"

He was pressing, but Jack decided to give him some leeway. "Molly—my friend Molly Byrne—and I decided to go up to Cabbage Key for the weekend. We left Saturday morning and came back Sunday after lunch."

"You own an Island Packet 370, correct?" Mr. Carter looked up at Jack, waiting for an answer that Jack knew he already had.

"That's correct." If Mr. Carter was going by the book, then Jack would, too.

When it was obvious that Jack wasn't going to say anything else, Carter looked down in his notebook.

"About what time did you and Ms. Byrne arrive there?"

"Around three p.m."

Again, Carter waited for more, and again, Jack wasn't going to play.

After a few more questions and short answers, Carter closed his notebook.

"Mr. Davis. May I call you Jack?"

"Sure."

Carter spread his hands palms up as if asking for forgiveness. "Jack. I'm afraid we've gotten off on the wrong foot. I'd like to apologize for my blunt manner. This is an intense and unusual investigation that was dumped on me less than twenty-four hours ago. Right now, I'm not sure what I can say about it and what I can't. I don't know who's on first. Hell, I don't even know what game we're playing and what stadium we're in.

"What I can tell you is that we found an abandoned rental sailboat anchored just off Useppa Island. On board was some interesting and expensive hi-tech surveillance equipment. This is not the kind of equipment used by a private investigator trying to nail a suspicious spouse's partner, if you get my drift. We're trying to figure who the person was and why he was there. The boat was left as though the person was certainly planning on returning fairly soon. We also found a small waterproof waist belt along the mangroves that seemed to go with the boat and the person. So anything you could tell me about what you and your friend saw could be of enormous help to us."

Jack could tell the man was under a lot of pressure. He appreciated him apologizing and coming clean, so he told him everything he could remember about the weekend. Although he told him about going onboard, he left out the part about the items he took. He was careful not to embellish anything and keep it as factual as possible.

"That's all I can tell you. I wish I could tell you more," Jack said.

"Thank you. I really do appreciate it. It was helpful."

"I know you're not allowed to tell me much of anything, but can I ask you a question?" Jack said.

Carter nodded as if to say *go for it, but I don't know what I'll be able to say.*

"Do you think there was any possibility that guy was following us?"

Carter froze in the middle of closing his notebook. It was obvious the thought hadn't occurred to him. If it had, he was playing it close, Jack thought. Special Agent Carter thought a long time before replying.

"Why would you think he might have been following you?"

"Mr. Carter, I don't know. He probably wasn't. But he anchored next to us. And I heard that the equipment was surveillance equipment, so who was he watching?"

Carter watched Jack for a moment before speaking. He rephrased his previous question, "What reason do you have to think that someone may have been watching you? Is there something else you'd like to tell me?"

"No, no reason I know of. It's just a little creepy, okay? I mean, I'm up there with my friend and this guy anchors next to us. He comes over for a beer and disappears while we're up there. And he's following or watching somebody? Just a little unnerving, that's all."

Carter studied Jack for a moment. "I understand. As I said, we don't know who he is or what he was doing. But if you think of anything at all, please give me a call." He slid another business card toward Jack on the desktop. "This one has my cell phone number on it."

As soon as Carter left, Jack called Molly. "Have you heard from a—"

"Special Agent Carter?" Molly finished his question. "He's on his way to my unit. I'm meeting with him in fifteen minutes. I tried to call, but you didn't answer your phone."

Funny, Carter never mentioned talking to Molly.

"Because I was talking to him. He wants to know about the sailboat. I told him about everything but the phone and the key."

"Don't worry. I figured as much," Molly said.

"Meet me at Ray's tonight after work. I'll buy."

"Damn right you will. You ask, you pay. See you there." She hung up.

Jack took the phone out of his backpack and looked at it. It was a basic flip phone, nothing fancy. It was some brand he didn't recognize and it looked like one of those cheap, prepaid phones you see at the convenience stores.

He found the power button and turned it on. He pressed the key for contacts, but none were stored on the phone. That was odd. He figured out how to get recent calls and looked at the list of numbers. There were only a few numbers. Jack wrote them down and turned the phone back off.

The first number was a Fort Myers number. He went to his computer to a reverse phone number lookup site. He entered the number and Beach Marina came up. On his office phone, he dialed it.

"Beach Marina," the voice on the other end answered.

"Yes, I wanted to talk to someone about renting a small sailboat."

"You need to talk to Sonny. He handles all the rentals, but he's on the water checking out a boat. Can I get your number and ask him to call you?"

"That's okay. I'll check back with him later. Thanks."

Jack hung up the phone. He decided to drive out to the beach later and see what he could find out.

Around three o'clock, Jack walked out of his office and told Barb he had an outside appointment and probably wouldn't be back this afternoon. He walked down to his boat and changed clothes. He put on shorts, an old t-shirt, and his well-worn deck shoes. For good measure, he put on a ratty Tampa Bay Bucs cap to complete the picture.

When he got near Beach Marina, he parked on the street and walked down to the office. An older woman was sitting behind the counter, most likely the one he spoke with on the phone.

"Can I help you?" she asked.

"I was looking for Sonny? Wanted to talk to him about a rental."

"He's out back, working on a boat. You can walk through here if you like," she said, motioning to the door on her right.

Jack thanked her and walked through the door out to the dock. He saw a guy about his age in the back of a power boat, looking at the outboard with its cover removed. He walked down to the boat.

"Hi, how's it going?" Jack said.

The man heard Jack and looked up. "Not bad. This damn motor's driving me crazy."

"I'm Jack. You must be Sonny." Pointing back toward the office, he said, "She told me I could find you back here."

"Yeah, that's me. What can I do you for?"

Jack adopted Sonny's tone. He knew it well. It was the tone of someone who had worked with his hands on and around the water all his life. Jack could have been Sonny.

"You know that Catalina you rented out this past weekend? The one that was abandoned up at Useppa? I think the same guy who stuck you is the same guy who owes me some money. Average size and build, short brown hair?" Jack described the man he'd seen in the sailboat.

"Hell yeah." Sonny took off his cap and wiped his forehead with his forearm. "That son of a bitch. Came out here, rented my damn boat, took it up to Useppa, and left it. Now the fucking Marine Patrol has it and I can't get it back for another two or three days."

Jack picked up the patter. "I hear you. I did a little work for that asshole and now it looks like he skipped out without paying."

"No shit. If you find him, tell him I'm keeping his fucking deposit, but he still owes me."

"Yeah, well, I was hoping you could help me out with finding him. What name did he use with you?" Jack asked.

Sonny chuckled. "Robert Smith. I thought it sounded fishy, but he gave me a Kansas driver's license that matched. It was probably a fake."

Jack shook his head. "He gave me the same damn name. What a fucking con man. By any chance did he give you an address?"

"Yeah, some damn address in Kansas. Matched his driver's license. I'll have to go up to the office and look it up. Damn cops have already been out here earlier this week. I gave it to them."

"Yeah, but you know how much good that does for somebody like us," Jack said, shaking his head.

"Ain't that the truth." Sonny climbed up out of the boat. "Come on, I'll get it for you." Sonny looked around to make sure no one was listening.

"I got something else that might help. I told the guy I needed a local address. He gave me the address of some condo downtown. I wrote it down on a piece of paper, but didn't give it to the cops. I was hoping to go down and pay him a little visit, know what I mean? But I'll give it to you. At least I got his damn deposit. You got nothing. Maybe you can get something out of the bastard."

Inside the office, Sonny found the rental form and turned it around so Jack could see it. As Sonny had said, the address was in Kansas. Without saying anything, Sonny pushed another sheet of paper across for Jack to see. It was a handwritten note. The address was in Molly's building. 714, Palm View Condominiums.

Jack's hand was shaking slightly as he copied the address onto a piece of paper, even though he didn't need to. The time of the rental was 12:30 Saturday afternoon.

"I know I ain't supposed to give you this, all that privacy bullshit, so keep it to yourself, okay?" Sonny said.

"Thanks, man, I will. I really appreciate it. I'll let you know if I find the asshole." Jack shook Sonny's hand and walked out.

Driving back to Fort Myers, Jack thought about what he'd discovered. Robert Smith had a condo in Molly's building? And he'd rented the sailboat not long after he and Molly had left, which meant he had to know where they were going. So how did he know? The only time they had discussed it was in Molly's condo that Thursday night. How in the hell . . . ?

Molly's condo had to be bugged. That was the only explanation. Smith had been following them and somehow overheard their conversation. There was no way it was a coincidence that Smith rented a boat and ended up next to them Saturday, or that he had a condo in Molly's building, or that he'd been masquerading as a homeless man. That also explained what happened to the things in the storage unit. Jack and Molly had discussed that in her condo that Thursday evening.

By the time Jack got to Ray's, Molly was already at their table.

"We need to find a new place," she said.

"I've been thinking that, too. Just not the same ... without everyone."

"I'm assuming you wanted to discuss our visit today from our friend Special Agent Carter?" Molly said.

"Among other things. But, yeah, what did you think about him?"

"Mr. Personality. He's like a poster child for the CIA or something, or should be."

Jack laughed. "I think central casting would love him for a movie role. What did you tell him?"

"Same thing as you, I imagine. I left out the part about the phone and the key, as you so subtly suggested. I just said that you went over to the boat to check, you came back and told me that you found no one on board."

"Thanks. We're good."

"But why didn't you tell him about the phone and the key? I mean, don't you think this has gotten to the point we need to turn everything over to the police?" Molly asked.

"No, not yet. Because as soon as we do, we're out of the loop. I want to get to the bottom of this. You really think the G-man poster child, as you call him, is going to share anything with us?"

Molly seemed to consider what Jack was saying. "You're right, doubtful. But just to play devil's advocate here, aren't they better equipped to get to the bottom of this?"

"Certainly better equipped, but not as motivated. Besides, we don't know who's pulling strings here. We've already found out Chuck Thompson isn't on our side. Advanced Cardiac Meds and HealthAmerica have deep pockets, and we don't know who's on whose side. My vote is we keep everything to ourselves as long as we can. Along the way, maybe we can find somebody we can trust. But right now, I don't trust anybody but you. Especially after what else I found out today."

Jack was making a passionate plea, and Molly knew it. Deep down, she agreed. They both wanted to nail Richard's killer and expose ACM. That was what was important. And he was right. Nobody was as motivated as the two of them.

"Okay, Sherlock." She held up her fist, and Jack bumped it with his. "What else did you find out today?"

"I know who took the stuff in the storage unit and how he was able to do it."

"Really?" Molly was impressed.

"Robert Smith."

Her eyes widened. "The guy up at Useppa?"

"Yep. Probably a fake name. And I found out where he lives."

"Well, he had a Palm View keychain. Don't tell me he's my neighbor. And how did you manage all that?"

"You can call me Detective Davis." Jack puffed up.

"You're so full of shit."

Jack glanced around to make sure no one was listening. "I went on the Internet and looked up a telephone number that was on the phone I took. It was Beach Marina.

According to their website, they have a Catalina 22 for rent. So I went out there to talk with them, see if I could get any information."

"Please enlighten me as to why they would tell you anything?" Molly asked.

"You forget. I grew up on the water. But for the grace of God, I could've been the guy I talked to out there at the marina. So I bonded with him. Told him the guy owed me some money and convinced him it was the same person who stiffed him. He gave me his name and address. Guess where the guy lives?"

Jack didn't wait for an answer. "He has a condo on the seventh floor of your building." He let that statement sink in.

"What? The guy who was on the sailboat next to us has a condo one floor below me? You're kidding me, right?" Molly practically levitated off her chair.

"That's not all. The guy rented the boat at 12:30 Saturday afternoon."

"Not long after we left. So what?"

"Think about it. He had to know exactly where we were going."

Molly was still trying to figure it out. "How did he know that unless . . ." She was doing the math in her head. "He listened to our conversation Thursday night. In my condo." She was getting pissed. "My condo is bugged?"

He nodded. "That's the only way," he said.

"So that explains how he found out about the storage unit. Thursday night was when we figured out the answer to Richard's cryptic message."

"You got it. He was listening to every word we said. And he probably followed us out there when we went to the unit."

"That asshole. What am I supposed to do in the meantime?" Molly asked.

"I ordered one of those electronic detection devices off the Internet. It should be here tomorrow. It looks like Smith has disappeared, so I doubt he's listening. Unless—"

"Unless someone else has taken his place. Jack, this is getting too close."

"I know. I know. Just one more night. Soon as we get that black box, we'll find the bugs and take them out. You can stay with me. Or I can stay at your place."

She didn't say yes, but she didn't say no.

"So this guy was following us?" Molly asked.

"I don't think there's any doubt. Smith had to be working for ACM or HealthAmerica or both. The trick is to find out who his connection was."

After a couple of beers, they decided to go over to Molly's and get on the computer using the condo's Wi-Fi. They went out to the pool area on the river side of the complex and found a private table over in the corner in the shade.

Jack took out the piece of paper where he'd written down the numbers from Smith's cell phone. He knew the last number Smith called was Beach Marina. He didn't recognize the area code on the next number. They went online and did a reverse number lookup. The number came back as a cell phone in Atlanta, GA. For $14.95, the website offered to tell him who it was registered to. Jack tried a couple of other websites with no luck. He wasn't sure he trusted the $14.95 offer, but he went back and put in his credit card number. The cell phone number came back as unlisted. That was fifteen bucks wasted.

Jack wanted to call the number and see who answered. Molly convinced him that would probably not net anything and might scare the other person. If they called, they didn't want to call from either of their cell phones. They needed another phone to use. Jack said he'd go down the street to a convenience store and pick up a prepaid phone. He convinced her that it would be worth a shot and pose no risk to them.

When he got back with the phone, they called the number. Molly had her head next to Jack's and was listening. It rang, and a deep male voice with a Southern accent answered.

"Hello?"

"Hello. Who is this?" Jack figured it wouldn't hurt to ask.

"I think you have the wrong number," the voice on the other end said.

"Wait. Don't hang up. I work with Mr. Smith." It was a long shot, but Jack figured it was worth it.

The man on the other end hesitated. The number of people who had this number could be counted on one hand. He knew his contractor sometimes identified himself as Smith, but this could be a coincidence. But he hadn't heard from him in almost a week. Unusual, but it had happened before. "Who am I speaking to?"

"Richard."

"Richard who?"

"Richard Melton."

The man holding the phone froze. What the hell kind of prank was this? He knew that Melton was that troublesome pharmacist in Fort Myers. But he was "gone;" at least that's what Smith had told him. He needed time. After a long pause, he tried to keep his voice steady.

"I'm afraid you have the wrong number. I have no idea who you're talking about. Goodbye." He pressed End and disconnected the call. He looked at the number and didn't recognize it. He decided to call Smith. He scrolled to the number and pressed Send. The phone rang, but no answer. It rolled over to voice mail. He heard Smith's voice say, "Leave a message."

"Call me." Something strange was going on, and he had a feeling that trouble was brewing.

Jack set the disposable phone down on the table. "He was too clever to identify himself. But he recognized the name when I said Smith. And he recognized Richard's name, I know. You could hear it in his voice."

"Now what do we do?"

Jack held up the key he had taken from Smith's sailboat. "Let's go see what's in Smith's condo."

"You're kidding me, right?" asked Molly. "And exactly why do we want to do that?"

"I don't know. Maybe there's something in there that would help us."

"And what if someone else is up there in his condo?" Molly couldn't believe what they were about to do.

They got on the elevator in the lobby and pushed seven. Just before the doors closed, a well-built man slightly taller than Jack got on the elevator with them. The stranger had on a tropical shirt and shorts. Underneath the Red Sox cap, he was wearing sunglasses. He glanced over at the elevator panel, then looked ahead, crossing his hands. Jack and Molly looked at each other. The only button pressed was seven.

"Excuse me," Jack said, pressing the button for nine. He looked at the stranger. "I'm sorry, I pressed the wrong button."

The stranger, still wearing his sunglasses, looked at Jack and said nothing.

When the elevator stopped on seven and the doors opened, the stranger got off. As soon as the doors closed and the elevator started moving again, Jack and Molly both exhaled.

"I've never seen that guy before," Molly said. Her voice wasn't much louder than a whisper.

"I didn't recognize him either, but that was a weird coincidence. I think we'll pass on going to Smith's place right now."

They went up to the ninth floor and, as soon as the doors opened, Jack pushed the button for the lobby.

Back at the same table in the pool area, they sat down.

"Are we just getting jumpy or what?" Molly asked.

"I'm not sure. It's unreasonable to think that we'd recognize everyone in your building. We don't even know if he went to that condo."

"And I sure as hell wasn't going to get off on seven and find out. Now what do we do?"

"We've got to get in that condo. See if there's anything there that could help us. Maybe Smith took everything from the storage unit there before he followed us up to Useppa?"

"Right. Or maybe Smith's buddy is in there waiting for us to come in. Then what?"

"We can knock on the door or something, make sure no one's in there."

Molly just shook her head. "Did it occur to you that if someone is inside, they might choose not to answer the door? Or if we do go in, someone might come home while we're inside, trapping us, I might add? Some sleuth you are. Forget it—we're not going inside that condo."

"You never did answer my question," Jack said, changing the subject.

Molly looked at him, stood, and held out her hand. "Let's go upstairs for a minute, then go get something to eat."

He took her hand and stood, figuring he wasn't going to get an answer. She surprised him by putting her arms on his shoulders and looking him in the eyes, her face inches from his.

"I'm staying with you tonight, on the boat," she said. "I just need to get a few things first."

TWENTY-FOUR

Jack was sitting in his office, going through budgets for some of the departments. He had his red pen out and was marking questionable areas. Just as Chuck had promised, corporate had asked for another fifteen million dollars in reductions. This round was going to hurt.

His desk phone rang, and he picked it up.

"This is Jack," he answered.

"Mr. Davis. Good morning. This is Special Agent Carter with FDLE." All business.

Jack stiffened. "Hello. What could I do for you?"

"I was wondering if you could come down to the office and answer a few questions." It didn't sound like a request.

Jack looked at the stack of departmental budgets he had yet to go through. "Sure. Would tomorrow be okay? I've got a ton of work yet to do today."

"I think it would be better if you come this afternoon."

There was a long silence on the line. Now Jack was worried. "Do I need to bring an attorney?"

There was another pause on the line before Carter answered. "I'm sorry. I can't advise you on that. All I can tell you is that we need you to come down here this afternoon to answer a few more questions relating to the missing person case we discussed the other day." He waited for Jack's answer.

Jack looked at his watch and said, "Four thirty okay?"

"Our office is at 283 First Street, fourth floor. I'll see you then." He hung up the phone.

Jack put the phone back on the desk set. This didn't sound good. Carter wanted him on his own turf for some reason besides convenience. If Jack had been totally innocent, he probably wouldn't have thought twice about it. But he'd taken Smith's phone and condo key.

He opened his desk drawer and fished around until he found what he wanted. He pulled out the business card Walter Dobbs had given him and dialed his cell phone number. To his surprise, Walter answered after only two rings.

"Walter Dobbs."

"Walter, Jack Davis here. How are you?"

"Jack." The voice warmed. "Good to hear from you. I'm fine, how are you?"

"Well, to tell you the truth, I'm not sure. Have you got a few minutes?" Jack proceeded to give him a short sketch of what had transpired, ending with the phone call he'd just received from Special Agent Carter.

After a few questions to Jack, Dobbs assessed the situation and took control. "I'll meet you there at four thirty. Do not say anything to Carter or anyone else until I get there, understand?"

"Absolutely. Thank you, Walter."

"No problem. Remember, not a word until I arrive. I'll see you there."

Jack hung up the phone. He was relieved to have Walter take charge. He realized that he hadn't discussed payment and wondered how much someone like Walter Dobbs charged. He decided not to think about it right now.

At twenty minutes after four, Jack walked into the FDLE office in Fort Myers and asked for Special Agent Frank Carter. Walter was nowhere to be seen. Jack signed in as requested and received a VISITOR badge. In a few minutes, Carter walked out and escorted Jack back to a small conference room. Another agent, introduced as Clara Gibbs, was there waiting on them.

"Have a seat, Jack. I appreciate you coming down on such short notice." Carter was all smiles and seemed to be putting on a show for Gibbs. "We just wanted to ask you a few questions."

"Not a problem, Mr. Carter. But I've been instructed by my attorney not to say anything until he arrives."

The smile vanished from Carter's face. He looked at Gibbs and then at Jack. "Your attorney? Where is your attorney?"

Before Jack could answer, someone knocked at the conference room door. Gibbs walked over to open it. As soon as she did, Walter Dobbs walked in with his briefcase. He stuck his hand out to Agent Gibbs and said, "Walter Dobbs. I'm Mr. Davis's attorney."

Jack noticed the look of utter shock on Carter's face as he struggled to maintain his composure. The situation had just spun way out of his control, and he was furious.

After the introductions were complete, Walter sat next to Jack. He clasped his hands together on the table and waited for Carter to begin. The script hadn't called for this, and Carter was desperate to salvage the meeting.

"Mr. Davis. Can you tell us where you were on the afternoon of June 11?" Carter asked.

Jack started to answer, but Dobbs placed his hand on Jack's arm. He leaned over and whispered in Jack's ear. "Only answer the question after I tell you it's okay. And just answer the question, no more."

Dobbs turned toward the agents. "Could you be more specific about the time, please?"

Carter was frustrated, and they had just started with the first question. "Around three p.m." Carter's voice was ice.

Jack looked at Dobbs. Dobbs nodded and Jack said, "I was on a boat anchored off the southern end of Useppa Island."

"Were there any other boats anchored there at that time?"

Jack started to answer, caught himself, and looked at Dobbs. He nodded.

"Yes," Jack answered, remembering Dobbs's instructions.

Carter shook his head and exhaled. After finally establishing that one of the other boats was the Catalina 22, he asked Jack if he'd gone onboard that boat.

Jack looked at Dobbs, and Dobbs shook his head.

"Mr. Carter, I'm afraid that my client isn't going to be able to answer any more questions at this time. I didn't have the opportunity to talk with him prior to this impromptu meeting, so I'm sorry to say that this meeting is over until I've had such time to confer with my client about his involvement in your investigation."

Carter lost his composure. "Let me tell you something, Mr. Dobbs. I can hold your client for twenty-four hours if I please. And if you continue to refuse to let him cooperate, I just might do that."

J. Walter Dobbs remained calm and unruffled. He straightened his cuffs, looked directly at Carter, and called his bluff.

"You may indeed, Special Agent Carter. But, if there's no substance to be found for holding my client, which I strongly suspect is the case, I'll have you in front of a judge before you know it. And my next call will be to the Commissioner's office. So I would think long and hard before resorting to such drastic measures."

Dobbs's eyes bore into Carter as he waited for a response.

Carter was cornered and had been out-maneuvered. He was very familiar with who J. Walter Dobbs was and knew he was close friends with the Governor and the Commissioner of FDLE. This wasn't the battle to pick. The best he could do to save face at this point was to insist that Jack not leave the area without notifying his office and point out they still had further questions for him.

"I can assure you my client has nothing to hide and will be available. If you wish to ask him further questions, I would request that you contact me directly," Dobbs said as he handed both of the FDLE agents his business card. As he turned to walk out, he stopped, as if he had an afterthought. He looked back at Carter.

"One more thing. I also represent Ms. Molly Byrne. So if you're thinking of contacting her, I can save you the trouble. Again, just contact me directly."

Carter looked at Gibbs and shook his head, disgusted.

On their way out of the building, Jack said, "I think we may have really pissed those two off."

Walter just laughed. "Serves them right. They were trying to sneak in under the radar to question you. You have time to come by my office and tell me what's going on?"

"Sure."

They walked the block over to Walter's office, where Jack sat down and told him the whole story, including what happened that weekend at Useppa.

"Taking the phone and key could be problematic, but I think we can finesse that one. Let me dig around and find out what I can. I'll call you in a couple of days. I don't think they'll be bothering you again, but if they should, give me a call. And please let Molly know. I'd hate to have her disavow any knowledge of me representing her."

Jack laughed. "Thanks again, Walter. And thanks for including Molly."

Jack got up to leave and hesitated at the door. "About your bill . . ."

"Taken care of. Don't worry about it. I'll send you a bill for expenses, if any, but my fees are gratis. I told you, if you needed anything to call. I meant it."

Jack shook his hand. "That's a relief. I was thinking I was going to have to sell Left Behind to cover your hourly rate."

Walter laughed out loud and slapped Jack on the shoulder. "We couldn't do that, Jack. Then who would I have to take me out sailing again? I'll be talking to you. Don't worry, everything will be fine."

On his way back to the marina, Jack pulled out his phone and called Molly. "Busy?" he asked when she answered.

"Not really. Just paying some bills. What are you doing?"

"I just left Walter Dobbs. It's been an interesting day, to say the least. Why don't you meet me at Carlos Cantina and I'll tell you about it?" Carlos was a Mexican restaurant next door to Ray's; not as good a view and lacking the ambience of Ray's, but also lacking the memories.

"Carlos sounds good. We haven't been there in ages. I'll meet you there."

"See you in a few."

TWENTY-FIVE

When Jack got to the boat, he changed clothes. Grabbing his ever-present backpack, he headed toward Carlos.

On the way, Jack remembered the electronic bug detector should be here and stopped by the marina office. As soon as he walked in, Mike pulled out a box with a UPS label on it. It was addressed to Jack.

"I guess you're looking for this," Mike said.

"Yes, I was. Thanks, Mike." He put the small box into his backpack and went to the restaurant.

Molly was standing inside the door, waiting for him. He gave her a big hug, and the hostess took them to a table outside. When their waiter came over to take their order, Molly asked for a Sam Adams, but they didn't have it, so she ordered a Tecate with Jack.

"You'll have to convert," he said.

She smiled. "I can manage. I was getting tired of Sam Adams anyway. I'm glad you called—it's a little creepy sitting around my place, knowing someone could be listening to everything."

"It is a little weird. That's why I suggested meeting here. I have the bug detector in my backpack. Soon as we leave here, we'll take care of those little devils. Call me the exterminator." Jack laughed again.

Molly shook her head. "You're sick."

"I know. But you still love me, right?"

She had to smile when he said that. "Yes, I do. Don't know why. So, tell me what happened today. What were you doing with Walter?"

"Long story short, I got called in for interrogation by Special Agent Frank Carter. Smelled like a trap, so I called Walter and he went with me. Good thing. Frank and his buddy were going to put the squeeze on me. More questions about our weekend up at Useppa."

"Great. So does that mean I'm next on their call list?"

"I don't think so. Walter pretty much blew up their plan. By the way, he's also representing you if anyone asks."

"Really? So tell me how can we afford Walter Dobbs? Doesn't he charge like a bazillion dollars an hour?"

"Not to us. He told me that he'd only bill out of pocket expenses—no fees for his time."

"Wow. I'm impressed. So he's a good guy after all."

"He is. He's a good friend, I'm sure of that."

"Did you tell him everything? The phone and all?" she asked.

"Yeah. The phone may be a problem. Walter said he'd check out some things and get back to us. He said not to worry."

"I just want to get those damn listening devices out of my place so I can get back to normal."

"Well, let's take a look at this thing."

Jack took the package out of his backpack and opened the box. Inside was the bug detection device he'd ordered yesterday off the Internet. He didn't know much about such stuff and hoped this one would be sufficient. It better be. The handheld device had cost him two hundred fifty dollars plus an extra thirty for expedited shipping.

It was about the size of a cell phone, although three times the thickness. There was a collapsible antenna on top and a series of red lights on the front. He pulled out the small manual that came with it and quickly scanned it for operating instructions. After putting the batteries in, he put the device and instruction booklet back in his pack.

"When we get to your place, let's try to keep the conversation as normal as possible while I look for the bugs."

They walked over to Molly's condo, where she opened the door and they walked in.

"How about something to drink?" she asked.

"Sounds good."

He took the detection device out of the bag, extended the antenna, and turned it on.

Molly looked over his shoulder, nodded, and walked into the kitchen to get their drinks. Jack walked into the kitchen, passing the device along appliances, cabinets, and counters. They continued to try and carry on some semblance of a normal conversation.

As he walked to the dining room table, several red lights came on. He moved it around the table, but there was no change. When he moved it near the single light fixture hanging down over the table, the thing lit up like a Christmas tree and started flashing. He set it down on the table and examined the light fixture. After a few minutes, he held up a tiny black device between his fingers for Molly to see. She nodded. He took it into the kitchen and wrapped a towel around it. Placing it on the floor, he ground the heel of his shoe into the towel and heard plastic crunching.

He continued to search the condo. When he walked into her bedroom, he paused, looked at her, and twitched his eyebrows. She covered her mouth to keep from laughing out loud.

After finding no other surveillance devices, he pronounced her place clean.

"We probably should check your boat, too," she said.

"Good idea. I didn't think about that, but wouldn't hurt to check it." Jack laughed. "It didn't seem to be a problem last night."

She blushed. "You distracted me."

"You complaining?"

"Not at all. I still wonder how he got in my place," Molly said.

"Probably not that hard to pick the lock during the day. Don't forget, he had a unit downstairs, so he knew what kind of lock you had. And there would have been no reason to question him being in the building."

"Thanks. That really makes me feel safe and secure."

They both laughed a nervous laugh and decided to go out on the balcony. When they got to the door, Molly stopped and held her arm in front of Jack.

"We didn't check the balcony," she said.

Jack nodded. "You're right. We probably should, just in case."

He walked back over to the bag and brought out the bug detector. Turning it on, they walked out onto the balcony. First, he checked the table and chairs. Nothing. He held it up near one of the outside lights. Again, nothing. But when he walked over to the other side of the balcony and held it near the other fixture, it lit up. He smiled and handed it to Molly. Looking underneath the cover over the light bulb, he found it. They took the tiny listening device back into the kitchen, where it met the same fate as the other one.

Back on the balcony, they sat at the table and relaxed once again.

"Maybe you should consider a new career," Molly said.

"No, thanks. I don't have the nerves for this." He held up his hand that was still shaking. "I don't know how people do this for a living."

They discussed what to do next. Jack still wanted to go into Smith's condo on seven, but Molly would have none of that.

"We do have pictures of the stuff we found in the storage unit," she said.

"Let's take a look at them."

Molly plugged Jack's phone into her computer and downloaded the pictures she'd taken in the storage unit. She pulled up the images and enlarged them as much as possible. Jack wrote down the information as they scrolled through the pictures multiple times, making sure they wrote down everything visible.

When they finished, they looked at the list.

"We have a link between Vic Chaney and Michael Taylor," he said.

"And between them and the ACM plant in Mexico."

"Manny spelled it all out."

"Yeah, but Manny's not around to testify."

"True, but with everything here . . . They can't cover all of this up; it's just too big. I'm thinking it's time we brought in the professionals. But first we need to check out Smith's condo."

"Are you nuts?"

"Molly. I need to do something with that phone. Why don't we check out Smith's condo and put the phone in it. Eventually the cops are going to find out about his place. When they do, the phone will be in it. Nice and tidy, don't you think?"

She hesitated before answering. He knew she hated the thought of going into that condo.

"Why don't you just pitch it into the river?" she asked.

"I thought about that. But I want the police to get the information off it. There's probably more stuff on the phone they could use, so I'd hate for it to be lost at the bottom of the Caloosahatchee. And I can't very well share it with them." Jack eyes were pleading.

"This is against my better judgment—"

"We'll be in and out in five minutes. Tops."

She nodded. "Okay."

Jack got Smith's phone out and carefully wiped it clean of all fingerprints. He wrapped it in a clean hand towel and put it into his pocket. Molly had a box of latex exam gloves in her bathroom, and they each stuck a pair in their shorts.

The plan was go down to the seventh floor. If the coast was clear, Jack would put his gloves on and knock on Smith's door. If nobody answered, Jack would open the door with the key while Molly stayed a safe distance away. Once Jack had determined the unit was empty, then Molly would put her gloves on and join him inside. If someone was in there, Molly would go for help.

They took the elevator down to the seventh floor. No one was on the elevator with them, and as they stepped off the elevator into the hall, there was nobody to be seen in either direction. As soon as the elevator doors closed, they walked down the hall toward Smith's unit. Molly stopped a couple of doors away while Jack put on his gloves. He walked up to the door marked 714 and knocked. No answer. Molly kept looking up and down the hall, hoping no one would emerge. She listened for the elevator, but there was no activity.

Jack knocked again. Still no answer. He slipped his gloved hand into his pocket and pulled out the key he'd taken from Smith's sailboat, hoping it was the right one. Inserting it into the lock, he turned it and felt the latch unlock. He looked one more time at Molly. She nodded, and he opened the door to Smith's unit.

It was dark inside. He felt for a light switch and located the row of switches on the right hand wall. He flipped them all up and several lights came on. There was no sound from inside. As fast as possible, he looked in all the rooms. The condo was laid out like Molly's, which was convenient and made it easier. There was no one there.

He went back to the front door and peeked out into the hall. Molly was still standing by herself in the hallway. He motioned to her. She pulled on her gloves as she walked to the condo and inside. Jack eased the door shut.

"Nobody home," he whispered. For the first time, he looked around the apartment to see what was there. It was furnished, but had the appearance of a place that was unoccupied. There was no sign of any personalization. They made their way to the dining room. A black box a little larger than a shoe box sat on the dining room table. It had several knobs and dials and a round antenna sticking up from the back. Plugged into the box was a pair of headphones on the table. The chair was pulled out from the table as if someone had just left. But there were no lights on anywhere on the box, and it appeared to be turned off.

"This had to be his listening station," Jack said.

There were papers scattered on the table. The FedEx envelope from the storage unit was there. Jack saw the documents they had photographed. He was careful not to disturb anything. He grabbed Molly's arm and pointed.

"Look," he said. It was a note from Manny to Richard. That hadn't been in the briefcase at the storage unit. He started to pick it up, and Molly grabbed his arm.

"No. Leave it. Take a picture, but leave it for the police," she whispered.

He nodded and looked at the other papers without touching them. One was attached to a legal pad and had handwriting on it. It appeared to be notes that Smith or someone had written.

He nodded, took out his phone, and snapped several pictures of the table. He checked the images to make sure they were legible before he put the phone back in his pocket.

Jack reached in his other pocket and pulled out Smith's phone wrapped in the towel. Taking no chances, he wiped it down once more for good measure and carefully set it on the table near the console.

"Let's get the hell out of here," Molly said.

Halfway to the door, someone outside knocked on it. They froze, then looked at each other.

Shit, Molly mouthed to Jack, not uttering a sound.

Grasping Molly's hand, Jack tiptoed to the light switches and turned them off. The person outside knocked on the door again. Careful not to make any noise, Jack put his eye up to the peephole and looked through it.

It was a college kid wearing a Pizza Man shirt and earphones, singing along to the music. He was holding a large cardboard pizza box. The kid knocked once more. When no one answered, he decided to check the address on the delivery slip. He looked down at the slip of paper, then up at the door.

"Oh man, wrong floor," the kid said out loud to himself. He turned and hurried away.

Jack waited to hear the sound of the elevator. Once he did, he turned the lights back on.

"Pizza guy. Wrong address. No big deal," he said.

Molly slapped his arm. Hard. "Let's get out of here. Now."

Jack eased the door open and stuck his head out. The hall was clear. Molly switched the lights back off, and they closed the door. Jack locked it back and put the key into his pocket. As fast as possible, they took the gloves off and went back to Molly's condo, taking the stairs this time to avoid running into anyone at the elevator.

Safely inside Molly's condo, Jack started laughing. "That scared the crap outta me. I'm still shaking."

Molly could only shake her head. "How I let you talk me into things, I'll never know. I thought I was going to pee myself when I heard that knock on the door." She started laughing, too. "What are you going to do with the key?" she asked when they quit laughing.

"It's going in the river, never to be seen again. I don't want anything else to do with Robert Smith or whoever the hell he was."

"I'll second that. How long do you think it'll take the police to find his place?"

"Not long. I'm surprised they haven't been here already. They've probably already been back out to Beach Marina."

Molly looked at him. "So we're going to let the police handle it from here, right?"

Jack hesitated. "Except for one thing. I want to talk to Chaney. For Richard."

She softened at the sound of their friend's name. "Jack. This is bigger than us. We need to let the cops handle it."

"We will. We'll give everything we have to Budzinski, I promise. But first I want to pay a visit to Chaney."

"What are you going to say to him?" she asked.

"I don't know. I just want the satisfaction of telling him face to face that Richard figured it out."

Jack knew where he'd heard the voice before. Chuck's office. It was Vic Chaney. That was who answered the number he took off Smith's phone.

"What's the matter? You look like you just saw a ghost," she said.

"Heard one is more like it. Remember when we called that Atlanta number from Smith's phone? And I told you the voice sounded vaguely familiar?"

Molly nodded.

"It was Chaney."

Her mouth opened, and her face turned pale, but she didn't say anything.

"I heard him talking to Chuck that day in Chuck's office. That was where I heard the voice."

"Are you sure?" Molly knew by his expression he was, but part of her wanted him not to be.

"No doubt. I may not be good with names, but I have this uncanny knack for remembering voices. It was him."

"When are we going to see him?" Molly asked.

"Soon as I figure out how."

He picked up on Molly including herself, but figured now was not the time to argue with her.

"I'm beat. We need to get some sleep. Why don't you get whatever you need and let's go back to the boat." Jack got up and moved toward the door.

She didn't argue. "Give me a few minutes."

When they got back to his boat, he unlocked it and they went below. He got the bug detector out and checked everything. It was clear.

"Looks good. Glad there wasn't one in there," he said, grinning and nodding toward the forward berth.

Molly blushed, but smiled.

He held the key to Smith's condo up. "I'm going to get rid of this. I'll be right back."

Jack walked out to the end of J dock. He could see the channel marker not far away. It was quiet and no one was around. Few boats were out on the river this late and none within sight. He could see the reflection of the bridge lights on the water.

He held the key in his hand. After checking once more to make sure no one was around, he threw the key as far as he could toward the middle of the river. It made a small splash and was gone.

He was glad to be rid of that, and hoped that was the end of their encounters with Robert Smith. He just wondered who else was out there looking for them.

Jack turned around to go back to his boat. He scanned the marina area as he walked and saw only Hank, the security guard, making his rounds. Jack knew him well, and felt more comfortable with him around. Hank was not your stereotype overweight, dim-witted rent-a-cop. He was ex-military, recently retired, but still in good shape and sharp as could be. Not much escaped him.

They were safe on the boat, Jack felt, and he was glad Molly was here with him. It was amazing, how comfortable that had become in such a short period of time. Although they had agreed to take things slow, circumstances had accelerated the pace, with neither complaining.

When he got to his cabin, she was sitting up in the berth, reading. She set the book on the nightstand next to her.

"Done," he said. "Let's hope that's the last of him." He took off his clothes and crawled into bed next to her, snuggling up close. She turned out the light, put her arms around him, and they drifted off to sleep, holding each other.

TWENTY-SIX

The next morning Jack was sitting in his office when his phone rang.

"Hello?"

"Jack? Hi, this is Mary. Chuck wanted to know if you had a few minutes to come up to his office."

"Sure. When?"

"Would now be okay?"

"I'll be there in five minutes."

Jack hung up the phone, wondering what this was about. Probably more budget cuts from corporate, he guessed. He grabbed his notebook and headed upstairs.

When he got to Chuck's office, Mary told him to go on in. Chuck was on the phone, as usual, and motioned for Jack to sit down. He finished his call and hung up the phone.

"Thanks for coming up. I only need a few minutes. I've been thinking about the Clearart issue." He leaned back in his chair and spread his hands. "You really think there's a problem, don't you?"

Jack was caught off guard, not expecting this from Chuck. He still suspected Chuck of being aligned with corporate and wasn't sure how to answer.

"Well, yes, but like I told you, I don't have any proof. I thought you had decided to drop it?"

"I had. But it keeps bothering me. I checked around a bit and there's no indication that ACM is doing anything with it. Now I'm starting to wonder if they're covering something up. If there is a problem, we need to light a fire under them."

Jack was surprised at this turn of events. "So . . . what are you suggesting?"

"I think we need to go to Chaney with it, get him involved and put a little pressure on them. He called this morning. He's coming down to his house on Sanibel this afternoon to spend a few days. I was thinking you and I should ride out there and talk to him."

Great, Jack thought. That was the last thing he wanted to do.

He needed to buy some time and think this out. He tried to keep a straight face and calm demeanor.

"You sure? I mean, you were concerned before about not having anything concrete to give him." Jack was stalling and hoped it didn't show.

"Still am. But if there's even a hint of a problem, Chaney will want to get in front of it. He doesn't like surprises."

Yeah, right. Speaking of surprises, he realized poor Chuck didn't have a clue about what he was getting into. Chaney and the president of ACM were in this up to their necks. Jack was sorry he misjudged Chuck, but he couldn't figure out a way to decline Chuck's offer without raising suspicion.

"Okay. But can we hold off for a couple of days? That would give me a chance to summarize everything we know into some type of cogent report. At least have it organized. It would be easier to sell that way," Jack said.

"Good idea. I'll go ahead and call him, just tell him I need an hour of his time in a few days. Let me know when you have the report ready." Chuck stood to signify the meeting was over.

"Will do. Thanks, Chuck."

Jack walked out of the office and back downstairs.

When he got to his office, he shut the door and called Molly on his cell phone.

"Hey," he said. "I just left Chuck's office. We were wrong about him."

"What do you mean?"

"Chuck doesn't know anything. He called me in to tell me he thinks ACM isn't doing anything on Clearart, and he wants to go ahead and take it to Chaney."

"Even with no proof?"

"Yes. He checked up on ACM, so he wants to stir the pot."

"Wow. So he has nothing to do with any of this?"

"Nope. Not a thing. He's going to be shocked when it all comes out. But he still thinks Chaney is a good guy. Speaking of Chaney, he's coming down to Sanibel this weekend."

"You said we'd turn this over to Budzinski."

"We will. I want to go by to talk to Walter this afternoon and discuss it with him. I'll give you a call after."

Jack ended the call. He left work a few minutes early and went by to see Walter Dobbs. Walter told him to just bypass the reception desk and come straight up to his office.

Walking into Walter's office, Jack was still amazed at how big it was. It had to be the largest office he'd ever seen.

It was even bigger than the CEO's office at the insurance company in Jacksonville where Jack had worked.

Walter seemed genuinely glad to see Jack. They chatted a few minutes before Jack got down to business.

"I'm not sure how to tell you this, but the phone and key I took from Smith's sailboat are no longer a problem."

Walter's eyebrows arched. "Oh? How so?"

"What I tell you is confidential, right?" Jack asked.

"Totally. Unless you're about to tell me that you're going to commit a crime."

"We put the phone back in Smith's condo. Wiped clean of any prints, of course. And the key is at the bottom of the Caloosahatchee River. The cops will find the phone when they find Smith's condo. And the loss of the key is a non-event. In both cases, no harm, no foul."

Walter pondered what Jack had told him. At last, he spoke. "Well, that certainly makes things a lot neater as far as you're concerned. As long as they can't tie you to the phone or his condo."

"We were careful. We never used the phone; in fact, kept it turned off. No one saw us go in or out of the condo. We wore gloves, too. I suppose they could still do some sort of television forensic magic and maybe find something."

Walter laughed. "Maybe, but they would only resort to the hi-tech stuff if there was some reason to believe a serious crime had been committed there. From what you've told me, that doesn't seem to be the case."

"One other thing. Molly and I want to take everything we have to Budzinski. Wash our hands of it. Let the cops pursue it from here."

"Hmm. I'm not sure we can cut Carter and FDLE out of it at this point," Walter said. "Why Budzinski and not Carter?"

"One, I don't trust Carter. Two, I'd like to make sure that Richard didn't die in vain. I think Budzinski wants that, too," Jack said.

"I have to agree with you. So what are you suggesting?"

"I've thought about it. There are two separate tracks here. First, Carter is investigating a person's disappearance at Useppa. We ran into this guy up there and that's all we know about it, right? Nothing more. We've never seen the man before or after. We don't know who he is or what he was up to. We meet with Carter, answer his questions, and we're done with him."

Walter nodded.

"Second is what we have on Clearart. All of the stuff Richard put together. That's what we want to take to Budzinski. We think it may have something to do with Richard's murder. We don't link Smith to it at all because we don't know. We keep Smith out of it. If he was involved, that's for the police to find out."

"That seems to be awful close to the line, Jack. I have to say I'm not entirely comfortable. You two have put it together and so will they. Why not give everything, except for the phone and key, of course, to both of them? Tell them there may be a connection, so you just wanted to give them everything together. That way, the only lie is the omission of the two items you took, which I agree is inconsequential. What's the downside?"

Jack considered what Walter said. Maybe he was right. That strategy would be less risky. "Okay, I trust your judgment. But I want you to be there."

"Of course. In fact, I'll suggest we all meet here."

"Can you set it up for tomorrow?"

"I think so."

The next day, Jack and Molly met over at Walter Dobbs's office. Lieutenant Budzinski and Special Agent Carter were already there. A court reporter was there to document the meeting.

Walter got things started. "I appreciate everyone coming in on such short notice. My clients, Molly Byrne and Jack Davis, have information potentially relating to the death of their friend, Richard Melton. It's a complicated story and may also have something to do with the missing person you're investigating." He pointed to Carter.

Dobbs continued, "I advised them to share it with both of you simultaneously and let you do your jobs. Please feel free to ask questions as we go."

Jack started with Peter's heart attack as a way of introducing how Richard got suspicious. They explained Richard's curiosity and their meetings about the subject. They spoke of the break-ins at each of their places and why they didn't call the police. When they got to the part about the contents of the storage unit missing, Carter spoke up.

"Why didn't you call someone?"

"For what? We were in a storage unit rented under a false name—I still don't know what name Richard used—looking at information implicating corporate officers of Advance Cardiac Meds and HealthAmerica. So you're telling me if I had walked in complaining that someone had stolen it, you would have taken me seriously?" Jack asked Carter.

Carter didn't answer and seemed content to let it go.

When Jack told of searching their apartment and finding listening devices, Carter again wanted to know why they hadn't called him.

Molly answered this time. "I wanted the damn things gone. I didn't know who was listening and why. Honestly, I didn't care. But I wanted my privacy back as soon as possible. Jack found the things and destroyed them. That was all I wanted."

"That could have been dangerous," Carter said.

"I realize that now. But surely you can understand."

Carter and Budzinski each asked a few more questions, clarifying the story in places. Three hours later, they said they had what they needed.

"So what do you do now?" Jack asked.

Carter spoke first. "We're still trying to determine the identity of Robert Smith. We're close. Once we do that, I think it'll open a few doors for us and hopefully for the lieutenant here," he said, nodding to Budzinski.

"My interest is this Smith character. All of the other stuff is interesting, but way over my pay grade. Drug companies peddling bogus medicine is out of my league. My primary interest is finding out who killed your friend. Based on what we've heard, Smith looks like a good fit," Budzinski said.

"Any other questions?" Walter asked. "Mr. Carter, I trust that has answered your questions about my client's knowledge of that weekend at Useppa Island?"

Carter nodded. "We're just trying to pin Smith down. Your clients were the last people who saw him."

"Any idea what happened to him?" Jack asked.

Carter looked at Budzinski, then back at Jack. "I can't say too much because it's an ongoing investigation. But I don't think you have to worry about Robert Smith anymore."

Jack could tell that Carter wasn't going to say more. Everyone stood with Carter and Budzinski walking out. Molly and Jack stayed behind to talk with Walter.

"I think that went extremely well," Walter said.

"So you think we're done?" Jack asked.

"I think so. They may come back with some questions later on, but I think they have plenty to go with at the moment."

"Do you think the other piece will ever come up?" Molly asked, referring to the information they had left out.

"I doubt it. As Jack said, no harm, no foul. Let them do what they do best."

That night, on the boat, they argued about Jack visiting Chaney.

"You can't just show up at his house. Jack, the guy's dangerous!" Molly was not backing down.

"Okay, okay. I'll call him, see what he says."

"How're you going to call him? You think he's going to take your call?"

Jack smiled. "I still have the number from Smith's phone."

"Damn, you're stubborn."

"And I bought another disposable phone." He pulled it out of his pocket.

Molly crossed her arms as he dialed the number.

"Hello?" Chaney answered.

"Vic? Don't hang up. I'm calling for Robert Smith. I know you know who I'm talking about."

The voice on the other end didn't say anything, but didn't hang up.

"I've got the package that Manny Garcia sent Richard Melton."

"Who is this?" the voice on the other end said.

"I'm a friend of Melton's. I want to talk to you about a deal."

"I'm listening."

"Not on the phone. In person." Jack knew he had to convince Chaney to trust him.

"Look, I'm not a cop and I'm not recording this. I've got documents that could hang you and Taylor, documents that prove MexC is not effective. I obviously have your private number. If I'd wanted to, I could've just given it all to the cops. But if I do that, there's nothing in it for me."

There was a long pause on the other end of the line. "Maybe we should talk. You know where I am?"

"Yes," Jack said.

"Bring the package here. Alone. Eight o'clock tomorrow night."

"I'll be there." Jack hung up and turned to Molly. "He wants me to come to his house and talk."

TWENTY-SEVEN

"I still don't think this is a good idea," Molly said.

It was dark, and she was driving. They were going across the Sanibel Causeway to Vic Chaney's house. Jack had gotten the address from the year old *Fort Myers Magazine* article.

"We have to, there's no other way. Look, if we don't give that stuff back to him, he won't quit. Do you want to worry about people like Robert Smith for the rest of your life? Don't get me wrong. I hope Chaney burns in hell for what he's done. But the truth is we can't win. We have nothing to tie him to Richard's murder. The most we could do is maybe cause him some embarrassment, but he'll just get some big shot attorney and—"

"Oh, I agree. But what if somebody else is there? Seems awful risky to me. I wish you had at least told Walter." She was worried. Vic Chaney wasn't someone to be trifled with.

"I couldn't, Molly. He would've never let me come."

"Chaney's dangerous, Jack."

He started to say that was why he wanted to bring his gun, but didn't want to get into an argument with her. Molly had persuaded him not to bring it and Jack had reluctantly agreed. Her logic made sense; Chaney was expecting him and there should be no reason for guns in his house.

"I told you. If I'm not out in fifteen minutes, then call Budzinski, Carter, 911—everyone."

They were on Periwinkle Way and turned left on Casa Ybel Road, which turned into West Gulf Drive. Chaney's house was on West Gulf Drive. Jack watched the numbers as they got closer. All of the houses were on the right side of the street, but with an unobstructed view of the Gulf. Most were set back from the road, with fences and trees to block the view from passing motorists.

"That's it." Jack pointed to the large gate with the numbers lit up. The gate was open. A wrought iron fence tastefully covered with shrubbery ran along the road and was connected to two large brick pillars that flanked the driveway. Molly pulled over alongside the road and stopped just before getting to the driveway.

She reached over and put her hand on Jack's. "Be careful."

"Fifteen minutes, no earlier."

Jack got out of the car with a manila envelope and walked toward the driveway. He walked down the curving driveway and soon saw the house. Stopping next to a tree that would partially conceal him, he got his bearings.

The house was spectacular, setting some fifteen feet off the ground. He could see that it was a little cattycornered on the lot, probably to better leverage the view and privacy. Parking was underneath, and he saw a late model BMW parked there. No other cars were there. A porch ran across the entire front of the house. He remembered that from the magazine article. As he recalled, the view from up there was awesome.

The main entrance door was roughly in the middle of the porch. Lights on each side of the door were on, but no other lights on the porch. To the right, there were windows and French doors facing the porch, but no lights on in the part of the house that he could see. On the left at the far corner of the house, there were lights on. The entire corner was glass. From here, it looked like a study or library. He could see bookshelves toward the ceiling.

He tiptoed up the steps and, when he got to the porch level, turned left. The magazine picture didn't do it justice. What a view. The moonlight was reflecting off the calm Gulf waters. Lighting flashed faraway over the Gulf, too far to hear the thunder. He wondered what a view like this would cost.

To his right he had a better view of the study on the corner. Next to the windows he could make out a telescope and a large globe. He walked a little closer, still staying in the shadows beside the house. In the middle of the room was a desk with a computer screen on one side. The desk was angled and faced the corner of the house. French doors were open and led to the deck.

As he got closer to the doors, he could see a flat panel television in the middle of a floor-to-ceiling bookcase to the right of the desk. It looked like CNN or one of the news networks was playing. He could hear the talking heads. Chaney was sitting at his desk, writing and not paying any attention to the television. No one else was in the room.

Jack walked through the French doors and cleared his throat when he entered.

Chaney looked up and stared at him.

Jack walked around to the front of the desk, threw the envelope on it, then held his hands up, palms out.

"Who the hell are you?" Chaney said.

"Not important, but since you asked, my name is Jack Davis. I work for you, here in Fort Myers at Rivers Hospital." He figured that Chaney already knew who he was, and if not, could easily find out.

"How do I know you're not recording this?"

"How do I know *you're* not recording this?" Jack replied. "Open the envelope."

Chaney picked up the envelope, opened it and removed the pages inside. He shuffled through them, skimming each page, then lay them on top of the envelope. "These are copies."

Jack nodded. "You think I'm stupid? That I'm gonna walk in here with the originals, you take them, and leave me with nothing? Or worse? Don't worry, the originals are safe."

"What do you want?"

"Simple. Leave me and my girlfriend alone. Forever. I don't want to go around the rest of my life looking over my shoulder for people like Robert Smith."

"That's it? Nothing else?"

Jack shook his head and sat in one of the chairs in front of Chaney's desk.

"I don't want your money, if that's what you're asking. It's blood money and we both know it." Jack pointed to the envelope. "That proves it.

"Don't get me wrong—I think you're scum of the lowest type. You're making billions selling worthless drugs to people. And you killed my best friend. If I had my way, I would've given that package to the cops. It would have been worth it to see you rot in jail. But that's not how things work. You'd hire some hotshot attorney and get off with a slap on the hand. And we spend the rest of our lives trying to avoid your hired help."

Chaney seemed to ponder the offer. "How do I know you don't keep copies?"

"You don't—that's my insurance. Anything ever happens to me or her, they automatically get sent to the press."

Chaney snorted. "Unacceptable. A few months from now, then you're back asking for something else, money next time. It never ends. I'm not stupid, either."

He saw Chaney's right hand move slightly as he eased open the top drawer to his desk. Chaney pulled out a black, semi-automatic pistol and pointed it at Jack. His hand was steady. Jack wasn't sure if that was a good sign or not. Probably not. So much for the no guns argument. It was easy to believe someone wouldn't shoot you until they were pointing a gun at you.

"I've got a better offer," Chaney said.

Jack shook his head. This wasn't in the script. Now he was sorry he told Molly to wait fifteen minutes.

Chaney leaned forward, picked up the handset for his desk phone with his free hand, and punched in a number. "Bring her in."

He turned the computer screen around so Jack could see it. In the top right corner was a feed from a security camera. It looked like it was on the front of the house, pointed down the front porch. Jack saw a man walking behind Molly, his hand at her back.

In a few seconds, the picture became real. A stocky, muscular man pushed Molly into the room. He was holding a gun to her back and motioned her over to the empty chair next to Jack.

Jack started to rise, but Chaney spoke. "I don't think that's a good idea, Davis. Max, here, he has an itchy trigger finger. You don't want to provoke him."

Jack eased back in his chair. "You okay?" he asked Molly in a low voice.

She just nodded. He could tell she was scared. So was he. This was not going the way he planned. Max, who was the size of a small truck, stood there pointing his gun at them.

Jack considered the situation. He didn't think that Chaney would pull the trigger, not in his own house, but Max seemed to be the real deal.

As if reading his mind, Chaney said, "Don't even think about doing anything stupid. Max is well-trained and he won't hesitate."

Chaney laid his gun on top of the desk, looked at Jack and said, "Now we have a real problem, wouldn't you say?"

When Jack didn't answer, Chaney chuckled. "Just a minute ago, you were all mouth. Here's my offer, and it's non-negotiable. I'm going to let you go. And you have exactly two hours to bring back the originals and all copies, understand? Meanwhile, your friend here will stay behind. My insurance.

"And don't even think of alerting the authorities. She and Max won't be here. You show back up with everything, and I'll tell you where you can pick her up."

Shit, Jack thought, this is going from bad to worse. He didn't have to ask what would happen to Molly if he didn't bring the documents. But he knew he couldn't tell Chaney he didn't have the originals; without that card, there was no need for him or Molly. He had to think of something quick.

"I can't," Jack said.

"What do you mean, you can't?" Chaney said, irritated.

"They're in a safe deposit box. Bank's closed, it'll be tomorrow before I can get them."

Chaney studied Molly, then shifted his gaze to Jack. "That so?" He picked up his gun and pointed it at Jack. "Max. Separate them."

Max pulled the chairs a few feet apart and turned them so they were back-to-back. Jack was now facing the bookcase.

Chaney got up and walked over to Jack. He was still holding the gun. "I think you're lying. So here's what we're going to do." He handed Jack a pencil and piece of paper. "Not a peep out of you. Max likes to cut things, and if you even breathe too loud, he's going to start carving on your girlfriend. Clear?"

Jack nodded.

"Write down the name of the bank and the box number." He looked over the top of Jack's head at Max. "Give her a pencil and paper."

Jack's chin sagged. They were screwed. Molly knew the safe deposit box was at Southwest Florida Bank, but she didn't know the box number. He shook his head.

Chaney grinned. "That's what I thought. I believe in second chances, Davis, but that's it. You just used yours. There are no more. Understand?"

Jack looked up at Chaney with hatred in his eyes and nodded.

For the first time since Max brought her in, Molly spoke. "Why did you do it?"

Chaney shook his head and looked down at Jack. "You two wouldn't understand. I've invested billions in ACM and

Clearart. And that prick scientist Garcia was going to ruin it for all of us."

"It didn't work. The MexC didn't work, and you and Mike Taylor knew it. And you kept selling it," Jack said.

Chaney was on a roll now. "So what? It wasn't harmful. It was old people that took it; they were going to die anyway."

"Richard Melton and Manny Garcia weren't old people. You killed them," Molly said.

Chaney's face tightened and he walked around to Molly. "I didn't kill anyone. Yet."

"You might as well have. Robert Smith worked for you. He did your dirty work."

Easy, Molly, Jack thought. This guy's a psycho, don't get him worked up. He couldn't see them, but from the sound of Cheney's voice, he knew he was in front of Molly.

"I hired Smith to take care of things and that's what he's always done. Just like Max, here. I don't tell them how to do their jobs."

Molly kept it up. "What, you were afraid of a pharmacist and a scientist? Some big shot like you couldn't handle them without killing them?" She laughed.

Jack shook his head. What in the hell are you doing, Molly? Damn, he wished he could see her, tell her to cool it.

Chaney's voice had an edge to it. "They got in my way. That's what happens to people who get in my way. You'd do well to keep that in mind."

He walked back around to face Jack.

"Your little friend here has a mouth on her. She needs to learn when to be quiet. If you don't get back here soon, Max may have to teach her a lesson. Enough chit-chat. The sooner you bring back the documents, the sooner I'll be done with the both of you."

Jack didn't like the way that sounded. He still hadn't figured out what he was going to do, but he was convinced that Chaney had decided to kill them. And he couldn't let that happen. Not without a fight.

"Freeze! Drop the guns! Now!" a voice shouted from behind Jack. He was still facing the wall and couldn't see what was going on, but heard a lot of commotion. Chaney started to raise his gun, then dropped it by his side.

Jack heard scuffling and footsteps, then a man with a FDLE windbreaker came over and handcuffed Chaney. Then he heard a familiar voice behind him. "You okay?"

"Yes, thank God you got here when you did," Molly said.

Jack turned his head around to see, still unsure about getting out of the chair. There was a small army of people, all with weapons. Tony Budzinski was standing in front of Molly and looked past her at Jack. "You okay?"

Jack exhaled and rose from the chair. Max was lying on the floor, hands behind his back in cuffs, another man in a FDLE windbreaker standing watch. Frank Carter was in the corner on his phone.

"I think. What the hell just happened?" Jack asked.

Molly stepped over to him, throwing her arms around his neck and hugging him so tight he couldn't breathe, almost knocking him down.

"Oh, Jack. I thought . . ."

He hugged her back with an intensity he couldn't imagine. His mind was racing, trying to piece together the events of the last few minutes. Still holding Molly, he looked over to Budzinski. "How—"

"Let's go outside," Budzinski said.

They walked down the steps and onto the driveway, where Molly and Tony filled Jack in. She'd gone to Budzinski, telling him of Jack's plan to confront Chaney. Tony called Frank Carter and they put together the operation. Molly had been wearing a wire.

At first, Jack was upset that no one had told him.

"You didn't think I was going to let you come out here to meet with Vic Chaney alone, did you?" Molly said, holding Jack's hand.

"It would've been nice to know."

Tony shook his head. "Sorry, Jack, but we felt it best to keep you in the dark. You'd be more believable to Chaney that way. We didn't think he would be crazy enough to do anything rash in his own house, so our plan was to contain everything here."

Carter walked over. "You did good, Molly. That took guts. Hopefully we have enough to put that sleaze away," he said with a nod to Chaney, who was being escorted out.

Carter looked at Jack. "Hang on to this one—she's a keeper." He walked back up the stairs to the house.

Molly smiled at Jack. "You should listen to him, you know?"

He nodded. "I intend to. And thanks. You saved my ass. I'll probably never say this again, but I'm glad you didn't listen to me."

TWENTY-EIGHT

It was a beautiful Saturday morning in Fort Myers, brilliant blue sky and a light breeze. Jack and Molly were sitting out under the bimini on Left Behind having coffee when Tony Budzinski walked up.

"Mind if I come aboard?" he said as he slipped his shoes off.

"How 'bout some coffee?" Molly asked.

"Thanks, I can always drink a cup." He sat across from Jack as Molly went below to get coffee.

"How you doing?"

"Not bad, considering I don't have a job, almost got us killed, and my best friend's murderer is probably going to get off. I saw on the news where he made bail."

Molly came back topside with another cup and a full carafe of hot coffee. She poured the lieutenant a cup and sat next to Jack.

"I got some news that may help. That's why I came by." He took a sip of his coffee before continuing.

"Just left Frank Carter's office. They found Robert Smith's place. Seventh floor of your condo building," he said, looking at Molly. "Surprised you didn't know that." He shifted his glance from one to the other, but got no reply.

"Anyway, his real name was Todd Lowery. Ex-military, apparently did dirty work for hire. We tied him to Richard Melton's murder." He let the news sink in.

"You did?" Jack was suddenly more attentive.

Budzinski nodded. "Found a note from Manny Garcia at ACM to Richard and matched fibers on it from the shirt Richard was wearing the night he was killed. They also found Richard's laptop and the material Garcia had sent Richard."

"So have you found Smith or Lowery or whatever his name is?" Molly asked.

"What was left of him, in the water off the south end of Useppa Island. Identification was difficult, but the cause of death was established as an alligator attack."

"Alligator attack?" Jack and Molly both said.

"Best guess is Lowery was headed over to your boat."

Molly and Jack looked at each other and exhaled. They remembered going for a swim late that night after they got back to the boat.

"So you see, sometimes there is justice. Your friend's killer didn't get away after all."

Molly put her hand over Jack's as a cloud passed over his face. "Smith may have done it, but Chaney pulled the strings. And he's free," he said.

Budzinski shrugged. "Maybe you did more damage than you realize."

"What's that supposed to mean?"

"Watch the news. You didn't hear this from me, but Chaney and Taylor are going to be charged. They've opened an inquiry into Garcia's death. ACM has closed down the plant in Mexico, recalled all of the stuff produced there. Gonna cost billions, I hear."

Jack smiled. "No shit?"

Budzinski finished his coffee, set the cup on the table, and stood. "Gotta run. Thanks for the coffee."

Jack and Molly got up and shook his hand.

"Thanks, Tony. For everything," Jack said.

"Just doing my job. I like to nail the bad guys just like you do."

They watched him walk back toward the main dock.

Molly put her arms around him and hugged him. "See? You were being too hard on yourself."

"Maybe, but we're still out of a job."

She kissed him, a long, lingering kiss. "We've got each other and a beautiful boat to live on. Complaining?"

His face broke into a big grin as he held her close. "Not at all. Let's just be more careful in the future when we go skinny-dipping."

Acknowledgments

Many thanks to all of my wonderful friends and family that have supported me over the years and listened to me threaten to write a novel. A special thanks to the following people for taking time to read my manuscript and offer much-needed feedback and support: Mary Jo Burkhalter Persons, Otis Scarbary, Cindy Deane, Shirley Scarbary, Clara Blanquet and Fred Blanquet. Any mistakes that remain are mine.

Last, but certainly not least, thanks to my granddaughter Breanna, who shares my love of reading and inspires me to write, and my wife June, for her patience and support.

Made in the USA
Lexington, KY
19 February 2013